FURTHER ACCLAIM

"One of the most purely, deeply thrilling, inspired, and inspiring American novels I've read in many years."
DENNIS COOPER

"*The Drop Edge of Yonder* is a book Fellini would have stolen and turned into a major film. Wurlitzer has a sly, subversive humor that is inimitable. I enjoyed this book immensely."
ALAN ARKIN

"A wild ride into the heart of the California gold rush. Wurlitzer's women make 'Deadwood' look like 'Bonanza.'"
ROBERT DOWNEY

"A wild adventure written by a bard who knows how to keep his audience spellbound by the campfire. And it's a subversive modern novel about the bounds of love and the discontents of civilized life. And it's also an invitation, delivered with an archaic smile, to meditate with a master on letting go."
JUDITH THURMAN

"I have never read anything like it. Every page transports the reader from the cerebral to the visceral and back again, until you start to feel that in the end there is no difference between the two."
SCOTT SPENCER

ACCLAIM FOR RUDOLPH WURLITZER

Nog

"*Nog* is to literature what Dylan is to lyrics."
JACK NEWFIELD, VILLAGE VOICE

Flats

"Wurlitzer will convince you in this stunningly successful book that this really is the way the world ends – not with a bang, and not with a whimper but with the light slowly covering all of us."
BOOK WORLD

Quake

"Wurlitzer is exposing the worst in people, a worst that phony, plastic Los Angeles had previously concealed.... A powerful, frightening book."
CHOICE

Slow Fade

"*Slow Fade* comes out of the space between real life and the movies and closes it up for good. A great book: beautiful, funny, and dangerous."
MICHAEL HERR

Hard Travel to Sacred Places

"Every scene, every word is underlined and meaningful, from the point of view of grief. Like morphine withdrawal, grief sensitizes the observer, since it cannot be denied. He is held right there. And like the Ancient Mariner, Wurlitzer holds his reader right there by his account."
WILLIAM S. BURROUGHS

THE DROP EDGE OF YONDER

a novel by
RUDOLPH WURLITZER

TWO DOLLAR RADIO
Since*2005

Visit *The Drop Edge of Yonder*'s official website at
www.ZebulonLives.com

Published by the Two Dollar Radio Movement, 2008.
Copyright 2008 by Rudolph Wurlitzer.

Cover photograph by Lynn Davis.
Cover design by Two Dollar Radio.

ISBN: 978-0-9763895-5-2
LCCN: 2007924062
All rights reserved.
First Printing.

Distributed to the trade by Consortium Book Sales & Distribution, Inc.
The Keg House
34 Thirteenth Avenue NE, Suite 101
Minneapolis, Minnesota 55413-1007
www.cbsd.com
phone 612.746.2600 | fax 612.746.2606
orders 800.283.3572

Two Dollar Radio
Book publishers since 2005.
"Because we make more noise than a $2 radio."
www.TwoDollarRadio.com
twodollar@TwoDollarRadio.com

Things are not as they appear.
Nor are they otherwise.

∾ Lankavatara Sutra ∾

THE DROP EDGE OF YONDER

THE WINTER THAT ZEBULON SET HIS TRAPS ALONG THE Gila River had been colder and longer than any he had experienced, leaving him with two frostbitten toes, an arrow wound in his shoulder from a Crow war party, and, to top it all off, the unexpected arrival of two frozen figures stumbling more dead than alive into his cabin in the middle of a spring blizzard.

Rather than waking him, the cold blast of wind from the open door became part of a recurrent dream: a long endless fall through an empty sky towards a storm-tossed sea.... *Come closer*, the towering waves howled....

He opened his eyes, not sure for a moment if the man and woman staring back at him weren't hungry ghosts. Frost clung to their eyebrows and nostrils, and their swollen faces were raw and crimson from the tree-cracking cold. The man wore a hard-brimmed top hat tied under his bearded chin with a long red scarf, along with a buffalo robe coated with slivers of ice. The woman appeared to be a Shoshoni half-breed. She was wrapped inside a huge army overcoat distinguished by sergeant stripes at the shoulders and, at the chest, two bullet holes, one over the other.

The man sank to his knees, swearing and choking from the smoke pouring out of the cabin's leaky fireplace and the overpowering stench of a nearby slop bucket. He spoke in a rasping whisper, as if his larynx had been smashed.

"I figured we be dead meat until the breed told me you was camped on the Gila. She knows things that ain't available to other mortals."

The man was Lobo Bill, an old trapper and horse thief, known for his wide range of windy tales and maniacal rages, that Zebulon had run into and away from in various saloons and hideouts from Tularosa to Cheyenne. When he removed his top hat, he exposed a face sliced on one side from cheek to jawbone, as if neatly quartered by a butcher's knife.

Lobo Bill nodded towards the breed, who was standing with her back to the wall, staring at Zebulon with huge, empty eyes. "She ain't one for words, but when she does open her flap, she packs a punch you don't want to know about. Even so, I owe her. She saved my bacon when a wolverine took after me. Axed it into quarters and sliced me up as well. I won her in Alamosa from a horse trader. A straight flush to his full house. A hand for the ages. She's half Shoshoni, half Irish. 'Not Here Not There' is what I call her, and I'm favored to have her, things bein' what they is these days, or ain't, depending on which way the wind blows, and even if it don't."

Lobo Bill and Not Here Not There took off their clothes. After their bodies thawed out, they collapsed on a pile of bearskins near the fireplace.

Zebulon spent the rest of the night stoking the fire and drinking from one of his last bottles of Taos White Lightning, pondering memories of Lobo Bill and all the other mountain lunatics he had known, and what he and they used to be, or not, and what he was meant to do, or be, depending on his view from the valley or mountaintop. It wasn't so much that the old mountain ways were played out, although that day was surely coming. There was something else that Lobo Bill and his breed had brought in with them, a mysterious presence or shadow that he was unable to define. Or maybe it was just the sight of two strange and lost figures snoring on his bed.

It was dawn when the wind died, along with most of his premonitions, enough anyway, to let him pass out next to his guests.

WHEN HE WOKE, A HARD, BRITTLE LIGHT WAS SPLATTERING against the cabin walls. There was no sign of Lobo Bill. When he questioned Not Here Not There, she shook her head and rolled her eyes back and forth, which made him think that Lobo Bill had either gone off to find his mules and traps, or he had decided to skip out altogether. Around him the cabin had been swept clean. The slop bucket had been emptied, his stock of flour, tobacco, whiskey, coffee, and dried jerky were stacked neatly in one corner, and split logs were piled up on either side of the fireplace.

The extreme tidiness of the cabin, together with Not Here Not There's sullen silence, made him uneasy, as if she were harboring secret thoughts or maybe, god help him, some ill-intentioned plan. Never mind, he thought. Whatever was meant to come would come, ready or not.

While they both waited for Lobo Bill to appear, Zebulon hunted for small game and prepared for the annual spring rendezvous by taking down and sorting the hundreds of muskrat and beaver pelts he had stashed in the crooks of several trees.

After three days Lobo Bill still hadn't returned. Most of the time, Not Here Not There sat on the bench outside the cabin, staring at the river and the dark blue ice that had begun to splinter into large moving cracks. In the evening she avoided looking at him as she cooked one of the rabbits he had shot.

After they ate dinner, instead of retreating to the corner she had chosen to sleep in, she joined him near the fire. Looking at him with a sly grin, she took his bottle of Taos White Lightning from him and drained the rest of it, then swayed back to her place across the room.

That night he was woken by her long nails scratching lines of blood down his stomach and across his groin, a violent gesture which she repeated even as she pulled him inside her, locking her legs around his waist as if she wanted to break him in two.

For the rest of the night, she dictated their furious passion on her own insatiable terms. In the morning she left the cabin without looking at him or saying a word.

Two days later she returned in the middle of a thunderstorm. Standing before him, she looked into his eyes as he removed her clothes and positioned her over the table, pinning her arms above her head.

When the door opened, he was plunging on inside her as if they had never been apart. When he became aware that Lobo Bill was standing above them with a raised hatchet, he decided that he might as well go out in the same way that he had been conceived. Part of him enjoyed the prospect, and he was damned if he was going to give Lobo Bill the satisfaction of an apology. He continued to thrust himself inside her with even more abandon, letting out a long mountain yell: "Waaaaaaaaagh!"

His fury broke the table, sending them both to the floor. Lobo Bill's hatchet missed Zebulon's skull by an inch and sliced a large hole in the middle of Not Here Not There's stomach.

Before Lobo Bill could react, Zebulon reached for a pistol inside Lobo Bill's belt and shot him between the eyes.

Unable to move or speak, he sat on the floor, watching Not Here Not There stagger through the door.

When he finally went after her, she was standing naked on a slab of ice halfway into the river, her hands trying to hold back the blood oozing from her stomach.

"You killed the only man that ever cared for me," she said. "And now you've killed me."

They were the first words that he had heard her speak.

As the ice sank lower, carrying her downstream, and the black freezing water rose over her legs and hips, she called out to him again: "From now on, you will drift like a blind man between the worlds, not knowing if you're dead or alive, or if the unseen world exists, or if you're dreaming. Three times you will disappear to yourself and all that you know, and three times you will –"

She said something more, but he was unable to hear the words as she slowly sank beneath the ice.

WHEN THE DAYS BECAME LONGER AND FORMATIONS OF geese and ducks flew overhead, Zebulon cinched his pelts on the backs of his two mules and rode off on his horse. He was a tall, raw-boned man drifting through the mountains in greasy buckskins, with matted yellow hair falling over his shoulders, his gnarled trunk scarred top to bottom from knife and arrowhead wounds, as well as wounds secret and unimaginable.

That year the rendezvous was held along the Purgatory River, at the end of a narrow valley dotted with clumps of cottonwood and stunted alder. As Zebulon walked his horse towards the sprawling camp of half-starved Indians and drunken mountain men, he was confronted by an ancient Arapahoe squaw wearing a top hat and a dirty brown blanket thrown over a long red skirt. In one hand she held a large war club made of an elk's horn, in the other, a rattle. As he guided his horse around her, a luminous veil of smoky light shivered down her body. He thought of Not Here Not There, staring at him with angry, accusing eyes. As he looked closer, her shape dissolved into a mulatto woman with high cheek bones and finally, into the frozen death mask of a white-haired Mexican crone.

The Arapahoe laughed at his fear. Shaking her rattle, she circled him three times until he finally lost consciousness and fell headfirst off his horse. When he struggled to his feet, his body covered with mud, the Arapahoe was gone as if she had never been there in the first place.

He continued towards the camp, his spirits revived by long whoops and gun shots as the assembled traded pelts for supplies, swapped horses, gambled, and brawled. He had earned the right to let it all bust out, he promised himself, no matter that tight-assed company agents were offering only two months credit for supplies – including whiskey, coffee, and gunpowder – that no mountain man, particularly this one, could live without. Or that he knew the talk around the campfires no longer would be about who had been scalped or gone under or who had done what to whom and for what. Nossir. On this particular night he was in no mood to hear about the collapse of the fur trade, or the booming California gold rush, or the wave of ignorant flatlanders that were spreading across the mountains like a plague of locusts, or the last days of the free-trapper, when a mountain man could ride wherever he wanted and perform any sort of mischief that suited him. A way of life that was being replaced by sinkhole towns and know-nothing Eastern greenhorns honking the arrival of civilization and the dictates of the Sabbath – none of which, at least for him and his kind, were even remotely possible. Nossir, he announced again. This mountain lunatic was going to sink his teeth into what was directly in front of him and chew the pleasures of this particular rendezvous to the bone. Ready or not.

After he accepted a low cash offer for his pelts, he drank himself towards oblivion. His spirits raised to the frothy brim, he engaged in a tomahawk throwing contest followed by several rounds of three-card monte, then a hurried poke with a Pawnee squaw, and, with a dozen other mountain desperadoes, a wild free-for-all in the greasy mud that came to a sudden end when a crazed Polack tried to bite off his lower lip.

"Hoorah fer mountain doin's!" Zebulon shouted, smashing the Polack's nose halfway into his skull and kicking out what was left of his teeth. The two men then staggered arm in arm to join other lunatics sitting around a fire, smoking and drinking fire-water by the bank of the swollen Purgatory. They drank straight through the night, the river roaring past them high on the spring flood as they stuffed sloppy buffalo innards down their wet throats, singing and swapping a winter's worth of windy lies and tall tales.

The next morning he hoofed his way through a drum-thumping, fiddle-scratching fandango, then played poker around a torn blanket spread over the frozen ground. He won more than he had any right to, considering that he was unable to make out the numbers on the cards.

"Bad is best," he yelled, slamming down one winning card after another. In previous years, he wouldn't have stopped until he had lost his entire winter haul and found himself buried in debt to the Fur Company. That was the all-or-nothing code that he had always lived up to. Another year always came around, and when his pouch was finally empty and his body bruised and broken, he would head back to the mountains to hunt and heal himself and move on, to drift wherever the wind and his raw instincts took him. It was a grand free-for-all life that he took for granted, one that he never thought would end. But this year was different, and he had just enough presence of mind to sell one of his mules and ride out before he lost it all. Things end, he told himself as he pondered his options. Stealing and raising horses – he was skilled and experienced for that, enough to secure a cattle ranch on the headwaters of the Green. Or maybe he could make a stab at the California gold rush, even though that greedy stampede was at the bottom of his possibles list. In any case, he wasn't getting younger; hell, he was near thirty-five, or was it forty? He had never counted the years and his folks had never bothered to tell him. But one way or the other, he was riding down a river of no return on a leaky raft, a sloping drift headed for the rapids unless he figured out how to change. His mind was wandering, his body wasn't what it used to be, and more and more he felt the ominous presence of a dark shadow looming up behind him.

~ ~ ~

On his way back to the mountains, he planned to give himself the luxury of a pause in Panchito, a squalid high-desert settlement that he had hid out in more than once – gut shot or on the run from a war party or a round of horse thieving from one of the sprawling Spanish ranches south of Santa Fe. It was a place where he could wet his beak and lay out with a seasoned whore without worrying about being drilled in the back or skinned in a crooked poker game.

Two days outside of Panchito a storm slammed down from the north and twice he was blown off his saddle by gusts of ice-blue wind and sleet that slashed against his cheeks like razor blades. Not able to make camp because of the rocky terrain, he let his horse and mule drift beyond boundaries or any sense of direction. Several times he looked back as if he were being followed, but nothing moved beyond the heavy scrim of falling snow. When he finally reached a sheltered hollow he picketed the horse and mule and burrowed into a snowdrift, covering himself with a buffalo robe.

The next day the storm passed and he continued on through heavy drifts, his moccasins and leggings frozen solid, the eyes of his half-dead horse and mule covered with icy sleet. In the evening the skies parted and he could see the Sangre de Cristo Mountains, their cold vermilion peaks promising a measure of deliverance, enough anyway, to keep him plowing on towards Panchito and a rest-up in the town's two-bit cantina.

The promise of refuge ended with a low rumble followed by a rushing mass of up-rooted trees, rocks, and snow that swept him off his horse as easily as a matchstick tossed over a waterfall. Running, tumbling head over heels, he rolled along the edge of the boiling avalanche until he landed in a deep drift.

Half-conscious, he lay spread-eagled on his back, waiting for a second eruption or last exhale, whichever came first. He wasn't exactly a stranger when it came to facing the misty beyond, or the *jornada del muerto*, as he had heard death referred to south of the border. There had been other times: when he'd been lost and half-frozen in a blizzard, wounded in more than one saloon shoot-out, nearly scalped by an Apache war party, fallen headfirst off a butte, to name a few.

He was interrupted by a second avalanche that sounded, as it roared upon him, like a dam busting loose. Slammed forward, more dead than alive, he crawled towards a small clearing of spruce and cedar, where he managed to construct a crude wickiup out of fallen branches.

He woke to find his horse staring at him with bewildered eyes. A mile away he found his mule, its legs sticking straight up inside a huge drift.

A DAY LATER HE REACHED PANCHITO, A FORLORN CLUSTER of adobe buildings grouped around a cantina. Inside the moan of biting wind, he heard the distant maniacal chords of a runaway piano, punctuated by bursts of mindless laughter.

An empty stagecoach was pulled up in front of the cantina. Near the stagecoach a small bandy-legged man, wearing a sheepskin coat and a whore's feather boa around his neck, was doing his best to mount a horse. Halfway into the saddle, his foot slid out of the stirrup and he fell headfirst on the frozen mud.

He looked up at Zebulon through glazed, shifty eyes. "I seen you somewhere."

"I don't think you did," Zebulon said.

The bandy-legged man tried to mount his horse again and then gave up. "Maybe you come in last night with Hatchet Jack," the bandy-legged man said. "Folks say that half-breed weasel-head should be tarred and feathered. Not me. I'd give the bastard a long rope and a short drop."

Zebulon dismounted and pushed past him into the cantina.

Three oil lamps hanging from a rafter cast a dim light over the narrow low-ceilinged room. Hatchet Jack sat at the bar wearing a red and white Mexican army coat and a black bowler with a raven feather slanted over one side of the brim. A scar shaped like a long *S* ran down his left cheek from a wound Zebulon had carved a long time ago.

Hatchet Jack looked at him through one blue eye, one black.

"You're a hard buzzard to track. I looked for you at the rendezvous, but you had already lit out. They told me you was ridin' a hot streak but quit while you was ahead. That didn't sound like you."

"It was a hard winter," Zebulon said. "I'm holdin' on to what I can."

"I ain't askin' for no hand out," Hatchet Jack said, "if that's what you're thinkin'."

The piano player's gnarled fingers rolled over the broken keys with mechanical precision. Further down the bar, two played-out whores sat staring at a rattlesnake coiled up inside a glass jar. When the piano player struck a dissonant chord the snake shifted its head back and forth looking for a way out.

Zebulon poured himself a shot from Hatchet Jack's half-full bottle of Taos White Lightning, a slug that burned into his gut like a branding iron. While he waited for Hatchet Jack to say what was on his mind, he focused on three stuffed moose heads lined up on the wall behind the bar. All of their marble eyes except one had been shot out, and their antlers and heads were punctured by tomahawks and darts.

"I need help with your Pa," Hatchet Jack said. "I want his forgiveness."

Forgiveness: it was a word Zebulon had never used before, much less thought about.

"It's been seven years since you been up to see them?" Hatchet Jack said.

"More like two."

Hatchet Jack shook his head, pouring himself another shot of Taos White Lightning. "Last time I rode up I went all the way *loco* and then some. The week before, an Arapahoe war party had buried Pa up to his neck in a swamp with the water rising. Me bein' of mixed blood didn't help. He told me not to call him

Pa. Said he never should have taken me in after he won me in that poker game and he wanted me gone. That's when I cleaned his plow."

"You cleaned Pa's plow?" Zebulon asked.

"I told him to dig a hole and go fuck himself. Those were my words. Then I took off with his big sorrel horse and a mess of his traps."

"How did Ma take it?"

"She brained him with an ax handle before he could smoke me. Said she was glad to do it, but that she'd look forward to when I took off and didn't come back. Which is what I done. Until now."

Hatchet Jack downed another shot of Taos White Lightning. "I been told to make it up to him by an old Mex *brujo*. Name of Plaxico. You wouldn't know him. After I left the mountains I rode straight to the end of myself, doin' the usual bad mischief before I signed on with him. He has big medicine, that old man. Big sack of power. Learned me all about the spirit world. What to do and not to do. How to find and hold on to your power without sellin' it on the cheap. He said someone put a curse on me after your Pa took me in and that if I wanted to shake it loose I'd have to make it right with him."

"How do you aim to do it?"

"Damned if I know."

"What kind of curse?"

"Somethin' about being stuck between the worlds. Not knowin' which end is up. He went on about a woman. When I asked him about that, he wouldn't say."

"Pa will plug you just for showin' up," Zebulon said, not wanting to know any more about curses.

"Unless you ride up there with me," Hatchet Jack said. "I'm askin', Zeb. This one time. You be the only one that knows how to stretch the blanket with the old bastard."

"I used to know how to stretch it. No more."

Hatchet Jack shook his head. "I went to a whole lot of trouble stealing a prime horse and a bunch of traps to give back to him. Thing was, I got taken bad in a game of stud. A full house to some white nigger's straight flush. I lost the horse and the traps and everything else."

He paused. "Look. I'm ridin' the rump of somethin' I don't know about and I need your help."

When one of the whores banged her shot glass on the bar, Hatchet Jack signaled the bartender to give her a refill.

"That's how it goes," he said. "Ever since I poked her, she been on me like the last squirrel of winter. I'd be better off spendin' time with Ma Thumb and her four daughters."

The piano player pounded out another tune. The back of the room was full of all-or-nothing gamblers, along with three heavy-lidded *vaqueros* sitting on the floor against a wall, drunk or half-asleep. Four other men sat at a table, speaking in whispers as they looked Zebulon over. Out-of-work ranch hands, Zebulon figured. At the next table a large-bellied rancher was playing poker with the stagecoach driver, a busted up man with a handle-bar mustache and a soiled patch over one eye. Behind them a man sat slumped over a table; either drunk or possibly dead, his face lay across his forearms and a black cape was draped across his emaciated shoulders. A woman sat next to him wearing a dark green high-busted dance-hall dress and long silver earrings that drooped in a long bow to her neck. Her bronze high-toned face, as luminous as ancient rice paper, was framed by spills of medusa-like hair, blacker than black. Zebulon had never seen anyone like her, not even in his usual rut of Denver whorehouses known for specializing in mixed colors. She was smoking a long Mexican cheroot and appeared, as she looked over at him, more weary than curious. Or perhaps she was just bored.

"Spooky," Hatchet Jack said. "They come in on the stage, goin' south to old Mex. Looks to me like the old rooster owns her. Or maybe it's the other way around."

The woman removed a deck of cards from her purse. Cutting the cards with one hand, she spread them on the table for a game of solitaire. The first card up was the queen of hearts, which she quickly buried in the deck.

"Are you goin' to help or not?" Hatchet Jack asked.

Zebulon's eyes were on the stagecoach driver and one of the *vaqueros* as they sat down at the woman's table. "Right now I need to skin some cards and rest my bones."

Hatchet Jack started to object, then changed his mind. Picking up the bottle of Taos White Lightning, he headed slowly up the stairs. After a short consultation, the two whores knocked back their drinks and followed him.

Zebulon considered and then rejected what it would mean to join them, then downed another shot and walked across the room to a battered billiard table, its patched green covering stained with spilled whiskey and vomit. Sliding around the table like a two-step dancer, he maneuvered the cue ball around the table just to prove that he still could. Then he made his way over to the woman who was dealing a hand of poker to the *vaquero* and stagecoach driver. "Room for one more?" he asked.

She kept her eyes on the cards. "There's always room for one more: as long as one more ends up one less."

She spoke with what he took to be an English accent, along with a softer, more spaced-out inflection that Zebulon figured came from some kind of African lingo.

He placed a stack of silver dollars on the table.

"A word of advice," the stagecoach driver said. "Delilah don't take prisoners."

"But I do take prisoners," Delilah replied, looking at Zebulon with the hint of a smile. "It's what I do after I take them that causes problems."

"I second that statement."

The black-cloaked man sitting next to her raised his head,

revealing a small-boned face highlighted by a thin mustache and long pointed goatee streaked with white.

"I suggest caution if you don't want to find yourself falling over a cliff," he mumbled, his head slumping back to the table.

They played seven-card stud, nothing wild. The betting remained more or less even, with no one falling very far behind except for the *vaquero*, who bet every hand as if it was his last. When the *vaquero* finally lost his stake, he bowed his respects to the woman and left the room.

"I am privileged to fill the empty space," the black-cloaked man said, looking at them as if he had no idea where he was or what space he was meant to fill.

Most likely a Rusky, Zebulon figured, having heard the accent before. Either that or a Turk or Polack.

From the moment that Ivan, as Delilah referred to him, sat down, Zebulon suspected that she was dealing off the bottom: It was the way her fingers manipulated and spread out the cards with practiced ease, cutting the deck with one hand while knuckle-rolling a stack of coins with the other.

Her precise movements cast a spell, a dreamy ritual, and no matter how much he tried to resist, he found himself unable to break or even interrupt it. As the night wore on and the hands flowed back and forth with no clear winner, he surrendered to a strange sense of relief. It was as if he had been through this before, in the same dimly lit cantina with most of the oil lamps burned out, listening to the same restless chords from a banged-up piano with cracked and missing keys, the same row of moose heads with their eyes shot out, the same low murmur of betting and raising, the same slap of shuffling cards whose numbers and faces had become so bent and rubbed that they were barely visible. He was dimly aware that he might be in trouble because winning and losing no longer seemed to matter, as if the results had already been decided.

The game was watched over by the bandy-legged man and

a few drifters and ranch hands, all of them making side bets. Hatchet Jack, who had come downstairs with the two whores, was watching from the end of the bar.

When Delilah turned over three kings, beating his three jacks, Zebulon's loss emptied most of his pouch, sending him back to the billiard table, where he won three games from one of the ranch hands and then two more from the bandy-legged man, more than doubling his money.

When he returned to the table, Hatchet Jack walked over and sat down opposite Delilah.

The new arrivals caused Ivan to slam his hand on the table with such force that a glass jumped and shattered on the floor. "All the way to the end, gentlemen," he said. "No exceptions or discounts allowed. So says one who comes and has already gone and is yet ready to come again."

"You're crackin' wide open, Count," the stagecoach driver said. "I know the signs."

"Not cracking, my friend," Ivan replied. "More a glimpse from the pit of darkness into the terror of endless space. That happens at the end of a long night when one is bored and foolish enough to abandon the reins of control."

"I say you're bluffin'." Hatchet Jack pushed his money into the center of the table.

"Bluffing, you say? Well, well, well." Ivan stacked twenty gold eagles next to Hatchet Jack's raise. "What is life if not a bluff? I see your call and raise you one-hundred silver dollars."

When Delilah and Zebulon matched Ivan's raise, Hatchet Jack threw down his cards and walked over to the bar.

As Delilah dealt the last of the cards face down, Zebulon noticed a shiver run down her sleeve into the tips of her fingers.

Ivan turned over three aces.

The stagecoach driver turned over a ten of spades, adding to the two that were on the table.

Delilah produced a queen of hearts, filling out a straight flush to Zebulon's full house.

As she gathered in the biggest pot of the night, the bandy-legged man staggered towards Zebulon, waving his pistol. "I remember you all right. You're that same mountain scum that stole my bay horse in Galisteo. You and that breed."

"I never been to Galisteo," Zebulon said, reaching for his pistol.

Before either of them could fire, three shots from the other side of the room blew out two gas lamps and one of the windows.

The last thing Zebulon remembered was staggering out of the cantina and trying to make it down the street before he collapsed.

ZEBULON DIDN'T SEE THE STARS SHOOTING ACROSS THE SKY like silver bursts of rifle fire, or the goat feeding on garbage next to him, or the Mexican kid sitting on the lip of the arroyo waiting to steal his boots.

"*Quién es?*"

He turned over on his back, his head pounding as if it was locked inside a giant church bell.

"*Quién es?*" the kid asked again.

Who was he anyway? And where was he? And where was he going? He sat up, wiping the dried blood from his eyes. A man lay next to him, surrounded by smashed bottles and scraps of rotting meat. There was a hole in the man's forehead and his matted yellow hair fell in bloody strands over his face. Zebulon looked closer. There was something familiar about the man's fringed buckskins and torn moccasins and the fact that he was clutching the queen of hearts in one hand. Zebulon watched a fly crawl across the man's cheek. It was a long journey, the way the fly was crawling, then stopping, then crawling on. From life to death, he thought, and back again. And how was he doing on this journey? Was he dead or alive, or was he trapped between the worlds like a blind man? When he shut his eyes and opened them again, the man was no longer there.

He remembered a full house and a queen of hearts, a shot followed by more shots, then staggering out of the cantina and falling headfirst into the arroyo. He took a deep breath. He wasn't dead. Not that it would be so bad to be dead, the way things had been going.

The goat's chewing made him think of his Pa. Or maybe it was the smell of stale urine. If the old bastard was still alive, he and Ma would be getting their winter pelts ready to sell. He ought to ride up and help them. Anything to be shut of this town of aging outlaws and second-rate card cheats – one of whom had tried to kill him. Or was that another time in another town?

"*Quién es*?" the kid was asking.

On the road to nowhere. On the drift ever since he had left his family in the Sangre de Cristo Mountains five years ago. The goat stepped closer, staring down at him with dull insolence, as if to remind him that his string had run out. "Not hardly," he muttered. Not yet. Just to make sure, he raised the Colt and fired a bullet through the goat's eye. One way or the other, he was back. The stinking garbage and the dead goat and the way the Colt felt in his hand convinced him of that, enough anyway, to stumble past the Mexican kid who was sliding back on his haunches as if he had seen a ghost.

~ ~ ~

He staggered down the deserted street towards the cantina. Above the moaning wind, he heard the faint chords of a piano.

The stagecoach was gone. His horse wasn't where he had hitched it and he mounted the first one he came to. Before he could ride down the street, the bandy-legged man staggered out of the swinging doors to take a leak, an act that was causing him trouble with one arm wrapped in a sling.

Shaken, he looked up at Zebulon. "I swear you're dead, only you're on my horse. Listen. It was a long night, and I didn't see what went down. But it weren't me that smoked you. I tried. Sure. But I got nicked before I called you out. It might have been that whore, the one that dealt the straight flush. She and that ferriner that owns her. Take my word, they're some devilish act, them two. Slicker'n three-headed snakes. When she won that last hand, all hell broke loose. What I recall anyways. Like I said, I wasn't in the best of shape."

The man's confused, cloudy eyes reminded Zebulon of the goat.

"I'll take your horse," Zebulon said, "for settlement. And maybe I'll blow off your trigger finger for tryin' to take me out."

The bandy-legged man looked back at the saloon where the two whores were laughing at him through a broken window. There was no help from either of them.

His hand shook as he raised his pistol. "No one takes a horse from me, or even thinks about it. And I never jacked it. It was that ferriner or one of them *vaqueros* or ranch hands at the billiard table. Or that breed. Hatchet Jack. Ask him. He's in there now. I can take a loss. Hell, that's my middle name. Lost and never found. If you don't believe me, we might as well slap to it here and now."

"It's your call," Zebulon said. "But if you dry-shoot me, do it with your whizzle in your pants."

He dismounted and pushed past him into the cantina, not giving a damn one way or the other.

"No sense to it," the bandy-legged man said to the two whores. "The man come back from the dead. What do you want me to do, send him straight to hell again?"

Inside the cantina, the only signs of a shoot-out were dark stains on the floor, a few smashed chairs, and a blown-out window.

Hatchet Jack was sitting at the bar, a bandage wrapped around his head.

Zebulon shoved Hatchet Jack's money towards the bartender, motioning for a bottle of Taos White Lightning.

"No hat size to this town," Hatchet Jack said. "Only thing left is to get shut of it."

"Who shot me?" Zebulon asked.

"You don't recall?" Hatchet Jack rolled a shot glass between his palms. "When I went over to the bar I heard someone, I don't recall who, sayin' the woman was dealin' off the bottom – snakin' a queen of hearts straight flush to your full house. Or maybe it was the other way around. A bunch come in the door and I was too pissed and likkered to notice. Next thing, I'm cold-cocked. When I come to, you was gone and I went upstairs and slept it off. I don't recall the rest. Who gives a damn. We're still on the dance floor, ain't we? More than some."

"You see anything?" Zebulon asked the bartender, a squat man with a bushy mustache and wide red suspenders.

"Not a thing," he replied. "I was out back haulin' likker stock. When I come in, it was all over and everyone had cleared out. I don't remember. Hell, that was two nights ago."

"Anything can happen in two nights," Hatchet Jack said. "Or one, for that matter. Or none."

"You been here two nights?" Zebulon asked.

Hatchet Jack poured himself another shot. "Like I said, I was upstairs. Now everyone's zippered up or rode off. You might have noticed I ain't in the best of shape myself. If someone don't try to plug you, he might settle for me. And that ain't why I rode down here. How about it? You want to ride up to see your Ma and Pa? It ain't like you got anything better to do."

"Tell me one last thing," Zebulon asked. "Did you throw your loop over that bay horse in Galisteo?"

"Hell no," Hatchet Jack replied. "I snagged a zebra dun. The bay wasn't worth a bag of rocks."

When they pushed through the swinging doors, the bandy-legged man was sitting on a bench. He didn't look up when Hatchet Jack rode down the street, followed by Zebulon riding the bandy-legged man's horse.

HATCHET JACK AND ZEBULON RODE NORTH ACROSS THE high desert towards the Spanish Peaks of the Sangre de Cristo Mountains. Two days later they reached the cabin, a hard little stand at the end of a steep valley, quilted halfway to the roof with drifting snow.

Nothing much had changed. The cabin's roof still had most of its shakes blown off, the makeshift corral hosted three starving mules, and a curl of smoke drifted up from the chimney like a lonely question mark. After they walked their horses over the ice-covered river that snaked in front of the cabin, Zebulon hollered a long "Halloooo." When there was no answer, they secured their horses inside the sagging corral and pushed through the stiff door of buffalo hide.

An ancient stern-faced woman sat behind a three-plank table in patched red long johns, pointing a shotgun straight at them. In front of her a torn deck of cards was spread across the table for a game of solitaire. Brown streaks of tobacco juice ran down her chin, and a thin curtain of gray hair fell over one side of her ravaged face.

"I thought it was your Pa come back," she said to Zebulon. "I was lookin' forward to smokin' the old grizzle-heel straight to hell."

She looked him over top to bottom. "A bit off your graze, ain't you, son? Last I heard you was hangin' out with flatlanders and gold-suckin' Argonauts.'"

"I was, Ma," Zebulon said. "No more."

"You sure are a sorry piece of used up sod," she went on. "You look like a damn ghost. Beat-up and thinner'n a snake on stilts."

"I'm comin' around," he reassured her.

"You might be comin', but you ain't yet around."

"Howdy, Ma," Hatchet Jack interrupted.

"Howdy yourself," she replied, spitting a thick stream of tobacco juice in the general direction of a copper spittoon. "And don't *Ma* me. Use my Christian name or put your scrawny half-breed ass back on the trail."

"All right, Annie May." Hatchet Jack picked up a bottle of whiskey from the table and took a long pull, then handed the bottle to Zebulon.

"You got some big fat *cojones* comin' back here," Annie May continued. "Last I heard you was down on the Brazos rollin' steers and makin' mischief."

"No future in steers these days," Hatchet Jack said.

"I'll vouch for that," Zebulon said, pulling off his bloody shirt and dropping it on the dirt floor.

"I'll just bet," Annie May said, shooting him a weary glance. "Vouchin' bein' a particular specialty of yours. That and poochin' stray women."

She turned her head towards Hatchet Jack. "What brings you here?"

"I need to get square with Pa," Hatchet Jack said. "I mean, Elijah. Finish my account with him."

"You gone to Jesus, or just *loco*?" the old woman asked.

"He's become a healer," Zebulon explained.

Annie May cackled, slapping her arthritic knees with her palms. "Well don't the sun just shine. You're too late, Mister Healer-Dealer. He took his sorry ass to Californie. Who knows where? Now you got me to deal with."

"It ain't the same."

"The hell it ain't. The horse and traps you stole were mine the same as his. By rights I should plug you for thievery and be done with you."

Hatchet Jack shrugged. "That's up to you. I still got a horse to give back, even if I lost the traps."

"We'll eat," she said firmly. "Then speculate."

She sighed, shifting her gaze to Zebulon, who was slicing up a pair of his Pa's pants with his bowie knife.

"To think you're all I spawned," she said. "All that I care to recollect anyways."

She picked up the bottle of whiskey, studying his bloody chest. "What happened to your pump?"

"I guess I been shot."

"You guess?" She hobbled over to him and poured the rest of the whiskey on his chest, an act that made him howl more from witnessing the last of the bottle than from the acute pain. He shuddered as she carefully wrapped a strip of pant leg around his chest.

"How come there ain't no bullet hole?" she asked.

"I wondered about that," he said.

"Might be the slug passed through you. Who done it?"

"Most likely a pecker-head sneakin' a card off the bottom." He nodded at Hatchet Jack. "That's what he says, anyway."

"You was there?" she asked Hatchet Jack.

"I come in after the show was over," Hatchet Jack said.

Satisfied with her nursing skills, Annie May stood up. "Don't neither of you burden me with your sad stories," she cautioned. "Or what you done or ain't done or what you're goin' to do. I'm too old for that bullshit."

She took down a tin of biscuits and a slab of jerky from a sagging shelf. After she dropped the food on the table, she sat down, lit up a curved ivory pipe, and watched Hatchet Jack and Zebulon eat.

"Raise many pelts this winter?" Hatchet Jack asked, chewing hard on the jerky.

Annie May shrugged, then let loose another streak of tobacco juice, missing the spittoon by a foot. "I floated my share of sticks, but the haul was damn thin. Not much beaver, a few muskrats and otter, the odd fox. Hardly worth the trouble. Far as I'm concerned, the mountains be finished. Leastways for this old sow."

They passed around a second bottle of whiskey. When the bottle was empty, Hatchet Jack and Zebulon lay down on a pile of pelts, too tired to pay attention to the rats sniffing across the floor for crumbs.

Annie May closed her eyes and continued to smoke, enjoying the smell and presence of two snoring men. When the memories of a newborn son and a mountain lover who wouldn't quit threatened to overwhelm her, she stumbled off to her own bunk in an add-to behind the stove.

~ ~ ~

The next morning Zebulon cleaned out a weasel nest underneath a rafter while Annie May sat by the window, watching Hatchet Jack sort out her meager display of pelts, then cinch and slap them over the backs of two emaciated mules.

"Never thought I'd see both of you at the same trough again," she said. "Not after what Hatchet pulled with your Pa. Not to mention your Pa with him."

"He's askin' forgiveness, Ma. That ain't easy."

"Forgiveness ain't in my possibles bag. If your Pa was here, he'd give him a taste of forgiveness upside the head."

Zebulon opened the door and threw out the weasel nest, looking at Hatchet Jack who was kneeling on the ground, carefully shoeing one of the mules.

"Hatchet's pulled me out of a few scraps and shoot-outs," he said. "I owe him for that."

Annie May shrugged. "You always were a sucker for idiot kindness. Truth is, your heart slammed shut when Pa brought Hatchet back and he tried to drown you in the river. I had to pull you out by your hair. Ever since then, you'll take any bone thrown to you."

She sighed, not remembering how much Zebulon had been told about Hatchet Jack.

"I'll tell you some things Hatchet picked up from your Pa," she said. "Dealin' off the bottom of the deck. Settin' someone up and draggin' him to hell and then tellin' him he done the opposite. For spite and pleasure."

"He's slick all right," Zebulon acknowledged. "I'll give him that."

"Never mind," she went on, as if she was having second thoughts. "He's still kin. I raised him almost the same as you, a fact that calls for some measurement, if not in the eyes of the Lord, then from you and me. Poor lost-and-found half-breed bastard."

She took a deep breath before she finally said what was really on her mind: "Tell you one last thing, son. After I sell my pelts, that's it for me. I ain't about to wait for my last days stretched out in a low-rent room over some dumb flatlander's store."

"Maybe I should pack you down to old Mex," Zebulon suggested. "Let the sun warm your bones. Fix you up in some little *hacienda* with a front porch and a cantina down the street. There are worse ways."

"What the hell would I do in old Mex? Chew my sorry cud with all them bean and chili-eaters? Nossir. When I take my carcass to the misty beyond, the sky will be my blanket and I'll have a mountain to lean against and a jug to pull on. That'll be enough."

He had grown up hearing this statement, or at least variations of it, and depending on her mood he always gave the same reply:

"You brought me into the world, Ma. I'll see you out."

This time she interrupted him: "I didn't raise you for false sentiments, son. You do what's in front of you and I'll do the same."

THE FOLLOWING MORNING THEY ALL RODE OFF INTO A SOFT spring rain. They took their time, as Annie May was in no hurry to be shut of the only place she had known for thirty years, a place she was beginning to realize she would never see again.

That night they camped among the crumbling ruins of an abandoned *pueblo*, the wind howling around their fire like a chorus of grieving widows. Halfway through a meal of Annie May's remaining biscuits and dried jerky, Hatchet Jack stood up, his head swiveling back and forth.

An ancient Mexican stood in the shadows, his nearly toothless face marked by an empty eye socket. His skeletal frame was wrapped in torn leggings and a long white cotton shirt.

"You leave a trail like a wounded buffalo," the Mexican said with a soft Spanish accent.

"Plaxico!" Hatchet Jack exclaimed. "How did you find me?"

"I didn't find you. You found me."

"But —"

"Your problem is that you think too much. And not enough."

Without another word, he turned and disappeared.

Spooked by the old Mexican's ghostly appearance, Annie May paced back and forth, raising her arms against the elements: "Hurrah fer mountain doin's and all the old warriors in all the times! My boys and I, we come in peace and we'll leave in peace and we'd be grateful if all you dead and dyin' red niggers and bean-eaters put the stopper on your salutes. One day soon I'll pitch my tent inside the big circle. But not now. Not this night."

Zebulon and Hatchet Jack joined her, shuffling their feet around the fire, faster and faster as they hollered their mountain yells: "Waaaaaaaaagh…! Waaaaaaaaagh…! Waaaaaaaaagh!"

Collapsing on their backs, they finished the last of the whiskey as they sang an old family song:

> *Old Long Hatcher gone under on the north Platte,*
> *Found him a bar but the bar laid him flat.*

Hatchet Jack reached into his pocket and removed a paper bag full of penny candies. Popping half of them into his mouth, he threw the bag to Zebulon, who took a fistful and passed the bag to Annie May, who gobbled up the rest.

"We're markin' the bush on sacred ground," Hatchet Jack said. "Plaxico might make us pay for that."

Annie May sighed. "You seen one old buzzard around these hide-outs, you seen 'em all. The hell with him. I'll settle for a healing. What about it, Mister Healer-Dealer? Can you strut your healin' stuff? Got me a bad knee, shoulder ain't right, arrowhead been stuck in my leg for ten years, teeth gone or rotten, sluice line to my gut plugged up. Not only that, but I'm spiteful with bad notions."

"I can handle that," Hatchet Jack said, showing no confidence at all.

"Check out Zeb while you're at it," Annie May suggested. "He's tough to figure, shot up with no bullet in his pump. Like he don't know if he's here or down under."

Hatchet Jack shook his head, not wanting to go ahead with any of it. "I never done two straight up. I always been the helper."

"Yoke us up anyway," Zebulon said. "Never mind the windy complaints."

Hatchet Jack poked their shoulders and cheeks with his forefinger, blowing tobacco smoke over their heads and shoulders and into their faces. Then he stood up and opened his arms to include the night sky and the black clouds drifting beneath a quarter-moon like a procession of giant bones.

"Old Father," he cried out, "don't contrary me now!"

Arching his neck and head, he shut his eyes and sank to his knees, pounding his fists on the earth.

The wind stopped as if turned off by a spigot.

Annie May shook her head in wonder. "I'll be stripped naked and fried in goose grease. Maybe the boy ain't such a lyin' shuck after all."

As the wind rose again, Hatchet Jack disappeared into the darkness. Just when they thought he had run out on them, he returned.

"Plaxico says it's all right to join him."

They followed Hatchet Jack down a steep path, descending a series of narrow, winding steps that led to a stone platform lit by a fire and a single torch set into a cliff. Beyond the platform, a deep canyon separated two mountains shaped like pendulous breasts.

Plaxico sat cross-legged on one side of a large circle made from white flour mixed with corn shuckings and colored stone beads. Above him on the crumbling walls, mounted warriors threw lances at running mountain lions and antelopes.

Hatchet Jack motioned for Zebulon and Annie May to sit opposite Plaxico, then took a position at the lower end of the circle, behind an altar of flat stones. On one side of the altar, a statue of the Virgin Mary had been placed next to an eagle feather and a brightly colored Kachina doll. On the darker side, the skeleton of a rattlesnake circled a human skull. A dozen tomahawks, as well as swords and hunting knives, were stuck in the ground in front of the altar.

Hatchet Jack stood up. "This medicine is from old Mex. It

raises the dead and then some. It has the power to cozy up to the underworld of the snake, the middle world of the mountain lion, and the higher world of the eagle. I never tried it, but that's what I been told. So here goes."

Plaxico sat behind the altar pounding a flat drum and chanting an incomprehensible prayer. He broke off a few times to yell instructions in Spanish to Hatchet Jack, who motioned for Annie May and Zebulon to stand at the top of the circle. Then he approached them holding a hollowed-out gourd in both hands.

Hatchet Jack drank, then offered the gourd to Zebulon, who drank and passed it to Annie May. After she drank, she handed the gourd to Hatchet Jack, who handed it to Plaxico, who finished what was left. After a consultation with Plaxico, Hatchet Jack pulled a long curved sword out of the earth and rushed straight at mother and son, yelling and dancing around them as he slashed the sword above their heads.

Annie May and Zebulon stood as if their feet had been nailed to the ground as Hatchet Jack replaced the sword in front of the altar and collapsed by the fire. Behind him, Plaxico swayed from side to side, shuffling around the circle, moaning and shaking his rattle.

The medicine roared through their bodies in noxious waves until they sank down on all fours, vomiting and heaving until nothing was left inside them. They stayed that way until the first light of dawn shuddered over the horizon. As the mountains grew bolder and more defined, Annie May cried out at a long parade of skywalkers moving towards them over the snowy peaks. Some were *conquistadors* and mountain men, others Hopis, Navajos, Zunis, and Apaches. All of them were raising their arms to greet the rising sun. Behind them, bringing up the rear was Annie May's long-dead brother. He was followed by her mother and father and then the preacher of her youth, who used to terrify her with fiery sermons on sin and repentance, and who now seemed, as he looked over the valley, sad and confused. The sky shifted and the parade dissolved as she saw an image of herself as a young girl standing in the middle of a field of tall, wavy grass, a bonnet pulled over her head, her bare feet planted on the black earth, crying out in fear as an eagle glided towards her in slowly decreasing circles. Her mother watched from the door of their homestead as the eagle gently lifted her up in its talons and flew her across the grassy plains into the foothills and mountains beyond. Fragments of her life appeared one after the other: her first shoes; her marriage bed; the long white beard of her father as he stood behind the mule on the last furrow of a plowed field; her husband, Elijah, whirling her around a dance floor, then carrying her on his shoulders through the door of the cabin he had built for her; and there was baby Zebulon crawling over the dirt floor. She wept and wept, haunted by the memories and the approaching shadow of her own death.

"Are we dead?" she cried. "Or does it just seem that way?"

Zebulon cradled her frail, broken body in his arms as Hatchet Jack, seized with his own visions and oblivious to her racking sobs and sudden peals of laughter, smacked the earth with his palms. "Who are my real Ma and Pa," he howled, "and why have they forsaken me?"

The only answer was the howling wind.

"Can you see the truth of it, boys?" Annie May shouted. "Life and death. The eagle and the washing up and the outhouse. The stove and the snow. The horse and the mountains and the 'baca juice. No doubt about it. The whole stew is only a passing, you and me and all the rest. The goddamn joke is on us, boys!"

Zebulon made his way to the edge of the platform. In front of him the mountains were undulating like three copulating snakes. He wept at the energies threatening to consume him, motherly and loving, violent and terrifying, a warm hissing breeze that flowed through the strangled knots of his being. He knew what he had always known and had always forgotten:

that he was composed of the same elements as the plants and animals and the rain, which was now spreading in thick sheets across the deep valley, followed by the sun and then a rumble of earthshaking thunder that suddenly transformed into the roar of a mountain lion. He was part of it all, a drop of water in the ocean, a crushed wild flower under the heel of an outlaw's boot, a sun-baked skeleton in the desert.

When Hatchet Jack loomed up in front of him, the vision dissolved into a vaporous fog.

For the rest of the night, mother and son slept in each other's arms, each comforted by the other's breathing. When they woke they were alone and the sun was shining directly above them as if through a huge prism.

Behind them, the altar was gone and the circle erased, as if none of it had ever existed.

Empty of thought or any emotion, they climbed up through the ruins until they found Hatchet Jack packing his horse. Plaxico sat against a crumbling wall, rolling a cigarette.

"I'm pullin' out." Hatchet Jack's hands shook as he swung into the saddle. "Some of the medicine worked and some went south." He looked at Plaxico, then at Annie May. "The spirits told me it wouldn't be a good idea to give you the horse."

"Who cares about any of it?" Annie May said softly. "It's all the same, horse or no horse."

They watched Hatchet Jack gallop off without a wave or a look back, as if pursued by a confusion of unknown mysteries.

"He talked to some of the spirits all right," Plaxico said. "But he choked on the rest. Too big a meal for a beginner."

And then he, too, was gone, disappearing back inside the *pueblo*.

ANNIE MAY AND ZEBULON SMELLED BROKEN ELBOW BEFORE they saw it. What had been a trading post and a few shacks only a year ago was now a long, rutted street dominated by pandemonium and open sewage. Drunken miners shouted back and forth in a dozen languages, a naked Chinaman crawled past them into an alleyway pursued by a screaming whore, half-dead oxen pulled overloaded supply wagons through mud and melting snow, past signs advertising wares at outrageous prices: Boots $30, Flour $35, Blankets $30, Washing $20. Every square foot of ground that was not lived on was cluttered with mining equipment, dead dogs, pigs rooting in piles of stinking garbage, wagon beds, spare wheels, barrels, and stacks of lumber, as well as makeshift corrals where mules and horses stood knee-deep in muck. Further away, on the banks of a swiftly moving river, hundreds of high-booted men – most of them Indians, Mexicans, and Chinese – squatted beside cradle-like gold washers and sluice boxes while others worked up a canyon in steep pits, hacking at the soil with picks and shovels.

At the end of the street, they reined up in front of a two-story trading post.

Inside the cavernous room, clerks ran back and forth filling orders in Spanish, French, and English for rifles, canned goods, farming equipment, wagon beds, and sacks of feed. A few of the older clerks waved to Annie May as she approached a plump young man perched at a high-top desk, adding up small sums inside a huge ledger.

Annie May pulled herself up to her full height, which was barely up to the level of the desk.

"I'm Annie May Shook, and I'm here to sell my pelts."

The clerk nodded, not looking up as he took off his glasses and rubbed his strained red-rimmed eyes.

Annie May rapped on the desk with the barrel of her shotgun. "I want both ears when I'm talkin', Mister. Where be the major?"

The clerk took his time placing his glasses over his nose. "Major Poultry sold out last winter. You'll deal with me now."

"Always was partial to the major," Annie May said. "Dealt with mountain folk straight up."

"Business is business," the clerk said with measured patience. "Whoever be the buyer or seller."

Annie May scratched her head, took out her pipe, began to light it, then shoved it back inside her buffalo robe. "All right, then. What be the price of pelts?"

The clerk looked down at Annie May as if her presence was an annoying fly. "The bottom has fallen out of the fur market. It will never come back. That said, I'll give you fifty cents a pelt. Take it or leave it."

She stared up at him, unable to comprehend. "The hell you say."

"The numbers come down from St. Louis, Ma'am. Trade or cash."

Her voice rose to a shout. "Two dollars a pelt, Mister St. Louis. And my usual loan on 'baca, cartridges, and flour. That's the way it's been for these thirty years, and that's the way it'll be. Nothing more, nothing less."

The clerk shut the ledger with a loud snap. "I'm afraid that's impossible."

"Well then, Mister St. Louis, let an old mountain sage hen

show you her possible bag."

Annie May waved her shotgun at the clerk, then at a window, then at a row of pickle jars.

The terrified clerk backed away, bumping into Zebulon who shoved him against a shelf of canned goods, sending him and the cans crashing to the floor.

This was more like it, Zebulon thought, looking around the room. This was what the old Spirit Doc ordered when he needed to stir things up. He reached behind the counter for a jug of liquor, uncorked it and took a long pull, then tossed it to Annie May, who caught it in one hand. As the clerk staggered up from the floor, she smashed the jug over his head.

"Hurrah fer mountain doin's!" she shouted.

Hauling herself onto a table, she fired her shotgun into the air. The pellets struck an overhead gas lamp that exploded when it hit the floor, sending a rush of flames roaring towards the ceiling.

"Hurrah fer mountain doin's!" Zebulon shouted.

He yanked off a large gold nugget that hung from a string around the clerk's neck.

"For settlement," he said.

Then he picked up an ax handle and knocked over a shelf of air-tights and smashed a window as customers grabbed whatever goods were close to hand and started for the door.

Zebulon found Annie May slumped underneath the table, a bullet through her chest. As he gently gathered her into his arms, a barrel of kerosene exploded behind them, collapsing the ceiling, blowing out windows, killing two miners, and setting the building on fire.

Zebulon carried Annie May outside and laid her on the sagging wooden sidewalk. Around them, a line of men were hand-rushing buckets of water to pour on the flames.

Annie May's voice faded to a whisper. "Deer is deer... elk is elk and this mountain oyster is a gone coon.... I done you wrong a time or two, son, as you did me... but that's family." She raised herself up, trying to see him as her eyes clouded over. "Always figured I'd go out the old way. Straight up and on my own breath.... But we caused a commotion in this town, did we not, son?"

"So we did, Ma," he answered.

"Did I ever tell how Hatchet come to be with us?"

"You never did," he replied, even though she had told him endless times.

"Pa won him from a Mex at a rendezvous down on the Purgatory.... Everything was in the pot, everything the Mex had – his traps, horses, pelts, and even little Hatchet as a throw in. No more than a stump, he was. When Pa palmed the last card, he got caught, which bothered him enough to carve the Mex up for callin' him out. Pa took Hatchet back with him out of guilt, and maybe because he thought he could use another hand. He was always one for slaves, your Pa...."

Her voice stopped and he thought she was gone, until he heard her again.

"Are you with me, son?"

"I'm here, Ma."

"All right, then. Hatchet was a weird boy. Always tryin' to drown you in the river. And then you tried to do the same to him, just to get even.... When you find your Pa... tell him.... Hell, don't tell him nothin'. He never did a damn thing for us except bring misery. And now he's trotted off to the gold fields. The old cocksucker."

She looked up, her eyes pleading with his not to ever let her go, and then she died.

He sat holding her as the lines of water buckets were passed back and forth. When the fire was out, the sheriff and the owner of the trading post, along with several clerks, surrounded him with drawn pistols. One of the clerks carried a rope with a noose tied at the end.

As Zebulon was pulled to his feet, Hatchet Jack galloped through the crowd, pulling a saddled horse behind him.

Shots were fired, but before anyone could mount up to follow, Zebulon and Hatchet Jack had disappeared down the street.

Ten miles outside of town they parted company, Zebulon for old Mex, Hatchet Jack for California, where he figured to make peace with Elijah.

WHEN ZEBULON REACHED THE HIGH DESERT, HE HESITATED, then rode back to the mountains. Two days later he arrived at the cabin in the middle of the night. His Ma's deck of cards was still spread out on the table. He removed a card and pushed it back into the deck without looking to see if it was the queen of hearts. What's done is done, he thought, lighting up her clay pipe and sitting down at the table. And none of it was coming back. No more mountain doin's. All gone. Forever gone.

Not able to sleep in the house, he went outside and built a small fire. When the first light of dawn prowled like a hungry predator over the mountains, he picked up a burning stick and tossed it inside the door. Then he walked around the burning cabin, yelling to his Ma his last mountain goodbyes: "Waaaaaaaaagh…! Waaaaaaaaagh…! Waaaaaaaaaagh!"

When he reached the end of the valley, he turned for a last look. All that remained was a thin cloud of smoke drifting into the sun.

From then on, it was a fast ride across the high desert towards Mexico, with a pause in Alamogordo long enough to hold up the town bank – an act that he performed with such careless disregard for his own safety that he not only escaped without a scratch, but with half a saddlebag of gold coins. Continuing south by southeast, he heard distant gunshots and shifted his direction, narrowly avoiding a band of White Mountain Apaches trapped inside a basin by a platoon of black cavalry. The next day he crossed the Rio Grande, then rode east across Chihuahua towards the Gulf of Mexico and down to Vera Cruz, where no one asked or cared who he was or where he came from.

In Vera Cruz he rented a room in the best hotel, spending his money on the sultry passions of a one-armed saloon singer who played with his broken spirit like a seasoned cat before a kill. Never mind, he told himself; Miranda Serenade, for that was her billing, healed the cravings of his body if not the confusions of his heart. Within a week, he had moved into Miranda's room above the saloon; his only excursions were nightly visits downstairs, where he gambled compulsively and bought wall-to-wall drinks after each set of his lover's sentimental love songs.

Miranda was pleased with him, at least for openers, as he was handsome and profligate enough to ease her constant insecurities about money and advancing age. He bought her a black pearl necklace and an elegant horse and carriage and filled her head with fanciful plans. The most prominent being a mad scheme he had overheard on the waterfront about a company of men led by a General Walker, all of them skilled adventurers planning to conquer Nicaragua – a conquest, he assured her, that was bound to be successful. She would be with him every step of the way, he promised, his muse, his fiery goddess, even his minister or queen of culture if that was her inclination. They would inhabit a palace in León or Granada, with all the finery of European royalty. She would have her own saloon, maybe two, and enough servants to satisfy every whim. If they grew bored running the country, they could retire to Madrid or Bahia or the new city of San Francisco, where half the planet now seemed to be headed. Or all three. It didn't matter. The choice would be hers. Of course, neither of them believed a word, his plans having been conceived after an afternoon of compulsive love-making followed by generous dollops of laudanum. Miranda's designs were more practical: an upscale milliner's shop for aristocrat ladies or a music palace in the center of town. Business first. Baby second. Love, if not exactly an afterthought, a distant third.

When his money ran out after an all-night card game, he was unable to face Miranda's wrath. Looking down at her as she lay sleeping in the black silk nightgown he had bought her that very morning, he kissed her for the last time and shut the door softly behind him.

Twenty miles into Texas, he noticed a wanted poster nailed to the side of a feed store:

Zebulon Shook Wanted Dead or Alive for
Bank Robbing, Murder, Arson, and Horse Theft.

It wasn't his reputation or fear of the law that made him return to Vera Cruz. The pathetic truth was that he missed Miranda Serenade, a raw and vulnerable feeling that he had never experienced before.

~ ~ ~

Miranda greeted him at the door in the middle of a steamy, claustrophobic afternoon. She was wearing her black silk nightgown and pointing a pearl-handled pocket derringer straight at his aching heart.

"You want to know who you are, Zeb-u-lon? One more fucking *gringo cabrón* asshole with a used-up firecracker for a dick and no heart."

When he told her that he was prepared to give her what she wanted, within reason, she said she'd consider it when he put something real on the table. Like money. Never mind his rotten used-up heart. She had given up on that part of him.

When he didn't answer, she slammed the door in his face.

He sat on a park bench and thought it over. Except for his horse and army Colt revolver and enough cash to last a week, he possessed nothing of value. He could always ride back to the mountains and try to rescue the family business. He had been good at the fur trade and was widely known and respected. But he had celebrated a last *adios* to that way of life, and there was no returning to what was forever gone. There was always the outlaw trail. With his new credentials as a wanted man, he could ride up to Arizona, where there was a local war going on. Or he could sign up with any number of desperadoes. Or he could disappear into the Far West, make his way to the Oregon territory, or Alaska where no one would have heard of him. And then there was Miranda. He could beg her for another chance, although if she was foolish enough to take him back, he knew that she would end up braining him with a frying pan. Or worse. Not to mention what he might do to her, heart or no heart.

Across the park a mariachi band was serenading a lavish birthday party in honor of a local politician. Further away, two Texas mercenaries leaned against the trunk of a cottonwood tree, sharing a bottle of mescal. He had run into them in a saloon a few nights previously, bragging about their knowledge of explosives and firearms and how much their specialties were in demand from various well-heeled banditos and revolutionaries. The older man, who went by the alias of "Salty Smith," was rumored to have broken out of the hard-rock prison at Yuma, killing two guards in the process before he joined John Wesley Harden on his last furious rampage through Texas.

The mercenaries weren't pleased to see him, having heard there was a wanted poster on his head and that he was one of those mountain lunatics who brought more trouble to the table than he was worth. After he took a slug from their bottle of tequila, he asked if they could put him on to a job. "Anything but cleanin' up saloon slop or runnin' errands for Mexican floozies."

Salty nodded, barely hearing the question, his attention directed across the park. He raised his hand towards a waiter standing at the edge of the birthday celebration. From then on everything slowed down. The waiter lit a match, cupping it in his hands as if it were a precious flame, while another waiter cautiously lifted up a large wooden box. The two mercenaries stood up, dusting off their pants as their eyes shifted across the park and down the side streets. Slowly, with studied nonchalance, they walked out of the park as a bomb exploded behind them, blowing up the politician and several guests. The act was followed by a line of men appearing on a rooftop, firing down at the crowd as they screamed and scattered in every direction.

Zebulon ran down a winding street, then turned into an alley as a platoon of mounted police appeared around a corner. Reversing direction, he stumbled into a crowded street full of cafés and clothing stores. A few people had stopped in the middle of the street to listen to the shots, which sounded, in the distance, like firecrackers. He ran past them towards the waterfront. Suddenly the shots stopped. Birds chirped from tree branches. Three young boys kicked a rolled-up ball of rope against a mud wall. Near them a vendor stood by a cart, calling out selections of fresh fish and crabs. Forcing himself to slow down, he walked on until he reached the harbor. When a cannon boomed a few blocks away, followed by more rifle shots, he turned into the door of a palatial three-story hotel.

The spacious high-ceilinged lobby was empty except for a well-dressed couple engaged in booking a room. Neither seemed aware of what was going on in the rest of the city. Zebulon picked up a newspaper and sat down in an armchair. Pretending to read, he was unable to stop glancing at the woman standing at the front desk with her back to him. A red silk shawl was draped across her shoulders, and her thick spill of black hair was as luminous as polished ebony. It was Delilah, the woman from the bar in Panchito.

Outside the hotel, a man was singing a plaintive song about a woman's soul that no one, not even the lover he was singing to, was able to comprehend. The man's voice made it seem as if he was drowning or committing suicide inside someone else's dream.

Zebulon stood up with no idea where he was going or what he wanted to do. He was halfway out the door when Delilah called out to him.

"I thought you were dead."

Her eyes focused on the Colt holstered around his waist, then shifted to the fifteen-inch Green River bowie knife tied to his right thigh, then to his Mexican trousers with silver buttons down the sides, his black sombrero, and finally, the bright blue serape that matched the color of his startled eyes.

"You seem to have recovered," she said. "My congratulations."

As he took a step towards her, she crossed both hands in front of her breasts. *Help me,* her gesture implied. *And... whatever you do, stay away.*

As impulsively as she had called out, she turned away, leaving him staring at Ivan, her companion that he remembered from the card game in the saloon. He wore a white flat-brimmed felt hat tilted over one side of his face and the same black cape was draped over his shoulders. Walking back and forth across the lobby in yellow hand-tooled leather boots, he banged a silver-handled cane on the floor, his voice rising as he argued in Spanish over the availability of the hotel's honeymoon suite, which, he claimed, he had booked three weeks before. The clerk threw up his hands, shouting that there was no record. *Nada. Nada. Nada.* There never was and there never had been. The only room was on the second floor facing the street. It was their choice. Take it or leave it. He had nothing more to say.

Zebulon walked across the room as if pulled by an invisible rope. "Give them what they signed up for," he said to the clerk.

"Or deal with one *malo loco gringo. Comprende?*"

Grabbing the clerk by the collar, he lifted him over the counter and dropped him to the floor. Then he removed the Colt from his belt and pointed it at the clerk's forehead, pulling back the hammer.

The clerk handed over the keys and yelled for a porter to carry the guests' luggage to the presidential suite *muy pronto*.

Before the porter could rush over, Ivan handed the key to Delilah, who seemed, by her controlled passivity, to have been through this kind of situation before.

Without a word, she picked up two bulging leather suitcases and hauled them up the winding staircase, leaving a bag and a wooden cello case behind.

The man in the black cape bowed to Zebulon. "I see that you found a way to survive." He paused, extending his hand. "Count Ivan Baranofsky. I would be honored if you would join me for a libation."

Zebulon's eyes focused on the woman's slender ankles and long muscular legs as they disappeared slowly up the stairs.

"I'll handle the bags," he offered.

"No need," the Count replied. "Delilah is very capable."

After a brief hesitation, Zebulon picked up the bag and cello case and went up the stairs two at a time.

He tried every door on the floor until he found her suite. She was standing at the window looking out at the harbor.

"Are you following me?" she asked, not turning around. "Or are you under the impression that I am following you?"

Her bare shoulders and the high sloping curve of her neck reminded him of a stalking crane.

"I follow what I hunt for," he answered.

"Then you consider me an animal?"

"I'm helping out."

"That's not all you're doing." She held him inside her gaze, then walked over to the bed where she untied the flaps of a hand-stitched leather suitcase.

"Would it amuse you to know that I'm an expert at capturing wild animals?" She removed a rattle from the suitcase and shook it back and forth, her eyes rolling as she circled around him, uttering a throbbing chant that seemed to be coming from the middle of her chest.

"I don't like being circled," he warned. "When I'm trapped I feel –"

"I know," she said. "You're dangerous."

She laughed and shook the rattle in his face, then threw it on the bed.

"If you don't return to the lobby, Ivan will come up and shoot you. He's famous for that."

"I can handle Ivan," he said.

"Are you sure?" Her question seemed to be directed as much to herself as to him.

When he couldn't come up with an answer, he shrugged and left the room.

~ ~ ~

Count Baranofsky was waiting for him in the lobby. Taking Zebulon by the arm, he led him into the hotel's cantina and ordered a round of whiskey at the bar. When the drinks arrived, the Count raised his glass, toasting Mexico, the United States, the brand new State of California, and finally Russia – but not the Czar, who, he proudly pointed out, had placed a price on his head. Then he asked if Zebulon was residing in Vera Cruz.

"Passing through," Zebulon replied.

"And so are we," the Count said. "Thank god our ship has arrived. We expected it six weeks ago."

Zebulon reached for a plate of fried squid and cheese enchiladas. "The woman you're with –"

"She's my attendant," Ivan said. "Or consort, depending on

circumstance and your cultural point of view. We were traveling overland to California, but once in Denver and faced with the prospect of a harsh winter, we decided to take a stagecoach to Mexico and sail around South America to California. We were looking forward to a pause in Vera Cruz but, I admit, not one this long."

"How's your pause been treatin' you?" Zebulon asked.

"Abominably. This is our third hotel. Each one more frustrating than the last. Sullen service. Worse food. Mosquitoes. Flies. Bed bugs. But despite the inconveniences, the city is not without its sultry charms; although, as we have learned only too well, it's a city given to unexpected vapors and violence."

The Count sighed, grateful for the opportunity of talking to a stranger that he would never see again. In pedantic detail, he described their voyage from Venice to New York, including the side streets and mercenary shops of Algiers, the restaurants of Málaga and Lisbon, and finally, the physical hardships of traveling overland to Denver – a journey that saw them nearly drowned crossing the Mississippi, attacked by Comanches, and almost killed in New Mexico in a barroom brawl.

The Count hesitated, not sure how much he should reveal. "An occasion, I might add, that you seemed willing to provoke."

"I don't recall what went down," Zebulon said. "I was trapped inside a nest of snakes."

"When you sat down at the table, obviously you were asking for trouble. Of course, I was well lubricated. And then we rode out on the stagecoach, so we never did find out what happened."

"You call her Delilah?" Zebulon asked.

"A biblical name; her actual name is too difficult to pronounce, some sort of East African jibber jabber. I met her in Paris, where she had the misfortune to be handmaiden to a French officer. She's part French, the rest Abyssinian, with a dollop of Babylonian and Egyptian and god knows what else. I would be lost without her. Fortunately I was able to free her owner from certain financial difficulties."

"You mean you bought her."

The Count laughed, delighted to be face to face with an authentic man of the West who was not afraid to say what was on his mind. "It wasn't commerce that dictated my involvement. More an impulsive demand of the heart."

Delilah glided towards them, waiting patiently until Zebulon pulled back her chair, a courtesy that he had never performed before, much less observed.

Without looking at the menu, the Count ordered a variety of hors d'oeuvres, followed by plates of burritos and chicken mole.

The Count's probing questions about the rituals and hardships of life in the mountains made Zebulon realize that he was being given an opportunity to sing for his supper, if not a way out of town, and he enthusiastically launched into a description of his adventures in California – all of which he invented, not having been there. Absorbed, they listened with fascinated attention as he created and embellished his own history. In florid, often long-winded detail, he described Indian raids and encounters with grizzlies; rabid wolverines and drunken mountain rendezvous, where the lies of lunatic trappers became truth, and the truth became lies; spring celebrations of their winter hauls that often lasted for a month or more, until everyone was talked out or dead or broke.

"Well now," he continued as they started in on plates of sugared apples wrapped in corn fritters. "Let me tell you, this coon's tasted his share of Californie and the Far West. Yessir. Been shot on the Oregonian Trail, scalped and left for dead in the high Sierras, froze my belly in more than one tailrace ditch, trapped the Gila and the Green, near drowned on the Columbia, raised more hair'n any coon you'll ever meet, was a barkeep in Hangtown, keel boatman on the Sacramenty, road agent, pit boss, company buster, buffalo skinner, teamster, logger, rail spiker; I done it all and then some. Been all the way to Alasky and the putrified forest, heard the opry in San Fran, scouted for renegade red niggers all the way to old Mex and on south to free Nicaragua with General Walker, parlayed my share of Chinee, Irish, and German bohunks, to name a few."

They stared at him, stunned by this compulsive torrent of strange, exotic words, hardly any of which they understood.

"But surely," the Count asked, "given the range of your extraordinary adventures, you must have searched for gold?"

"Gold, you say?" Zebulon wiped his face with the back of his hand and downed two quick shots, then one more. "Gold? This coon has picked more *oro* and Sonoma Lightning than you can shake a stick at. Made and lost more than one fortune. Even placed gold nuggets on the dead eyes of a Mex girl gut-shot in Sonora fer givin' a poke to the wrong customer at the wrong time. Gold was my music, my fiddle and my piana, all seranadin' the clink of pick-axes and the grind of shovels, washin' pans, and rockers – all shakin' for pay dirt. This coon gambled away more gold in three days than most pilgrims make in a lifetime. Yessir. I been on the Feather and South Fork and down to the Agua Fría, went bust on the Mariposa, struck pay dirt on Sullivan's Creek, bought me a saloon and lost it the next week in Placerville, struck a fat vein north of Virginia City and was robbed down to my boots by my partner; took me a year before I nailed his scalp to the church door in Sutterville. Spent every haul faster'n I made it. Call it what you want: greasin' the trail for salvation, or any damn thing. Now you take Tucker's Bend or Hangtown or any one of them half-assed shanty towns of blue-belly pilgrims not knowin' a pick or a shovel from a wagon wheel – all of 'em are bottomed out and gone back to where they come from. Good riddance, I say."

He looked at Delilah. "If you dream of gold, chances are

you'll wake up and all that's left will be the dream. And then not even that."

She nodded, as if she knew all about dreams.

Gaslights were turned on as the dining room began to fill up with customers, all of them stunned and excited from the day's events. On the street there was a sudden volley of shots that sounded like a firing squad. A dog barked and a lonely drunk sang a love song about a two-timing lover. Then silence.

Delilah pointed to the nugget hanging around Zebulon's neck, the same one he had ripped off a clerk's neck in Broken Elbow.

"Is that from California?"

"I picked if off the ground," he replied. "Go ahead. Take it. There are plenty more where that came from."

When he handed her the nugget, she hesitated, then gave it back.

"I prefer to gather my own," she said.

"Delilah, for god's sake," the Count said. "The man gave it to you from his heart. It's bad form not to accept such a spontaneous gift."

"Bad luck, too," Zebulon added.

Modestly, she bent her head, allowing him to slip the nugget around her neck.

"Then you're headed for California?" the Count asked.

"One way or the other," he said. "As soon as I gopher up enough chink for a passage. It ain't that easy for a *gringo* to find wages down here."

"Then you're not a guest at the hotel?" the Count asked.

Suddenly Zebulon wanted to get shut of this Count and his strange consort, or whoever she was. He was singing for his supper and waiting for a bone to be thrown his way, but hustling dumb foreigners wasn't a trick he favored, even though he had managed it more times than he cared to admit.

"Where on earth have you been?" asked a strident English

voice behind him. "I've been searching everywhere for you."

A tall emaciated man wearing a bright red serape, yellow sombrero, and brand new polished turquoise belt buckle stumbled towards them, accompanied by a local whore who was having trouble walking on one shoe.

"Don't you know there's a bloody revolution on?" the man asked. "Apparently some local politician was blown up in a park. Never mind! The ship is sailing on the tide, *compadres*! *Muy pronto*!

Zebulon knew the whore; she was an experienced and obliging professional that he had spent a few nights with before he had tied in with Miranda.

"Who's the dumb *gringo*, Lupita?" he asked in Spanish.

She shook her head, forcing a smile as she took off her shoe. "*Muy loco hombre*. Many bad habits. You don't want to know. As a favor to me, for all that I have given to you from my heart to yours, I am asking that you kill him. Or at least get him to pay what he owes me."

"What exactly is she saying?" the Englishman asked.

"That she can't live without you and that if you try to leave her she'll shoot you and then herself."

Lupita pulled on the Englishman's sleeve, stroked his cheek, and held out her hand until he reached into his pocket and handed her seven silver dollars. The transaction completed, she turned her tongue slowly inside Zebulon's ear, then hobbled back to the street.

As Zebulon started for the door, the Count took him by the arm. "I have a proposal that will relieve your financial dilemma."

Zebulon looked at Delilah, who was staring back at him, her eyes narrowing, as if she had been seized by a premonition.

"If you guide us to the gold fields," the Count went on, "I'm prepared to pay your passage to San Francisco. First we will travel to Sutter's Fort to meet Captain John Sutter, whose courage I have long admired. I have had discussions with his wife in Switzerland about possible business ventures – ranches, commerce, that sort of thing. Then, after our visit with Sutter, we will press on to the gold fields. I assume you've heard of Sutter?"

"Heard of Sutter?" Zebulon said. "Everyone's heard of Captain John Sutter. When they found gold on his land, it bumped off the whole damn stampede."

Delilah turned to Ivan. "Are you sure about this offer, Ivan? You know what happens when you act impulsively."

"Absolutely, I'm sure," the Count said, his voice rising. "We need an experienced man to help with supplies and transportation, someone who will protect us from dangers as they arise. A man like…."

"Zebulon Shook," Zebulon heard himself say, "*A su ordonez.* At your service. I'll take steady wages and a thirty-seventy split on whatever gold comes your way."

The Count hesitated, looking at Delilah as she considered the offer, then shook her head.

"Twenty-eighty," the Count said.

"Done," Zebulon replied.

The Count shook his hand. "The ship is *The Rhinelander.* German. Well appointed. You can't miss her: she's a three-masted merchant with a bare-breasted woman mounted on the bow and a row of three-headed snakes around her neck. A goddess favored by mariners. Or so they say. Our Captain informed me that she represents the beautiful woman in Greek myth that calms the cruel sea."

"Here, here," the Englishman said. "Although with a beautiful woman, one can't be too careful. Wouldn't you say? In any case, we welcome you aboard, Mister Shook."

From an adjoining room, Zebulon heard the *click*, *click* of billiard balls. Stepping around Delilah, he walked across the lobby and through the restaurant to a lounge hosting a billiard table.

He maneuvered the cue ball around the table just to prove that he still could. Then he put down the cue stick and, without a look at his new patrons, made his way out to the harbor.

THE RHINELANDER SAILED SOUTH OVER TURBULENT SEAS, her hatches loaded with supplies for the California gold fields. Zebulon, confined to his cabin with seasickness, was only dimly aware when the wind suddenly shifted to the west at gale force, tearing the rudder loose with a raw screech and threatening to punch a hole in the transom. After the ship's carpenter cut the steering lines the ship drifted for two days, finally ending up off the west coast of Florida.

When Zebulon finally appeared on the deck, the sea was a flat blue sheet without a ripple and the carpenter was fixing the rudder. Most of the passengers were grouped by the starboard rail, staring at a spit of land lined with tall undulating dunes shimmering beneath heat waves, their valleys dotted with mangrove and scrubby pine.

A voice spoke behind him: "A rotten ailment, *mal de mer*. Makes one loathe the sea. Much better for the world to be flat. Easier to sail off the edge and be done with it, wouldn't you say?"

The Englishman from the hotel in Vera Cruz extended a limp hand. "Archibald Cox. I don't believe we've been formally introduced."

Zebulon barely nodded, his attention fixed on Delilah, who was standing with the Count near the stern railing. She was wearing a white muslin dress that reached to her bare feet and a black scarf tied loosely over her hair.

"An odd duck, the Russian," Cox went on. "Used to be a military attaché at the London embassy. A bit much the way he carries on with that Egyptian whore, or whoever she's pretending to be these days."

He pointed to the poop deck where a portly figure in a cocked hat and black high-necked uniform was looking down on the crew as they prepared to lower a lifeboat. "Perverse old bastard, our captain. Always insisting on exercise and philosophy. Now he's ordering us ashore for a walk about."

They joined the Count and Delilah in the lifeboat, along with the first mate, three sailors, and the rest of the passengers: two middle-aged German merchants specializing in picks and shovels, a Polish clothing merchant, a Finnish soldier wanted in three European countries for forgery and arms dealing, and finally, a New York journalist hired to write a series of articles about the gold rush. All of them were curious about Zebulon, who, they had learned from the Count, was not only a legendary mountain man, but a veteran army scout, Indian fighter, and explorer.

The Count was the first to wade ashore. Kneeling on the ground in the imperial manner of a *conquistador* with Delilah holding an umbrella over his head, he intoned a solemn prayer.

He was interrupted by Zebulon, who had noticed three Indians standing on top of a dune, along with a towering Negro in cut-off sailor pants and a straw hat.

"We got company," Zebulon said. "Look up slow and easy and keep your irons lowered."

The Indians continued to stare down at them, their sallow faces pockmarked from typhus and parasites. All three, as well as the Negro, carried feathered lances and wore calico cotton shirts and beaded belts over their leggings and breechcloths.

When Zebulon raised a hand in greeting, they slowly walked

down the dune. Using sign language, he asked where they came from. After one pointed to the north, he questioned them in Kiowa, then tried a few words in Arapahoe and Sioux, none of which they understood.

Finally Delilah stepped forward and addressed the Negro in an African tongue. When there was no response, she tried another dialect, then two more until the Negro suddenly laughed and clapped his hands, telling her along with dignified pauses that even though the Seminoles helped him escape from Portuguese slavers when their ship ran aground, they had treated him as if he belonged to an inferior race, refusing to recognize him as a man of wisdom, especially when it came to war and agriculture. When he first saw her from the top of the dune, he was immediately aware that she represented an ancient and royal lineage and despite the fact that she was surrounded by obviously incompetent white men, he was sure that her journey, whatever its secret intentions, was not without courage and honor. He ended his speech by saying that he would be pleased to join her on the ship.

"He's an African chief," Delilah explained to the others. "Because the Seminoles are an ignorant people who don't treat him with the respect that he deserves, he wants to return to the ship with us."

"Absolutely not," the Count said.

The crew and the rest of the passengers, who had all become increasingly anxious, insisted that the ship was fully booked and that the Captain would never accept another passenger, particularly a black man without means, unless, of course, he would agree to become a slave.

Delilah advised the Negro that unfortunately all of the ship's passengers were obsessed with greed and conquest. Not only that, but she had been having ominous premonitions about the man she was traveling with – a man who, she confessed, had once owned her, but who now, even though he had finally released her from bondage, had become increasingly cruel and unhinged.

The Negro pulled himself up to his full height, his sad blazing eyes staring into hers. Perhaps she was right. If she was foolish enough to become involved with such confusion and venal behavior, he would be better off where he was.

He walked away, then paused and slowly turned back, asking if he could buy or trade for her. He had plenty of beads and skins to bargain with, as well as all the fruit the ship would need. He looked over at Zebulon. Not only that, but it was clear that she should run away as soon as possible, as one of the men she was traveling with was possessed by a very strange spirit, unlike any he had ever witnessed.

Delilah replied that having been given her freedom, she was no longer for sale and that if she ran away it would be on her own terms, no one else's.

The Negro nodded, not believing a word. Removing a handful of cowry shells from a small bag hanging from a string around his neck, he tossed them high in the air, then knelt to study the patterns they formed on the sand.

She was owned, he told her. But not by a man. She was owned by a curse.

Impatiently, the Count took her arm. "Are you coming, or do you prefer the company of a savage?"

When she hesitated he stomped after the others, all of whom – except for Zebulon, who had remained behind – were already halfway to the lifeboat.

"Would you consider abandoning the ship?" she asked, only half-joking.

"Not hardly," Zebulon replied. "Not when there's gold to be found."

The Negro, who had been watching their exchange, nodded abruptly to Delilah, then walked back over the dune with the Seminoles.

~ ~ ~

Zebulon and Delilah were in the lifeboat and halfway back to *The Rhinelander* when the Negro reappeared on top of the dune.

Bending a long bow, he shot an arrow in a high arc towards them, a flight that missed the lifeboat by less than a foot.

ZEBULON LAY ON HIS BUNK LISTENING TO THE SHOUTS OF
men climbing into the rigging. Hours later, the ship under
full sail, he heard sounds coming from the next cabin; they were
sonorous and melancholy chords from an instrument he had
never heard before. As he listened, he remembered the shape
of Delilah's ankles and the slow sway of her broad hips as she
stepped out of the lifeboat.

That night at dinner she was sitting next to the Count at the
end of a rectangular oak table supported at each corner by ropes
hanging from the ceiling. The Captain sat in the middle of the
table, expounding on his favorite topic: the world's obsession
with gold at the expense of freedom and happiness.

"Gold is a curse," the Captain pronounced, "a dangerous
mistress seducing everything in her path. I am now on my third
voyage to California. Going there is always hope fueled by
addiction and greed. Returning, all is loss and desolation."

Most of the passengers were no longer listening, having
heard this speech all the way across the Atlantic and into the
Caribbean.

The Captain shifted his focus to Zebulon, who represented,
among other curiosities, a new ear. "I understand that you have
been in California, Mister Shook. I'm curious why you have
chosen to return?"

"I guess you might say that my bucket sprang a leak."

"And now you are returning to fill your bucket?"

Zebulon nodded, his eyes gazing through a porthole at flakes of green phosphorous dancing across a black sheen of water.

"Gold is a blessing that provides the fuel that creates transportation and business," offered Artemis Stebbins, the New York journalist. "There's never been anything remotely like it in the entire history of the world. Thank god that this country is on a gold standard!"

"A blessing that will produce its share of casualties," the Captain added.

"The price we must pay," said Cox.

"I am happy to pay," the Finn said. "I want to be rich."

"If we don't risk, we die," added the Polish merchant.

"My brother and me, we have tried once before, and now we try again," said Heinrich, the oldest of the German merchants. "Otherwise what? Sell fancy shoes and women underwears?"

"There are those who would agree with you," the Captain observed: "businessmen, preachers, doctors, soldiers, criminals. Good men and bad, all running from their past. To what end? To die of cholera or be scalped or shot or driven mad with no one to say prayers over their unmarked graves. Why? I will tell you why: greed. Nothing else."

He looked around the table. "I sleep at night because I have chosen this ship to be my prison. Because of that choice, I am free."

"You are stupid," Heinrich said. "We are here. Where else are we? We go on. No one knows what will happen."

"Nothing ever moves in a straight line," the Count said, "even if man must be convinced that it does. Otherwise, he has no hope."

"Hope?" The Captain lit a cigar, pleased, finally, to be engaged in a stimulating conversation. "Man is not a shark, always moving forward. He goes backward. He holds his ground. By changing directions he avoids boredom, which, I submit, is the biggest curse of all."

"Curse?" the Pole asked. "What curse? I don't know any curse."

Zebulon felt Delilah's hand on his knee. When he reached down, his hand closed over a slab of butter.

"Always we search for new gods," Hans said.

"Otherwise we are donkeys," Heinrich replied.

"Better new gods than old demons, or the hounds of hell," added the Pole.

"A man needs a target," Cox insisted. "Otherwise he faces chaos."

"Chaos," the Count reached for Delilah's hand, "the mother of creation."

The Count exchanged his plate for Delilah's, which had remained untouched. "Why else would we suffer the stagnation and boredom of a sea voyage?"

"When I was young I sleep on a dirt floor," the Finn said. "I am cold and lonely. Cossacks kill my mother and father. When I find gold I am buying a woman and making a big house. I am having walls inside walls and never open the door."

"And you, Mister Shook?" the journalist asked. "What do you think?"

"A man traps what he can and heads for high ground," Zebulon replied. "If he's lucky, he gets to do it again."

The Captain nodded. "In my world, when a sailor tacks before the wind in the middle of a storm, he makes a deal with nature. Either that, or he finds himself at the bottom of the sea." He looked over at Delilah. "My dear Lady, as the only woman among us, I am curious to know your opinion."

"I have no opinion," Delilah said. "I surrender to what is given."

Cox lifted his wineglass. "A toast to a wise woman."

The Count struck his fork against his glass. "A song! A song from Delilah!"

"Here! Here! Here!" the others chanted.

She shook her head, her eyes pleading with the Count.

"If not a song, at least a poem," the Count insisted.

"I have no poems," she said, looking down at her plate, "and I have no songs." Then she stood up and, not looking at anyone, left the cabin.

The rest of the meal was spent in distracted chatter: "Will there be rain –"; "So humid –"; "When do we reach the equator –"; "Do the Germans or the Belgians make the best potato pancakes –"; "I detest French opera. So inferior to the Italians –"; "You can't improve on the Greeks when it comes to fish –"; "But the French… their bouillabaisse… impeccable –"

No one except the Count paid any attention when Zebulon left the table.

~ ~ ~

Zebulon was standing on the stern deck when the Count appeared, offering him a cigar. "Mexican, I'm sorry to say. Not up to Cuban standards."

"I never refuse a smoke," Zebulon replied, accepting the cigar.

"Such a melancholy overture," the Count remarked. "So different from the false promise of dawn. But then endings are usually more complex than beginnings, are they not…?"

He pointed towards the sun sinking over the horizon. "Look! There she goes. Like a wilted flower."

"Or a squashed tomato," Zebulon added.

"Or an Easter bonnet," the Count replied, surprised at Zebulon's use of metaphor.

"A thumb run over by a wagon wheel," Zebulon continued.

"A red sombrero," the Count replied.

"A smashed sweet potato."

"A splash of blood."

"So we agree," the Count said. "Everything, including nature, is impermanent, and you and I and everyone else are not what we appear to be."

"I wouldn't know about that," Zebulon said.

The Count pointed to a distant rainspout. "The banners of a retreating army?"

"Where is she?" Zebulon asked.

The Count shrugged, his eyes on the rainspout as it disappeared into darkness. "Waiting for me, I would assume. If not that, then perhaps she's jumped overboard. Leaving us with what, exactly? The remains of a great battle?"

Saluting Zebulon, he turned and went below.

~ ~ ~

That night Zebulon was woken by a sudden rain squall. *Come closer*, the wind and rain howled as the ship struggled over the waves, then shuddered and groaned into the troughs below; *come closer to a realm where life and death are the same.*

THE NEXT MORNING, AS ZEBULON PROWLED THE DECK hoping for a sighting of Delilah he was confronted by Stebbins, who had become convinced that a story about the exploits of the legendary mountain man would be the perfect opener for his series of articles about life in the Far West.

When he asked Zebulon for an interview, Zebulon hesitated, his eyes on the Count and Delilah as they appeared arm in arm on the other side of the deck, Delilah wearing a flowered dress and straw hat, the Count in yellow linen pants and a white shirt.

"It would be an honor," Stebbins insisted. "Particularly as you represent a disappearing breed of men who have gone where few ever have: men who have settled the frontier, who have fought and lived with Indians and experienced unimaginable hardships. My readers will be fascinated and thrilled to read about your adventures. And I'm the one to write about them. In fact, I'm the only one."

Stebbins produced a flask of brandy and handed it to Zebulon, who drained it before he spoke.

"I was raised by my Ma and Pa a thousand miles from any settlement. They learned me about red niggers and how to trap and build a fire in a blizzard. Went my own way and made do. I crossed Pike's Peak barefoot; lived with the Sioux and the Hopi; hunted buffler in the Black Hills; scouted for the army; lived with the Shoshonis, who called me Man Trapped Between the Worlds; sliced off more than one man's top knot; stole horses from the Comanche and Arapahoe; trapped with Jake Spoon, him that declared war on the Crow Nation; picked nuggets off the ground in Californie as big as your fist; rustled steers from Colorady to Texas; rode the outlaw trail and was proud of it."

He paused, looking at the Count and Delilah as they strolled towards them. When the Count said something, pointing towards him, Delilah laughed and turned the other way, only to have the Count draw her back again.

"I advise you to keep your secrets to yourself," the Count said to Zebulon as they approached. "Or you'll find your name on a wanted poster, or, even worse, the front page of a New York tabloid."

"I'll give you ten-to-one odds he's not a Count or even a Russian," Stebbins said as the Count and Delilah continued their promenade. "He's nothing but a flim-flam man. Take my word. I know men like him."

Before Delilah followed the Count below, she glanced once more towards Zebulon. *Come closer*, her eyes said once again, *and no matter what you do, stay away.*

Zebulon stared at a half-moon that had appeared over the horizon. Like a broken egg, he thought. Or a whore's earring.

AS THEY APPROACHED THE EQUATOR, THE SHIP ENTERED that inversion of sea and sky known as the doldrums, an oppressive zone of entropy inhibiting all movement and sense of time. The smell of rotten food permeated the ship. Sails drooped and clouds hung over the horizon like unwashed laundry. Not a dolphin or whale or even bird could be seen. In the suffocating heat, words felt as heavy as bricks and passengers and crew moved about the deck as if under water. When an elderly sailor lay on his back, staring mutely at the drooping sails, no one had the energy to come to his aid. In a rare gesture of compassion, Captain Dorfheimer allowed a dozen skeletal slaves to be led up from the lower depths of a cargo hold, where they had been chained to a bulkhead. Like uncorked ghosts they dropped on the deck, showing no emotion even when two of their companions, dead from malnutrition and the stifling heat, were unceremoniously tossed overboard. Until then, no one except the crew had known of their existence.

At night the passengers slept on deck, except for Zebulon and the Count and Delilah, who remained below.

Zebulon lay awake listening to the shifting tones of their muted conversations in an unknown tongue, words that were sometimes punctuated by shouts, followed by sighs and Delilah's exhausted sobs. When they were silent he imagined them making love. Once, just to make his presence known, he tried blasting a hole through the wall with his Colt, but when he pulled the trigger the chamber was empty.

On the seventh night of the doldrums, Delilah appeared in the cabin's hatchway, looking down on him as he slept. A bloody slash ran the length of her cheek and one breast had fallen out of her cotton shift. It was only when he felt her thigh next to his that he realized he wasn't dreaming.

They lay next to each other without moving, listening to the cello repeat the same monotonous scales over and over.

When the scales suddenly stopped, she placed his hand on her breast, whispering into his ear, "If I'm not there, and you're not here, then where are we?"

When the scales started up again, she walked out of the cabin.

~ ~ ~

That night at dinner the Captain observed that in all his many years at sea he had never encountered such a strange and difficult passage. He cautioned the passengers to keep within themselves, not to stare at the horizon, and to sleep as much as possible. From now on, water would be severely rationed and there would be one meal a day. As a reward for their endurance and patience, they would have an extraordinary celebration when they finally crossed the equator, quite different from the usual initiations imposed on those who had never crossed the line before.

When the Count began to laugh hysterically, Delilah helped him to his feet and led him below.

The rest of the meal continued in silence, as if any random remark might unleash the same demonic forces.

~ ~ ~

Days stretched into weeks. The boundary between sea and sky dissolved into a greasy smudge. The hours no longer clanged from the poop deck and the smell of unwashed bodies and laundry hung over the ship like a premonition of plague. The crew barely performed the most minimal tasks and finally, not even those.

Except for an occasional appearance on the bridge, wearing Chinese slippers and baggy French underwear, Captain Dorfheimer remained in his cabin, struggling over a letter to his wife that compared his situation to an accelerating whirlpool of tedium, a condition that made him feel as if he was descending into a black hole. He no longer referred to his charts, and at the close of each day the logbook was marked with the same comment: No wind.

Passengers slumped on the deck as if stranded inside a waiting room. The German merchants staked out a place on the stern, playing a game of chess, sometimes taking an entire afternoon to move one piece. The Pole walked back and forth, slapping his forehead, singing and muttering to himself. Neither German noticed when he picked up a knight from the board and dropped it overboard. The Finn talked to the bare-breasted goddess on the ship's prow, confessing his marital sins as well as his secret sexual fantasies. Cox read the opening page of *The Decline and Fall of the Roman Empire* over and over. Zebulon lay on his back, staring at the empty, relentless sky. Once Delilah's ankles drifted past and he heard her say to the Finn: "Have... you... ever... been... to... Iceland...?" And always there was Stebbins, whose imagination he continued to fill with accounts of Indian wars, Texas shoot-outs, and gun running in Mexico. Or maybe it wasn't Stebbins but the lethargic drift of his own mind-stream.

Despite the brutal heat he continued to sleep in his cabin, listening to Delilah and the Count. When they were silent he wondered if they had died, until one night, just to find out, he opened the door to their cabin. The Count was sitting on the bunk, Delilah mounted on top of him, her legs wrapped around his waist.

"Abandon all hope all ye who enter here," the Count said, quoting Dante as Zebulon backed out the door.

~ ~ ~

Another week passed with no hint of wind. Aching lungs gasped for air, bodies remained unwashed, faces were swollen and blistered, stomachs cramped with diarrhea or constipation.

On the twenty-third day of the doldrums, the Polish merchant appeared on the stern deck, wearing a blue suit and tie and carrying a wooden suitcase. Counting out loud he took twenty-three steps to the ship's railing, then twenty-three steps back, then twenty-three forward again. No one noticed when he swung his legs over the railing.

"Ladies and gentlemen," he announced in a loud, determined voice, "kings and queens, sailors and sea creatures, slaves and masters. This man no longer knows if he is dead or alive. Perhaps he is not even Polish. Perhaps this life doesn't exist or has never existed. Perhaps this is not a ship but a floating coffin. Perhaps we are dreaming and will wake up to find that everything is the same."

When he jumped overboard, there wasn't enough time or energy to lower a lifeboat. Soon all that remained of him was his wooden suitcase, which they watched all that day and into the evening, float slowly towards the horizon like a miniature casket.

The following morning, the Captain's eulogy was brief. "We are guests on this earth. We come and we go. No one knows when or how his time will come. We can only have faith and abide."

He nodded to the Count, who was seated next to him, his

cello poised between his knees. With a dramatic flourish the Count launched into a Bach suite, only to have two strings crack out like pistol shots.

As if a curse had been lifted, a faint breeze suddenly shivered across the water. Overwhelmed by this sign of grace, passengers and crew turned their swollen faces towards the breeze. The Finn shouted, pointing to a frigate bird hovering off the starboard bow. Cox sank to his knees. The two Germans raised their hands over their heads, reaching for handfuls of wind. Zebulon shook the Finn's hand. The crew hugged and slapped each other on their backs, then scurried aloft. Sails snapped and billowed and the ship began to move, slowly at first and then at a brisk five knots.

They crossed the equator under full sail. The Captain, true to his word, ordered a grand celebration, even providing a generous selection from his private stock of Chilean wine, Mexican mescal, and Spanish rum.

That night the crew appeared on deck in white jackets and stand-up collars. The passengers wore their finest European and New York clothes. The Count was resplendent in a combination Russian-English military uniform of red and black striping, Delilah elegant in a high-busted Parisian evening dress and white bonnet. Zebulon, accompanied by cheers, appeared in a leather overcoat that he had borrowed from the Finn, topping it off with an improvised hat made from sail cloth and a piece of the Captain's French underwear.

The Captain fired three pistol shots.

The passengers, except for Cox, who had crossed the equator before, were ceremoniously dunked into a large tub of salt water. After their bodies were smeared with red and yellow dye, they were made to crawl through a gauntlet where the crew spanked them with paddles. After a long, incomprehensible speech praising Neptune and local maritime deities, the Captain announced that Zebulon would be given a special sacrificial role, a decision greeted with wild cheers and foot-stomping approval.

After Zebulon's head was shaved, a blue circle was painted around his face, followed by two red lines across his forehead and down his cheeks.

When the Captain asked him to dance, Zebulon shuffled around the deck, crying out a vision prayer with two sailors prancing behind him, one playing an accordion, the other pounding an African drum:

> *Hee-ay-hay-ee… Hee-ay-hay-ee!*
> *The old people are sending me their voice.*
> *From far away where the sun goes down,*
> *My Mama the Earth sends her voice to me.*
>
> *Standing where the sun goes down.*
> *The old people are talking to me.*
> *My Mama the earth is calling me.*
> *The winged eagle where the Giant lives,*
> *Sends his voice to me. He's callin' me.*
>
> *All the old mountain spirits:*
> *They're all callin' on me!*
> *Hee-ay-hay-ee… Hee-ay-hay-ee-ee!*

He stopped in front of Delilah. "You are the spirit who lives where the sun goes down, who takes care of all the waters in all the lands. Tell me if that ain't true."

"If you wish it to be so, then it will be," she replied.

Taking a cigar from the Captain, she blew smoke over his face and head. Then she gave the cigar to Zebulon, who repeated the act on the Count and then on the rest of the passengers:

"Listen here, Wakan Tanka, Great Spirit!" he cried out, walking back and forth. "Listen to this man askin' to purify himself. Because of you the wind has come again and our journey goes forward. Now we're on the move! It's no flatlander or greenhorn that's callin' out to you. It's an old mountain wolf askin' for enough power and light to shake us all loose from where we've been stuck between the worlds. Is that too much to ask? Any way you look at it, it's a job that only you, the Creator, can handle; after all, Wakan Tanka, you're the one who gives the birds and fish the power to fly and swim…. Listen to this man, Wakan Tanka! Give us a sign. Let us know we ain't lost: *Hecheto welo!*"

Drums pounded and horns blared as the Captain, along with the crew and passengers, wept and sang and shouted their thanks through the night.

~ ~ ~

When Zebulon woke at dawn the passengers were still passed out on deck, all except for the Count and Delilah, who were standing by the ship's rail.

Suddenly the Count pulled Delilah's hair, jerking her head back.

"Foolish woman," the Count said. "After all that we've been through, you still cling to hope."

When Delilah slapped him across the cheek, he forced her to her knees.

"Confess your failures," he ordered her.

He pushed her chin to the deck. "Let me remind you: Failure to amuse, failure to polish my boots, failure to listen."

Her eyes found Zebulon, who was on his knees, staring back at her.

"Failure to refrain from ignorant betrayals," the Count continued. "Do you want more? I have several in reserve."

"No more," she said softly.

She pushed the Count with such force that he fell to the deck.

As Zebulon stood up and walked towards her, the Count held one of her ankles, then struggled to his feet and wildly tried to embrace her, kissing her neck and breast as they both cried and yelled at each other in Russian. When she broke away, he tried to reach out for her, but she stumbled and fell backward over the railing.

It was only when Zebulon had jumped in after her that he remembered he couldn't swim.

He sank below the water with closed eyes, his lungs bursting, as if his descent – a slow drop towards what he imagined to be a giant open mouth – was controlled by an unseen force. Or had he already been swallowed and was now being digested? The reality of surrendering to a black crush of water brought a certain relief: that he was finally facing what he most feared. It was a fear that he had never confronted, one that had been inside him ever since he had been a small boy, when Hatchet Jack had tried to drown him in the stream in front of the cabin as a way of making himself known to his new adopted family.

He was brought face to face with his own death, and suddenly life and death weren't the same. They were different and he had a choice, only it was too late.

As he began to lose consciousness from water filling his lungs, an arm underneath his chin pulled him upward towards the light.

"Lie still," Delilah instructed, holding his head above water.

But he felt only panic. He shoved her off. The sky was too empty and far away, with no beginning and no end.

As he sank down again she reached out for him but he pushed down on her head, trying to hoist himself up – an act which made them sink even faster, their arms and legs entwined, until she yanked his head towards her, smiling at him even as they were drowning. Somehow the maniacal gesture released his panic and he went limp in her arms, allowing her to guide him to the surface.

Treading water with one hand, she held him underneath his chin, comforting him like a frightened child. "I'm holding you.

Don't be afraid. If you fight me, you'll drown."

And so he floated, his body on hers, staring at the sky until a lifeboat appeared and they were pulled up over the side.

ONCE THEY WERE RETURNED TO THE SHIP THEY WERE GIVEN hot mugs of brandy and escorted below, where the Captain waited for them behind his desk.

"Count Baranofsky has been confined to his quarters," the Captain said to Delilah. "I am assigning you a spare cabin."

"What happened was between the Count and myself," Delilah replied. "No one else."

"Dear Lady," the Captain said. "Let me remind you that if it hadn't been for the heroic actions of Mister Shook, you would have drowned."

"I demand to see Count Baranofsky," she said.

"You will see him when we land. Not before. If we're graced by favorable winds, that will be in less than a week."

He turned to Zebulon. "I am ordering you to keep your distance with both of them. If you stray one inch, I'll have you arrested."

With an abrupt wave of his hand, he dismissed them.

As Delilah and Zebulon passed the Count's cabin, they heard his cello repeat the same scales over and over.

Delilah leaned her head against the bolted door. "Ivan?"

His voice was almost mute. "Did you enjoy your swim? Everyone else seemed to."

"We went too far," she said.

"Perhaps not far enough," he replied. "I would have jumped

in, except that I can't swim."

His fingers began a lingering vibrato, the bow sliding slowly to the end and then back again. "Do you remember that beautiful song we heard at the royal court in Vienna; the one in which the Maiden is confronted by Death?"

He played the notes, reciting the Maiden's plea:

> *Pass me by, o pass me by,*
> *Go wild skeleton!*
> *I am still young: go, dear one.*
> *And touch me not!*

He paused as Delilah sang Death's reply:

> *Give me your hand, o fair and tender form:*
> *I am your friend; I do not come to punish.*

They sang the last two lines together, the Count's cello rising in a mournful crescendo of grief and joy:

> *Be of good cheer! I am not wild,*
> *You shall sleep softly in my arms.*

"Which one of us will sleep safely in Death's arms?" the Count asked. "And who will play the part of Death, sweet Death? Or has that role already been assigned?"

He played a melancholy chord, then stopped. "I had a chat with the Captain. Everything has been arranged. All it took was a large donation to relieve his financial situation."

Delilah leaned her head against the door. "Ivan, I can no longer go on."

"With me or with the journey?" he asked.

"Both. As soon as we land I want to go back."

"Back?" he asked impatiently. "Back to where?"

"France, Egypt, Russia. Does it matter?"

"You know that I have been banished from those countries," he replied. "Listen to me. We go on or we perish. The Captain and I have discussed the situation. He agrees that a brief separation will benefit both of us. And now that the wind has started up again I'm quite content to be in the cabin. I see it as a kind of retreat. A gift and a privilege. Amazing how certain dramas affect one's state of mind."

As the cello repeated the first stanza of "The Death and the Maiden," she turned and walked down the companionway to her cabin.

~ ~ ~

She was sitting on her bunk, staring out the porthole when Zebulon appeared behind her. Not taking her eyes off the horizon, she allowed him to undress her, then lower her down on the bunk.

"Slowly," she whispered as he raised her legs over his shoulders.

"Too late for slowly," he said and plunged into her with such force that she cried out for him to stop.

He kept on even when she bit into his arm and chest.

Finally they collapsed and she rolled over on her stomach, her head on his thigh. For the first time he noticed the tattoo of a three-headed snake swaying up her back.

"When I saw you in Vera Cruz," she said, "I wanted you to rescue me... but just now, in the water, it was me that rescued you."

When he pulled her to him, she went limp inside his arms.

"Do either of us know how to surrender?" she asked.

Surrender? It was something that he had never considered.

He shut his eyes and she placed her hand on his stomach, then slowly moved it up to his chest as she leaned up to kiss him, positioning her body on his as she opened her thighs. Once he was inside her, she matched her breathing to his, dissolving his resistance and confusion. When they were both empty and her stillness had become his, she laid her head on his shoulder and wept.

She whispered into his chest. "When I first saw you, I thought you might be a ghost."

"And I thought you were a witch."

"I am a witch," she said.

He suddenly felt overwhelmed by anger and a confusion that he couldn't deal with.

"Did Ivan buy you?" he asked.

"I am expensive, if that's what you mean," she said evenly. "I have certain skills. I know how to deal with men. I speak English, French, and Spanish, as well as Russian and several African dialects. I cook and wash clothes."

"Who are you?" he asked.

She went on: "My mother was French and Abyssinian, my father Ethiopian and possibly Turkish. He would never say. They were killed when I was captured by an Arab raiding party. I was taken to Djoubouti on the Red Sea and sold to a French arms trader. He was cruel and he beat me, but he taught me about the world. We traveled through the Sudan, then across the Sahara to Egypt. When we reached Paris, Andre – that was his name – began to gamble and smoke opium. When he lost me to Ivan in a card game, he shot himself."

She propped herself on an elbow, looking down at him. "Ivan will do anything to save me. Even if it means losing me."

He stood up and pulled on his pants. She didn't look at him when he went out the door.

Later that night he appeared in her cabin. When he lay down beside her, he let her wrap her legs around his waist and slowly guide him inside her.

THE NEXT DAY CAPTAIN DORFHEIMER SUMMONED ZEBULON to his quarters. Delilah and the Count were already seated. Neither of them looked up as the Captain waved him to a chair.

The Captain cleared his throat before he spoke. "We have been discussing a painful situation. But I believe that we have arrived at a solution. No one has been hurt. Everyone appears to have forgiven one another, and I see no grounds for punishment or any kind of further restriction. However, because it is obviously awkward for all of you to live together in such close quarters, I've decided that as soon as we land, it would be best for Mister Shook to find another ship, one that will carry him up the coast to Panama, where he will be able to take a train to the Pacific and then a ship to San Francisco."

"If anyone leaves, it should be me," Delilah said.

"I thought we had reached an agreement," the Count said impatiently.

Delilah looked at Zebulon, then at the Count. "Why don't both of you go to California? If we all reach Sutter's Fort, then we can decide if we want to go on."

"Dear lady," the Captain protested, "you're contradicting everything that we have agreed to."

"I am not a *dear lady*," Delilah objected.

"You've obviously gone mad," the Count said.

"Are you referring to yourself?" she asked.

"You know very well what happened," the Count said.

"Do I?" she asked. "I'm not at all sure, except that you dictated the terms, as you always do."

When there was no answer from the Count, the Captain lifted a bottle of rum from a side table and poured them all drinks.

"I have a proposal," he said. "I'm prepared to wager five hundred dollars that Zebulon Shook will never arrive in San Francisco. That somewhere along the trail he'll disappear or find something or someone else that holds his interest. After all, he's a man whose fate has always been decided by the prevailing winds."

Delilah nodded towards Zebulon. "Do you agree?"

"Do I have a choice?" he replied

"At this particular moment, no," the Captain replied.

"How will I pay for my passage across Panama," Zebulon asked. "And then up to San Francisco?"

"That will be arranged," the Captain said. "A hundred dollars should be enough."

"I'll match the Captain's hundred," the Count said.

"And if you show up in San Francisco, I'll give you two hundred," the Captain promised. "With no strings."

"And if you don't show up, I'll do the same," the Count added. "A man with your tracking abilities should be able to find us."

"And if you find us," Delilah said, "you will have your job back."

"Double the offer," Zebulon said.

The Count looked at the Captain, who nodded his approval.

"Done," the Count said.

The Captain lifted his glass: "To long life, prosperity, and wind in our sails."

The Captain clinked his glass against Zebulon's, then did the same with the Count and Delilah.

"Have faith and abide," the Count said, saluting Zebulon as he went out the door.

~ ~ ~

Two days later *The Rhinelander* put in for supplies on the northern coast of Columbia. It had been raining for two weeks and the streets and the squalid collection of fishing shacks that were spread around the crumbling cathedral were covered with green moss and mud.

When Zebulon left the ship, Delilah was waiting by the gangway, oblivious to the sheets of rain slashing across the harbor. It was the first time they had seen each other since the meeting with the Captain.

"Take care of yourself," he said, as if she was nothing more than an acquaintance.

She pressed a gold necklace lined with rubies into his hand. "You'll get a good price. It belonged to the Czar's cousin."

He handed the necklace back to her. "You'll need this more than me."

She fastened the necklace around his neck. "If a person refuses a gift from someone to whom they are special, the one who offered it will die."

As he made his way down the gangplank, she called out to him: "I will find you.... You are no other than myself, even though I am not... now... you...."

The rest of her words were drowned in the rain and wind.

ZEBULON SPENT HIS DAYS WAITING FOR A SHIP ON THE veranda of the port's only hotel, a crumbling two-story wooden structure surrounded by wilted stalks of hibiscus and oleander. Occasionally he was joined by the sallow-faced manager of a nearby sugar plantation who spoke only three words of English: woman, gold, and money. Not that they could have heard each other anyway with the rain clattering like rifle fire across the tin roof.

When he wasn't drinking he shot billiards in the rundown lobby, an activity that he gave himself to with maniacal concentration despite a tilted table that sent all the balls rolling into the same corner. One afternoon he was interrupted from his hopeless activity by a piercing whistle from the harbor. Walking out to the veranda, he watched five men slog down the washed-out street towards the hotel, their heads lowered like penitents beneath the rain. Stumbling towards him, they collapsed on rickety whicker chairs. Their leader was a large white-haired man wearing a blue and red hand-tailored naval uniform with enormous epaulets hanging in clusters over a chest full of medals and ribbons. Tufts of hair splayed out of his nostrils, and thick sideburns ran down the side of his massive thick-browed face. Banging a fist on the table, he ordered one of his men to check inside the hotel, then shouted in broken Spanish for hot lemon water and rum.

Five minutes later the man returned. "He's not here, Commodore."

The Commodore focused on Zebulon, who was seated on the other side of the veranda. "We're lookin' for a short little bastard. William Walker. Green eyes, prettified, carries himself like some kind of poo-bah East Coast royalty."

"Haven't seen him," Zebulon replied.

"What?" the Commodore shouted. "I can't hear you! The damn rain."

"I haven't seen him," Zebulon repeated.

After drinks were served by a barefoot waiter, the men lit up hand-rolled cigarettes while the Commodore produced an oversized cigar.

"What the hell is there to do in this godforsaken place?" the Commodore shouted, waiting for his cigar to be lit.

"Drink," Zebulon said. "Shoot scorpions and monkeys. There's a billiard table."

The Commodore peered at him through heavy-lidded eyes. "Billiards, huh? You any good?"

Zebulon leaned back on his chair, propping his feet on the table in front of him. "Good enough for you."

The Commodore grunted, annoyed by the stranger's lack of deference or even curiosity.

One of the men stood up, peering through the rain. "They're comin', Commodore, but Walker ain't with 'em."

Three barefoot Indians passed the veranda, their eyes on the ground.

"Good god, man," the Commodore shouted. "Don't you know natives when you see them? What the hell is wrong with you?"

He turned back to Zebulon. "Where's this billiard table?"

Zebulon led him inside, followed by the others.

The Commodore stared at the billiard table. "You expect me to play on that contraption?"

"I don't expect anything," Zebulon said. "And I don't give a damn what you play on, as long as it ain't on me."

The Commodore laughed. He was almost beginning to like this ignorant drifter. Swiveling his huge head towards the doorway, he shouted at his men: "Get me my billiard table."

They reacted as if they hadn't heard him, a response that caused purple veins to spread across the Commodore's forehead. "I don't care how many of you it takes. I want my table in three hours. And if you run into that little runt, Walker, tell him he'll have to wait his turn to see Vanderbilt."

As the men disappeared into the rain, the Commodore stomped back to the veranda. Ordering another round of rum, he gestured impatiently for Zebulon to join him.

"How come you're hanging out in greaser country?" he asked as Zebulon pulled up a chair.

"Waitin' for a ship," Zebulon replied. "Headed for Californie by way of a train across Panama."

"I have a ship going to Nicaragua. You could get across that way, but couldn't afford the passage."

The Commodore sighed. "Walker is a big pain in the ass. I set him up down here, but as soon as he took over and declared himself president or king of Nicaragua or whatever the hell he now calls himself, he revoked my steamship license. So I ruined him." He paused, a look of satisfaction spreading across his face. "I got Costa Rica to declare war against him, and then I withdrew his funds. Now he's got a civil war to deal with. Two things I have no patience for are civil war and failure."

"I can see that." Zebulon felt comfortable with the Commodore's display of bull-headed fury and revenge. He had run into his kind before: half-assed generals slaughtering Indians just to satisfy a bunch of stuffed shirts in Washington, or big shots and cattle barons that hung around the lobbies of Denver hotels selling fake shares in made-up mining and lumber operations. It was clear that the Commodore was just another asshole from the East, set on driving a stake into whatever poor bastard or country stood in his way.

"And now he's asking me to help him take over the country again," the Commodore was saying. "Amazing how some people never learn their limitations."

"Why bother if he riles you that much?" Zebulon asked, not really listening—an attitude that only stimulated the Commodore's compulsion for candor.

"I'm trying out a new boat and I was headed down here anyway, although why the son of a bitch chose the rainy season to meet in this sink hole is beyond me. I have no patience for fools."

"So you said," Zebulon replied.

They drank in silence. It wasn't until after their third round of straight rum that the Commodore finally seemed to relax.

"It's been a week of failure and frustration. I feel like I'm stuck inside someone else's goddamn dream with no way out. You ever get that way?"

"From time to time," Zebulon replied.

"What's your business down here?"

"No business. Just movin' through."

"Going for gold, are you?"

"Thinkin' about it."

"Let me give you some free advice. The future of the United States of America is business, and smart business lies in transportation. I guarantee that I'll make more money in one year than all of you gold suckers put together. Don't get me wrong. I appreciate men like you who have the balls to push back the frontier. If America is about anything, it's about expansion. We took a big chunk out of Mexico. Soon we'll lock up the Pacific, Hawaii, the Philippines. Maybe even Japan if Admiral Perry makes the right moves, which I have my doubts about."

"I never thought about it," Zebulon said.

"Well, start," the Commodore said. "Never trust anyone.

And once you've made your pile, don't spend it. And always remember that –"

"– expansion is the future," Zebulon interrupted.

The Commodore nodded, pleased to have found someone who knew what he was talking about. "Maybe you're not as dumb as you look. And as for that puny little rail track across the isthmus you intend to travel on, that's for mail-order brides and amateurs, not heavy loads and commerce."

"And *heavy loads* is the name of the game," Zebulon added. "Except that I ain't carryin' a heavy load. Not even a light one."

The Commodore laughed. "You want a job? I can use a man who doesn't back down. Someone to put the boot to all the damn yes-men and hangers-on. Someone who's not afraid to ride for the brand."

"I already got a job," Zebulon replied.

"Well, quit."

They were interrupted by a solitary figure trudging towards them. Stumbling onto the veranda, he removed his rain slicker from his bony frame. After he unfolded a handkerchief and carefully wiped off his wire-rimmed spectacles, he shook out the water that had collected along the curved brim of his derby. Finally he presented himself to the Commodore with a half-bow.

"Always a pleasure, Commodore Vanderbilt," he said through pursed lips, as if pleasure was a meal he rarely tasted.

"I wish I could say the same, Ephraim," the Commodore said. "Where the hell is Walker?"

"President Walker is engaged in important matters elsewhere. He sent me instead."

"What kind of bullshit is that?" the Commodore roared. "Are you telling me that the son of a bitch is afraid to come down here and look me in the eye now that his pathetic game is over and done with?"

Ephraim Squier drew himself up to his full height, which

barely approached Vanderbilt's shoulders. "William Walker doesn't know the meaning of fear."

"No kidding? Maybe that's his problem."

The Commodore looked down at Squier's handmade English boots. "Where the hell did you get those whorehouse shit-kickers, Ephraim? Don't tell me. I don't want to know. The trouble with you pansy New Englanders is that you don't know when to quit. Every time you people go south of the border you embarrass the whole goddamn country."

"I didn't come all this way to argue with you, Commodore."

"Then state your case."

"President Walker has organized a second expedition in Mobile, Alabama, with the intention of sailing for Nicaragua within the month. He is firmly convinced that by the first of the year he will have regained control of the country. He has sent me to ask for help. He needs munitions and supplies as soon as possible."

The Commodore half-rose from his seat. "The man has gone mad!"

"Quite possibly," Ephraim Squier said. "Although that is not for me to say. In any case, I can agree that he is neither a statesman nor a diplomat."

"Was this your idea, or his?"

"That's difficult to say," Squier replied. "There are cultural and political complexities to consider, as well as weather, disease, and public opinion."

"Public opinion?" the Commodore shouted. "I don't give a rat's ass about public opinion! Never have, never will. Do you understand my meaning, Ephraim?"

"I understand, Commodore. Of course, even you must acknowledge that madmen are often successful."

"I acknowledge nothing," the Commodore said. "If you run across Walker, tell him that I hope he rots in hell. Let him know that I will do everything in my power to hinder his every progress."

Squier stood up and put on his derby and rain slicker. "Obviously, Commodore Vanderbilt, we have nothing further to discuss."

"My sentiments exactly," the Commodore said. "By the way, do you shoot billiards?"

Confused, Squier hesitated at the edge of the veranda. "It has never been a hobby of mine, if that's what you mean."

"Too bad, Ephraim," the Commodore replied. "Every successful man needs a hobby."

Without another word, Squier walked back into the rain.

The Commodore lit up another cigar and then smashed it out in the middle of the table. "I admit to a soft spot for Ephraim Squier. He's a decent family man that appreciates good food and stimulating conversation. But when it comes to worldly matters, his style trips him up. It requires a certain skill to play both sides against the middle. He's too refined and convoluted for his own good. But I'll hear from him again. His kind always comes back."

He took out another cigar, sniffing its length a few times before he shoved it in his mouth. "To put it bluntly, Ephraim's problem is a naive sense of integrity."

"You mean he ain't a man of his word," Zebulon said.

"That's not at all what I mean."

He looked at Zebulon as if seeing him for the first time. "What the hell do you care about any of this, anyway?"

"I don't," Zebulon said.

As the Commodore stood up to leave, a cart appeared through the rain, pulled by two horses. A twelve-foot billiard table wrapped in canvas stood in the middle of the cart. Ten men surrounded the sides and the rear of the cart, all of them pushing and swearing at the horses as they plodded through the mud.

It was another hour before the table was installed. Zebulon

had never seen anything like it. The legs were made of sculpted black teak and acacia, and the four leather pockets were embroidered with the Commodore's initials. A leather covering was stretched across the table like smooth polished skin.

"Now we'll have a decent game," the Commodore said. "Of course, I never play for fun."

"I got nothin' to put up," Zebulon confessed.

The Commodore thought it over, walking around the table and rolling a cue ball into each pocket.

"Tell you what, cowboy. If I win, you give me six months of back-breaking work in Nicaragua. My steamships only go so far up the lake and then it's overland. That's where you'll come in: getting the pilgrims to the Pacific. For each one that doesn't make it, you'll owe me another week of service, including burial. If you win, I'll give you free passage to Panama, plus a stateroom and as much food as you can eat. And I'll throw in twenty-five bucks for the train across Panama.

"Three months and it's a deal," Zebulon replied.

"Four," was the Commodore's counter-offer.

"Done," said Zebulon.

The game was Fall-Ball billiards: the winner, the first to make five hundred points.

They played through the night, the contest witnessed by the Commodore's men, as well as the hotel staff and the French plantation owner and his wife.

Before dawn, the rain stopped and hundreds of black-winged moths flew into the room, banging against the oil lamps. The Commodore, who had continued to drink heavily, was obviously tired, but he was determined to press on even though he was losing by fifty points. There was no way he was going to walk away from his own table, especially when he'd be leaving it to a down-and-out hustler with nothing left to lose.

As he lined up his cue ball, he was interrupted by the sudden appearance of an aristocratic dark-haired woman, her thin shoulders covered by an expensive white-laced shawl. She was followed by a heavy-set Negro carrying an umbrella and huge leather suitcase.

The Commodore motioned for her to sit down, then returned his attention to the table. Missing an easy carom by several inches, he banged his cue stick on the floor before he finally turned to her.

"You're late."

The woman removed her shawl, glancing imperiously around the room, as if she had stepped out of a Goya painting of Spanish royalty. Her refined features expressed the worldly exhaustion and arrogance of someone seized with loathing for the carnal and financial circumstances that had delivered her to such an improbable assignation.

"I come all the way from Cartagena on horseback through a monsoon rain and clouds of mosquitoes as big as your thumb, and all you say is that I'm late?"

"Wait for me upstairs, Esmeralda," he grunted. "I've booked a room. In fact I booked the entire floor."

"I prefer to wait on your ship."

"That's not possible."

"Don't tell me you've brought your wife with you?"

"Of course not."

"Then who?"

"That, my dear, is none of your damn business."

"Business? Is that all you ever think of, Cornelius?"

"Look around you, Esmeralda. Pay attention to the situation. I'm playing a game. I will join you when I am finished. Not before."

"Yankee pig-fucker."

She looked at Zebulon. "Who are you?"

When Zebulon shrugged, she stalked upstairs, followed by her servant.

Stimulated by Esmeralda's response and the anticipation

of what waited for him upstairs, the Commodore managed to conduct his cue ball around the table, making one difficult carom after another before he finally missed.

Zebulon finished off the match by making thirty-nine points on three shots, a victory that caused the Commodore to break his cue stick over his knee and throw a glass against a wall.

When he demanded another game, Zebulon refused.

"Wait for me," the Commodore said to his men, and marched up the stairs.

It was late afternoon before the Commodore joined Zebulon and his men on the veranda.

Esmeralda watched them from an upstairs window as they trudged back to *The Prometheus*, the largest and most well-appointed steamship in the world.

On board, Zebulon was given the master suite with a well-stocked bar, a dining table, and a full-length mirror over the huge round bed. The only time he saw the Commodore was through the half-open door of his private lounge. He was sitting opposite Ephraim Squier, a bottle of champagne between them, both of them too engaged in conversation to notice Zebulon as he strolled past.

The journey lasted a day-and-a-half over calm seas and leaden skies. When they docked in the steamy port of Colón in the middle of the night, Zebulon was the only passenger to disembark.

ZEBULON STOOD AT THE END OF A SAGGING DOCK, HIS clothes drenched from suffocating heat. Lightning cracked across the harbor, exposing a sodden collection of wooden houses and shacks. As he headed towards land and then down the waterfront, he passed mining equipment shoved between half-open crates of shovels, engine parts, coffee, hides, and tobacco. Canned goods, mixed with bundles of workers' clothes, were piled next to tin boxes full of medical supplies, each tin identified in large red lettering: TYPHOID FEVER, CHOLERA, SNAKEBITE, and MALARIA.

The only signs of security were two drunken soldiers sprawled against a train locomotive; around them, half-starved dogs were lurking in the shadows of storage sheds.

On the main street, black clouds of mosquitoes swarmed over rotting flesh and open sewage. Drunken prospectors guarded supplies with shotguns and rifles; others suffering from cholera, dysentery, and malaria were propped in doorways or sprawled across wooden planks.

Zebulon embraced it all: the smells and decay and violence, all the noisy chaos that marked a new frontier.

He stepped around a man in a top hat kneeling in the mud and spitting up thick clots of blood. Further on, a crowd of Jamaican laborers stood in the doorway of a burned-out house, laughing at a black whore as she confronted an opium-addled Chinaman who was struggling to pull up his pants. Their laughter stopped when the whore slashed a knife across the Chinaman's throat, then rifled his pockets only to come up empty.

The only hotel was locked for the night, a FULL UP sign posted on the door. Zebulon walked on until he found a sign advertising a fifty-cents-a-night patch of straw in a crumbling storehouse full of railroad spikes and spare parts.

At dawn he made his way to the train station, a large stone building at the edge of town where a wood-burning locomotive was hitched to eight canary-yellow carriages. At the rear of the train, men were loading supplies into two baggage cars. On all sides of the crates, names and mottoes were painted in red, white, and blue: HOOSIER, CALIFORNIA OR BUST, PILGRAM'S PROGRESS – CALIFORNIA EDITION, HAVE YOU SEEN THE ELEPHANT?

Most of the passengers were men except for a few exhausted wives already fed up with this so-called fast and easy crossing to the Pacific. Everyone was dressed for the great departure: the men in waistcoats, flamboyant shirts, fashionably tailored pants, and beaver hats; the women in ankle length full-skirted calico and cotton dresses, their sun-scorched faces covered with drooping straw hats and lace bonnets. Indians in white linen pants and straw hats worked through the crowd selling fruit, chicken, and papaya wrapped in banana leaves. A group of Argonauts, lubricated with cheap liquor, played violins and flutes and banged on homemade drums, singing:

> *Oh Susannah, don't you wait for me,*
> *For I'm going to California with a banjo on my knee.*

Thunder rumbled, followed by a violent rainsquall. As suddenly as the rain started, it stopped, leaving the street even more flooded and steamy.

The stationmaster strode into the middle of the street, firing an ancient musket: "All aboard," he shouted. "All aboard for the

Panama City Express!"

Zebulon found a seat next to an overweight Irishman, a former pub owner from Belfast with a hacking cough and rheumy eyes who wept with relief as the train slowly inched through the town, then chugged across a mangrove swamp through groves of palm trees and giant bamboo. From their open windows the passengers caught glimpses of red-breasted toucans and green and yellow parrots gliding through thick canopies of leaves. As the train pushed slowly into the jungle, they lost sight of the sky and were left with the screams of howler monkeys and the smell of the engine's wood smoke mixed with the fragrance of rotting leaves.

The Irishman lowered his head, unable to contemplate the display of abundant decay. "You won't see Irish on this run. They don't do well in warm climes. My mum and dad died in the potato famine of '46. When my wife ran off to Australia with a sergeant in the British army, I sold my pub and sailed for Boston. Worked as a bartender and baker, then got a job on the waterfront. Hated every goddamn minute, but saved enough for the gold fields."

They passed naked children staring at the train with huge empty eyes, then shacks covered with palmetto leaves, and further on, a funeral train stationed on a sidetrack where bodies were being lifted into two black carriages reserved for the dead. As Zebulon looked closer, he saw his own face staring back at him. Or was it Hans, the German merchant from *The Rhinelander*?

Suddenly there were yells and screams as the carriage swayed, then lurched back and forth and left the track.

"A washout," the conductor shouted, walking calmly through the carriage. "It happens, folks. We'll be up and running in no time."

The passengers stumbled outside to sit on the side of the tracks in front of a roaring torrent of brown water. Some had bruises and broken bones, but no one was seriously hurt. Where the bridge had been, there were now only two abutments of masonry, one on each side of the swollen river. Towards the other side of the river they could make out a spur and several iron girders protruding through whirlpools of thick green slime.

The conductor consulted with the engineer, then walked over to address the passengers. He presented a reassuring presence with his black silver-buttoned uniform and snap-brim cap set over a square face and neatly trimmed mustache.

"There's a settlement down river. We'll cross on canoes, then go the rest of the way on mules. No cause for alarm, folks. We'll be in Panama in a day or two. Maybe three. Once the river goes down, we'll ferry over everyone's supplies and get them to you in Panama. We've never lost anything yet."

The men talked among themselves or tried to comfort their wives, several of whom were openly weeping.

"Everything is under control, folks," the conductor repeated. "It will take ten days for a crew to pull the train back. Only thing to do is go on. Nothing to be alarmed about. A walk through a jungle paradise will do us all good."

Zebulon's entire body began to shake as his eyes lost focus and his brain felt as if it was about to explode. Stumbling towards the river, he sank to his knees and vomited.

He was barely conscious when the conductor and two male passengers lifted him onto an improvised stretcher. They carried him for over a mile until they reached a clearing where five bamboo huts were raised up on stilts over the flooded river. In the middle of the clearing a few Indians were waiting to trade bananas and yams for trinkets.

Zebulon was lifted up a ladder into one of the huts, where an ancient and toothless Indian woman wearing a muslin shift bathed his feverish forehead with a wet cloth, then poured green coconut water into his mouth from a gourd, followed by a bitter paste of root bark mixed with guava, lemon, and green chilies.

"Cholera," he heard a voice say before he passed out. "Or parrot fever. Most likely he'll be dead by morning."

He imagined a seagull soaring over towering waves. *Come closer*, the waves howled, and then he heard another sound, like a dress being ripped apart, and he thought of Delilah tearing at her heart. Or was it his heart?

"*Come, sweet death*," he heard her sing as the waves howled again. "*Deliver yourself to me.*"

HE LAY ON HIS BACK IN THE MIDDLE OF A DUGOUT CANOE. There was no hawk nor gull above, nor towering waves below, only the sound of the swollen river and then a scream from one of the other canoes as it rammed into a submerged log, throwing two Argonauts and an Indian into the water, their bodies sweeping over the rapids like a trail of wet laundry.

When they finally reached the far shore, several miles downriver from where they had started, Zebulon was wrapped in a strip of canvas and tied to a travois behind a mule. Once inside the jungle he was transferred to a stretcher. When the rotting vegetation became too thick, the Argonauts were forced to hack their way through the undergrowth with knives and machetes. Soon the light grew dimmer and then disappeared altogether. Poisonous plants brushed against the stretcher, dropping leeches and centipedes that left throbbing welts on his face and hands. Once when they stopped to bury someone, he heard a voice praying in an unknown language, and he wondered if the prayers and the grave were meant for him.

They spent the night in a small clearing where he was laid on a mat of cowhide and spoon-fed a thick soup that he immediately threw up. His feet had turned blue, and his fever had continued to rise even though his bones had stiffened and his teeth were clenched and then chattering from chills. Bats swooped overhead, feeding off insects half as large as his hand. Tree frogs croaked, and somewhere a jaguar screamed. In his delirium the jaguar's scream sounded as if it came from inside him.

He lost all sense of time, aware only that he was still being carried on a stretcher and that somehow the jungle was receding. Towards evening they reached the crest of a hill where a soft wind was stirring through clumps of bunchgrass. Around him Argonauts began to weep and offer prayers of gratitude.

The conductor propped him up. "Take a look. From sea to shining sea."

White clouds swept across a deep green valley. Further on, beyond a range of rolling green hills, he could see the Pacific. In the opposite direction, the Caribbean was visible over a thick roof of steaming jungle.

As Zebulon stood up, spreading his arms towards the two oceans, a large yellow butterfly circled his head, then two more, until his legs buckled and he collapsed.

~ ~ ~

He woke to groans and cries of pain. Around him men lay on rows of wooden bunks. He was on a ship, that much was clear, and for a moment he thought he was at sea again. Propping himself against a bulkhead, he looked out a porthole at a church spire rising above the red-tiled roofs of a town.

"Welcome to hell, pilgrim." It was the Irishman on the next bunk. "The only way out is feet first and a drop into the slop."

Zebulon sank back, covering his eyes with his arm.

"I went down right after you," the Irishman said, saliva drooling from his mouth. "But I'm too ornery to let a jungle bug get me. Most of the poor bastards in here aren't sure if they're dead or alive, and from the looks of you, you might not be either. Not that anyone cares."

Zebulon passed out, and when he opened his eyes, the Irishman's bunk was empty.

Hours later, or maybe it was a day or two, the doctor, a small man with a bulging alcoholic nose, made his rounds, followed by a nurse holding a handkerchief over her face against the stench of vomit, urine, and death. Once, she paused to tie a tag around the blue toe of an unfortunate who hadn't made it through the night.

"I was convinced you were dead meat when I first saw you," the doctor said, taking his pulse. "In fact, I even bet on it as you were being carried in. But you're one of the lucky ones. Not like some of your bunch who came in with cholera or typhoid fever. You're hard to figure. It might be a parasite. Whatever it is, it's obviously sucking all the life out of you. We'll keep you for a few weeks. Bleed a few ounces out of you to purify the blood. Throw in some camphor and hot-water emetics, mix in a little ginger and pepper and hope for the best. Maybe try calomel until your gums begin to bleed. Not much else to do. By rights you should be shark feed."

The nurse, a white thin-lipped Baptist with sparse tufts of gray hair across her skull, nodded her approval, convinced that anyone that ended up in this wretched hospital ship had been consigned there for God's punishment. As the doctor moved on to check the next patient, she bent her head towards Zebulon's ear: "You're under quarantine until we find out what's wrong with you. If you make an attempt to leave, you'll be shot out of hand. Nothing personal, but we have to guard against plagues. Those are the rules."

He slept away the days and weeks in a pool of night sweats, waking only to relieve himself. He was half-aware of being force-fed various foul medicines followed by water and a thin gruel that passed for soup. When someone tried to remove Delilah's gold and ruby necklace from his neck, he automatically reached for the knife he kept tied to his belt and slashed off the thief's hand. The act brought yells of approval from several patients, many of whom, in their deliriums, were on constant guard against pirate attacks and Mexican revolutionaries, not to mention the doctor and his nurse.

As long as it wasn't raining, which it was more often than not, he was encouraged to pass his afternoons on the upper deck, taking in the sun on a straw mat. One evening, as the sun was setting across the harbor, he noticed a ship sailing out towards the open sea.

It was *The Rhinelander.*

It was another month before he was given permission to go ashore, the doctor having finally dismissed his illness as "delusional."

A few days later he boarded a Portuguese whaler bound for the Bering Strait with a lengthy stopover for repairs in Mazatlán, before sailing on to Monterey and San Francisco.

WHEN THE WHALER SAILED INTO SAN FRANCISCO BAY SIX
weeks later, half the city was in flames and black soot-filled
clouds sagged over the water like shrouds. Through the flames
Zebulon could see the smoky silhouette of the shore and the
hills surrounding the city, where thousands of tents and canvas-
covered shacks were sprawled around iron buildings that had
been shipped in from the eastern states. The Captain and the
Portuguese crew were afraid to set foot on land, convinced that
the entire West Coast had been seized by a biblical conflagration;
a disaster brought on, they had no doubt, by the godless scum
of the earth who had deserted families, traditions, and religions
to rush off to the gold fields. The ship remained anchored in
the bay for six days until a squall drenched the last of the fires.
Finally, fears suspended, if not relieved, the ship made its way
towards a long line of wharfs, passing hundreds of deserted
vessels along the way.

Zebulon disembarked into a furious crowd of hawkers yelling
offers for supplies, whores, jobs, flop houses, peep shows, and
business deals. Now that his hooves were planted on earth, he
promised himself that he would never embark on a ship again.
Here was the Promised Land. Here was freedom from the past,
a chance to break loose. He let out a loud mountain yell, causing
a horse and wagon to bolt off the dock. Never mind Delilah
or Hatchet Jack or being trapped between worlds. Never mind

what his Ma or Pa or anyone else had said or thought or done. From now on, whatever hell awaited him would be of his own choosing.

He walked off the dock and shouldered his way into the first saloon he came to – three stitched-together army tents supported by empty crates and scrap iron. The bar was fashioned out of two wooden planks, each twenty feet long, propped up on empty whiskey barrels. Every inch was jammed with newly arrived immigrants and prospectors: Kanakas from the South Seas, Hawaiians, Cubans, Peruvians, Chinese, Russians, as well as all sorts of Europeans and foot-loose Americans. The only subject in the saloon was gold: where to find it, how to mine it, how to spend it.

He drank through the rest of the afternoon and into the evening, not moving except to relieve himself in a long ditch outside the tent. The more whiskey he consumed, the more he thought of Delilah, as if his exhilaration had given her an open invitation to invade him, and the more he tried to shut her down, the more present and haunting her spirit became.

When he finally staggered outside, it was dark and a soft mist was drifting over the waterfront and the hills. Not knowing where to go and preferring higher ground, he climbed a hill towards a collection of shanties and tents thrown together out of canvas, potato sacks, old shirts, and whatever else was available. When the mist turned to rain, followed by a violent downpour, he crawled into a shack. Inside, two men in red long johns sat near a crude stove made out of barrels, playing poker on a wooden crate. The older man's head was as smooth and shiny as a bullet. When he looked up at Zebulon, the tattoo of a sperm whale bobbed across his Adam's apple.

"Come far, partner?" the man asked.

Zebulon sank down by the stove. "Far enough to know better."

"You can say that again," said the younger man. He was rail

thin with a long, bushy mustache drooping over his sunken chin.

"We're lucky to have shelter," the older man said. "We threw together this pile two days ago in the middle of a rainstorm. Me and my boy aim to stay here until we put together a stake. Then it's hallelujah and off to the gold fields."

"I'll pay for the night," Zebulon offered.

The younger man looked at his Pa, as if waiting for a sign. When his Pa nodded, he threw his cards on the crate. The only card face up was the queen of hearts.

"I'll be goddamned. Lookee here. That old queen keeps floppin' up like a high-priced floozy."

"Don't mind my boy," his Pa said. "He ain't won more'n two hands all night. Him and me are Christians from the Church of the Holy Rapture. We're Pennsylvanians and proud of it. We work for the Lord and share what we have and don't gamble for money or drink hard liquor. We expect those we work and live with to help themselves to everything we got and we'll do the same."

"Fair enough," Zebulon said, and passed out.

When he woke the following morning the shack was empty. His money had disappeared, along with his boots, his Colt, and Delilah's necklace. All that remained was a half-a-pot of cold coffee.

Outside, a raw, wet wind blew off the bay. People were moving about in front of the tents and shanties, cooking breakfast and speaking in foreign tongues. Beneath the hill, beached on the shore like wreckage from a tsunami, were the hulks of schooners, brigs, paddle steamers, steamships, ferries, scows, and yawls. A few larger vessels had been converted to temporary saloons, others transformed into hotels or warehouses. One of them was *The Rhinelander*. All three of her masts were gone and a yellow and red sign was painted across her stern:

RHINELANDER HOTEL BEDS 75 CENTS.

He drank the rest of the coffee, then bound his feet with rags. Avoiding the still-smoldering embers, he stumbled down the hill past the charred remains of what had passed for shacks. When he reached *The Rhinelander*, his feet were bleeding and his pant legs were hanging in strips from his waist.

The deck was jammed with prospectors and refugees from the fires, all of them guarding their supplies. Not recognizing any of the crew or passengers, Zebulon went below.

Captain Dorfheimer lay spread out on the bunk of his cabin in a silk bathrobe, staring at the ceiling where a freshly painted galaxy displayed hundreds of stars circling around red and green planets.

Slowly, as if each cracking joint was causing him agonizing pain, the Captain gathered himself up and stumbled over to the chair behind his desk. Holding his head in his hands, he stared bleakly at Zebulon.

"How I fear and loathe the past when it arrives unannounced."

"I'm here to settle our account," Zebulon said.

Dorfheimer sighed, massaging the back of his head. "If only that were possible. My officers and crew have deserted me for the gold fields. Every last one. Left me to rot. Don't misunderstand, business will pick up. I have to hang on. Serve decent food. Provide fresh sheets. Then they'll pay double and I'll sail away from this cursed land, never, God help me, to return."

He opened his desk drawer, removing a page torn from a newspaper.

"Thanks to Artemis Stebbins, you're famous from Mexico to Alaska. My God, if I had known about the wild and violent crimes you've committed, I would have had you thrown overboard."

He handed the article to Zebulon, who glanced at it, pretending to read, then handed it back.

"Allow me," the Captain offered.

"No need," Zebulon said. "It's all lies."

The Captain folded up the newspaper and returned it to the desk drawer.

"Where are they?" Zebulon asked.

"Baranofsky ran into some trouble in a Spanish town south of here. I heard he was in jail. Stebbins will know about the woman. He hangs his hat at the Busted Flush, a café down the street."

"Are you going to settle up?" Zebulon asked.

The Captain shook his head. "Obviously you didn't hear me. Your passage and trip across Panama were paid for, which was far more than you deserved, given all the trouble you caused. Are you aware that there's a five-hundred-dollar reward posted on you, dead or alive? I should have you arrested."

"Settle up," Zebulon said, picking up a letter opener from the desk.

The Captain stumbled over to a chest. Pulling out an officer's uniform, he threw it at Zebulon. "My father's. A vice admiral in the Kaiser's navy. It will confuse the bounty hunters and vigilantes. Now leave. Go away and never come back, and I promise that I will never mention you to anyone, not even to myself."

Zebulon changed into a tight-fitting jacket with blue epaulets. Then he put on black pants that were six inches too short and had a broad red stripe running down the side, followed by knee-high boots. The whole assemblage was topped off by a cockaded admiral's hat and long sheathed sword.

Zebulon removed a pearl-handled revolver from the half-open drawer of the desk. Staring into a mirror, he blasted his image into flying shards of glass. Another bullet blew open the handle of a small wall safe.

After he removed seventy dollars in gold coins, a string of black South Sea pearls, and a gold-plated pocket watch, he shoved the revolver into his belt and yanked Dorfheimer to his feet. Dorfheimer shut his eyes, expecting the worst. When Zebulon embraced him, the gesture was so unexpected that the Captain collapsed on the floor, weeping and gasping for breath.

~ ~ ~

When Zebulon appeared on deck, he was greeted by shouts and applause from the assembled, everyone believing that Dorfheimer had been shot because of his overpriced accommodations and rotten food.

At the end of the gangplank, Zebulon turned to offer a salute to Dorfheimer, who was staring down at him from the bridge.

"I will see you in hell," Dorfheimer shouted.

"I'm already in hell," Zebulon replied.

Tossing the admiral's hat into the harbor, he pushed his way through the crowd on the dock.

IT DIDN'T TAKE HIM LONG TO FIND THE BUSTED FLUSH HOTEL, saloon, and Sporting Emporium, a three-story brick warehouse rising above a squalid row of one-story saloons, dry goods stores, and whorehouses. Inside, the cavernous space was jammed with sailors, gamblers, and prospectors, as well as the usual variety of thieves and entrepreneurs. There was no sign of Stebbins. In one corner, a crowd had gathered around a pit in which a wolverine was fighting a half-starved wolf. Across the room, two bare-fisted fighters were slugging each other into oblivion until the larger one, a three-hundred-pound Samoan, picked up his opponent as easily as a sack of flour and threw him against the wall, breaking his back.

When challengers were called for, Zebulon stepped forward – much to the amusement of the crowd, who, by the look of his uniform and stubby half-grown hair, took him for a runaway convict or crazed East Coast Argonaut.

Stripped to his waist, he was introduced as Admiral Doom, a champion of the Maldovian navy, undefeated in over a hundred bouts. Before the introduction was finished and bets were in place, the Samoan kicked him in the groin and tried to gouge out an eye. He struggled to his feet, only to fall back again as the Samoan raised his hands in victory. Waiting for the end, he experienced an unexpected stillness followed by a rush of energy that poured through his veins like water running through an open sluice gate. The release traveled up the length of his spine and launched him in a cold fury across the ring, where he pummeled the Samoan with blows to the head and body, followed by a vicious kick to the solar plexus. As the bewildered Samoan sank to his knees, Zebulon chopped down on his head. Then he broke his cheekbone with his forearm. The assault, as Stebbins wrote later in one of the San Francisco newspapers, lasted less than a minute and was as precise as an execution.

The crowd broke into hysterical foot-stomping approval: "Hurrah for Admiral Doom!" they shouted. "Doom! Doom! Doom!"

For his efforts, Zebulon received twenty-five dollars and a clean towel to wipe off the blood.

He pushed his way to a side room where drinks were served from thin rubber tubes that allowed each customer to suck out all the booze he could handle until he ran out of breath or passed out. As the liquor trickled down his throat he heard a song drift over the raucous din, a voice that entered his heart like the pointed end of a stake:

> *Black Town gals are plump and rosy*
> *Touch them and they'll sting like hornets.*
>
> *Black Town gals are lovely creatures*
> *Painted cheeks and sassy bonnets.*

Delilah stood on a wooden platform at the back of the room wearing a low-cut red dress. Her eyes were half-closed, her face caked with thick makeup. The newcomers in the room had never seen anyone like her or experienced a voice so penetrating and melancholy. As she sang, two fiddlers and an accordion player provided enough rhythm to keep her on course:

> *Think they'll marry white man preachers*
> *Heads thrown back to show their features*

Ha, ha, ha, Black Town gals!

Zebulon noticed Stebbins sitting alone at a table, rocking back and forth as he repeated the last line to wild applause.

His eyes narrowed as Zebulon sat down opposite him.

"I heard you been writing lies about me," Zebulon said.

Stebbins filled up his glass and pushed it towards Zebulon. "It's why I'm here: to satisfy the public's insatiable hunger and curiosity for frontier lore. And you, my friend, rank with the very best, thanks to my adventurously inflated prose."

He looked over at Delilah. "Lucky for me that she has contributed more intimate details about you than any scribbler could wish for. How you forget to take off your boots when engaging in the act of love, how you become violent when you lose at cards or billiards, or how you obsessively invent your past. All touching human fallibilities which help make a story appealing and accessible."

Zebulon walked over to Stebbins and lifted him off his chair.

"Extry! Extry!" Stebbins shouted, struggling to free himself. "Read all about it! Deranged mountain man goes berserk! Kills reporter for spilling the beans about his outlaw past! Read about his squalid love affair with an Abyssinian courtesan and a Russian count!"

Zebulon dropped him into his chair and sat down as Delilah launched into another song:

> *Oh, what was your name in the States:*
> *Was it Zebulon or Ivan or Stebbins or Bates?*
>
> *Did you flee for your life, or murder your wife?*
> *Say, what was your name in the States?*
> *I'd comrades then who loved me well,*
> *A jovial, saucy crew;*
>
> *A few hard cases, I'll admit,*
> *Though they were brave and true.*

Whatever the pinch, they'd never flinch,
Would never fret or whine —

Like good old bricks they stood the kicks
In the days of '49.

"A word of advice," Stebbins said, pouring a drink. "Choose an alias. Especially in San Francisco. Anything but Admiral Doom. Admiral Death has more punch. Think about it. After all, death is what people out here know about. Death and gold. Never Doom. Doom is the last thing they want to hear about."

They both turned to watch Delilah as she looked over at their table and began another song:

So I'll pack my clothing
And in search of him I'll go.

I'll cross the wide, wide ocean
Through storm winds and snow.

And never shall I marry
Until the day I die.

So I'll die broken-hearted
For my old mountain boy.

She sang the next verse in Portuguese, or maybe it was another song altogether, stretching out the vowels and ending each verse with a melancholy wail that traveled slowly up from her belly to her throat. By the time she finished, several men were openly weeping, unable to control their buried longings and fears. One man shot his pistol at the ceiling. Others stood on their chairs and cheered, throwing coins and nuggets on the platform, which were scooped up by the musicians, who took half for themselves before they handed the rest to Delilah.

Zebulon watched her weave slowly through the crowd, as if her fragile and weary body was struggling against a strong wind.

"How amazing!" she said to Zebulon as she sat down. "You've joined the German navy. And become an officer as well. Although your uniform does need some repair." She poured herself a drink. "Is it true that the Germans have plans to take over California and Oregon, as well as Mexico and Alaska? Or is that the English?"

He stared at her, shocked by how much weight she had lost and the deep lines around her mouth and eyes.

"I know," she sighed. "I don't bear close inspection. A girl's *joie de vivre* can so easily vanish when she has to sing for her supper." She shook her head. "And what about you? You don't look so well yourself."

She looked across the room where a waiter, no more than four feet tall, was maneuvering his way towards them, holding a tray over his black gnome-like head.

"I was hoping someone had stepped on him," she said wearily as the dwarf placed a bottle of whiskey and two glasses on the table.

Nodding at Zebulon, the strange dwarf spoke to Delilah in Portuguese.

"Toku is confused about you," she said to Zebulon. "I don't know why. Why don't you tell us, Toku? We have no secrets at this table. Very few, anyway."

The dwarf pointed at Zebulon.

"Tell your friend to stay away from games of chance," he said with a clipped English accent, "or he'll end up in a ditch. If you know what I mean."

"I don't know what you mean," she said.

He shrugged and picked up his tray. "You know very well what I mean."

"Do you plan to keep our appointment?" Delilah asked.

"When I am ready. Not before. Do you have any idea how difficult it is to find three guinea pigs? And not just any three guinea pigs. They all have to be the same age and color. And then there's the state of the moon, and various other elements that you have no knowledge of. If you ask me once more, or even look at me in the wrong way, you will find yourself talking to a stone wall."

He turned and walked back across the room like a drunken sailor navigating his way across a rolling deck.

"A friend of yours?" Zebulon asked.

"He used to be some kind of pet or court jester for the Captain of an English ship," she explained. "When everyone went off to the gold fields, he stayed behind. When he heard me sing, he told me that he had known me in a past life. He's African. Every time I ask him what tribe he's from, he tells me something different – Baule, Bwiti, Pygmy. Whatever he is, he has strange powers and sees things other people can't. I suppose I have an addiction for second-sighted people."

She started to gulp down a shot of whiskey, then thought better of it. Standing up, she steadied herself on the back of her chair, then slowly made her way out of the room.

HE KNEW HE SHOULD LET HER GO, BUT HE FOLLOWED HER anyway, keeping out of sight as she stumbled out a side door into an alley ankle-deep in mud. Once he thought he had lost her only to have her reappear and turn into a courtyard.

He stood in the shadows as she knocked on the door of a wooden two-story house with narrow windows protected by iron bars. Once again he felt presented with a choice. In the past, he had set his course by his instincts and certain signs: a shift in the wind, a campfire on the horizon, tracks in the snow. But now he felt only fear.

When the door opened and Delilah disappeared inside, he continued down the alley to the waterfront. He could ride south to Mexico, he thought. But he had already made that journey. And now there was a bounty on him. Wanted. Dead or alive. He would be better off trying his luck in the gold fields. He had taken enough from Dorfheimer for a decent stake. Or he could go on the drift, up to Oregon or Alaska. He knew how to exist hand-to-mouth. Riding fence, rounding up cattle, busting horses – none of it mattered as long as he was free and unknown. He looked out at the harbor where anchor lights were blinking from hundreds of ships. The whole place was on the gallop with orders to fill. If one direction didn't work out, there would be ten more.

The hell with her, he thought, then returned to where he had left her. He rolled a smoke in the courtyard, then stubbed it out and knocked on the door.

A Chinaman opened the door, staring at him through spectacles the size of bird eggs. A long black queue fell past his waist and his reed-like body was covered with a silk maroon robe.

Zebulon followed him into a claustrophobic low-ceilinged room lit by sputtering candles. In the dim half-light he made out a couch and a row of armchairs filled with shadowy figures that he figured were women for hire.

"You want?" the Chinaman asked and snapped his fingers.

A pubescent girl no more than fourteen rose up from a chair, clacking towards him on wooden sandals, a loose yellow shift hanging from her bony small-breasted frame.

"Young delight," the Chinaman said. "Small buds. Like peaches. Good for the heart."

His voice was oddly precise, as if he had learned English from a missionary.

"I'm lookin' for a woman," Zebulon said. "A mix. Not white or black. A long tangle of black hair."

The Chinaman shook his head. "Delilah not for sale."

"Not to buy," Zebulon insisted. "To talk."

The Chinaman smacked his hands together as if killing a mosquito. "Twenty dollars. But no touch. Only smoke."

After Zebulon paid, he followed the Chinaman into a back room that smelled of burned chestnuts. A low table held a lamp and several bowls filled with black opium paste. Emaciated men lay on their sides on narrow tiers of bunks, their heads resting on polished blocks of black wood. Delilah lay on a lower bunk, inhaling a long bamboo pipe lit by an old Chinese woman wearing a black high-necked dress.

"Are you dreaming me?" she asked with a smile as he lay down beside her. "Or am I dreaming you? Or are we being dreamed by someone else?"

She sucked at the pipe, then slowly exhaled.

"Where's my necklace?"

It took him a while to remember. "Stolen."

"I'm not surprised. Everything else has been stolen or taken from me. The only thing left is to invest in loss…. Do you ever ask yourself who belongs to whom…? Or why? Or why it is that most people prefer to rush towards their death rather than step out of the way?"

The old woman offered him a pipe, then held up a long wire with a smudge of opium resin on the end. After he lit the resin, she motioned for Zebulon to inhale. He repeated the procedure several times until he turned on his back, staring up at the ceiling.

Delilah's voice drifted over, like a leaf on a slow moving river. "If she rubs your feet, you'll float in the air."

He wasn't floating. He was a frog pinned beneath a giant thumb until he moved a finger back and forth in front of his eyes.

"I betrayed Ivan," Delilah said. "And I betrayed you. But if you had stayed on the ship, Ivan would have killed you. He tried it before. In New Mexico. Or was it Turkey?"

He remembered being a small boy and watching an eagle feather drift down from a blood-red sky and then land gently on his head.

"It's a sign," his Pa said after he shot the eagle. "I'm damned if I know what it means. Only that it's better not to think about it."

"Are you aware that dark spirits are searching for us?" Delilah asked. "For Ivan…. And for me…. And for you…. That's all they know how to do. They hunt for prey, and when they find it they swallow it, as if they intend to take on who they kill."

They lay side by side, legs and sides barely touching, smoking and slipping in and out of each other's dreams. He felt suspended somewhere between earth and sky.

"Or nowhere at all," he said to the fingers rubbing his feet.

The thought was pleasing, that of going nowhere at all. Never to move on. Never to hunt. Never to leave one place for another. Or one woman for another.

Her voice found him again. "After San Francisco, we rode north, Ivan and I.... So wild, so many rivers to cross and guns and horses. Ivan found more gold than anyone would ever need. Then he lost it all in a card game. He lost me, too.... So many men.... I was the only woman for a hundred miles... brutal men.... I never wanted to see you again.... You're wanted for murder... stealing horses... robbing banks.... A very dangerous man. When I saw you in that Mexican hotel I knew you were hunting me.... What I didn't know was that I was hunting you as well."

He curled up like a frightened animal, his arm over his eyes, his heart beating as if he was imprisoned inside a trap.

An old woman wrapped inside a man's button-down canvas jacket was bending down, holding a pipe, inviting him to inhale, to disappear into another dream....

"Men came from everywhere to hear me sing," Delilah was saying. "Then Ivan found me again. He always does, you know. And then he leaves."

Someone was playing a flute in another room and a woman was singing about love and a journey that never ends.

"Now Ivan will die. When he abandoned me in London, an Englishman took me in. A singing teacher. An aristocrat.... I have a certain weakness for aristocrats. So distant and unobtainable.... He taught me opera.... How to speak and read English.... Every time I tried to leave him, he became very cruel."

Across the room the Chinese girl was massaging the singer's feet, or maybe they were his own feet. Her scent made him feel as if he was lying in the middle of a garden. Or a cemetery.

"Ivan found me making love to the Englishman," she went

on. "He wanted to kill me. He had been in prison. In Russia.... They tortured him.... There are scars on his cheeks from cigarette burns. He's not a count, you know.... He's a spy and a scoundrel and a businessman. He smiled when he shot the Englishman through the head."

He wondered if Ivan had shot him in Panchito. Or had it been Delilah? Or someone else? Was he, in fact, dead, and dreaming his life and how it had been or might have been? He was on a journey. He was sure of that. A journey that he was unable to track, without a beginning or end, with no boundaries to guide him.

Her voice drifted back to him: "When my parents died, I lived with my grandmother.... She was over a hundred years old.... I had come to her in a dream before I was born.... Because I have mixed blood from many different races, she told me not to become trapped between worlds... I never listened to her, and now it is my fate... to learn how to die, over and over.... In my previous life I... I can't remember.... She told me to leave everything that I was attached to... even her, in order to be in the world but not of it.... When a Portuguese slaver killed my grandmother and took me away, I lost faith in God...."

In the middle of the night, or the next day, he opened his eyes.

Delilah was staring down at him.

"Do you know who I am?" Her voice was a faint whisper, as if shivering through the tops of trees. "I am the one that hunts for redemption in the darkest night, the one who is imprisoned inside dreams within dreams. Because I have lost my way, I am hostage to all that floats between the worlds. Including you."

HE FOLLOWED HER PAST THE LOST DREAMERS CURLED UP on their bunks and then down a narrow winding alley, stepping around buckets of waste tossed out of windows, abandoned mining equipment, and Argonauts passed out on soggy wooden planks.

On the waterfront they collapsed against a pile of grain sacks stacked against an overturned wagon, falling asleep with their arms around each other. In front of them, thick layers of fog spread slowly over the harbor's armada of abandoned ships and the rows of river schooners lined up gunwale to gunwale along the sagging exhausted wharfs.

They woke to a blaring trumpet and a pounding drum.

A dozen men wearing shiny black suits appeared through the fog, marching behind a woman in a red fez and yellow pantaloons, holding up a sign announcing the end of the world and the grand opening of the Paradise Hotel.

They sat leaning against each other, their bodies swaying like hollow reeds. The night had left them empty, without any sense of urgency or direction, free of all dreams and intentions. The fog had dissolved and the sun was spreading rays of light across the bay. On the street a small boy whistled as he pushed a ball ahead of him with a stick. A group of Brazilian sailors drifted hand in hand down the *embarcadero*, followed by a team of mules pulling a wagon loaded with mining equipment.

"I'm going on alone," she said. "I'll come back tomorrow and look for you in this same place. If you're not here, I'll know that whatever happened between us has come to an end."

He sat watching her as she stood up and, without a word, walked away from him. When she finally looked back, he stood up and followed her to the end of the *embarcadero*, then along a narrow grassy path that led through stunted windswept pine trees and thickets of wild rose bushes. Crossing a steep hill overlooking the sea, they stopped in front of a round hut constructed out of brush and torn canvas. In back of the hut, amulets and prayers written on strips of cloth hung from the branches of a towering oak tree. A wooden statue of a three-breasted woman guarded the hut's entrance. A smaller statue of a grinning monkey with a protruding belly stood behind it, the skin of a rattlesnake wrapped around its neck.

Delilah pulled a canvas flap over the hut's opening. "Welcome to my sanctuary. But if you go in, be warned. You might not come out."

She guided him towards a circle of round polished rocks on the edge of a cliff. Beneath them, long curling waves pounded on a rocky shore. As far as they could see there were no signs of life except for a full-masted schooner beating her way to the north.

They sat silently inside the circle. When the sun disappeared she left him, returning with a bowl of water and a cloth. Removing his clothes, she piled them outside the circle, then dipped the cloth into the bowl of water and washed each part of him.

She spoke as if she was instructing a child: "You have to be clean when you stand inside the circle. Otherwise you will disturb the spirits."

She handed him the cloth and bowl of water and took off her clothes; arranging them in a pile next to his, she allowed him to slowly spread the wet cloth over her body.

They were interrupted by Toku walking towards them. He

was dragging a heavy burlap sack and shaking a tambourine and wore a patched yellow-orange robe falling down to his ankles.

"I'm tired and very annoyed," he said, collapsing inside the circle. "You could have told me how long it would take to get here. And I need to be paid before I begin. My spirits won't work for nothing."

"Give him ten dollars," Delilah instructed Zebulon.

"Thirty," Toku replied. "And they're doing you a favor."

"Fifteen," Delilah countered.

After Zebulon paid him, Toku reached into his sack and pulled out three squealing guinea pigs and a curved scimitar. Squatting on his heels, he sliced their bellies into four sections, then poked his fingers through the entrails.

He looked up at Delilah. "You're confused about who is dreaming who. Your problem is that your dreams are controlling you, not the other way around. You no longer know how to stand on the earth. Too much hanging around the Dream Palace and follwing lost men."

"I could have told you that," she said.

"But you didn't," he replied.

He wiped his hands on his robe and jumped out of the circle, shaking his tambourine. Then he jumped back and squatted on his haunches, poking a stick through the entrails again.

"I see a prophecy, which is more than I expected to see, given your cloudy spirit. You will have a son, but he will never know his father. There's something else that I don't understand. Something about never being able to be in one place for longer than a few days."

He pointed at Zebulon. "That will be true for you, too. Not that it's any of my business."

"What is your business?" Zebulon asked.

Toku flopped on his back, cackling like a chicken as he slapped the ground. "Business? My business is making business. Why else would I be in this country? One day I'll have enough to buy a restaurant. And then a hotel. Maybe I'll even go back to my country and invest in a kingdom."

He took a pair of dice from his sack and rolled them over the ground, muttering an invocation in a foreign tongue.

"When you were a small boy, someone tried to drown you. Maybe it was your brother. The one who is not your real brother. Or maybe it was your father. Whoever it was, you're living inside a big confusion. Ever since then you've been afraid of water. Water means death to you, and until you die to who you think you are, you won't be able to live. Make sense? You'll always be on the move, trying to find out who you are. Like the rest of this crazy country."

Toku poked through the entrails again.

"Did someone shoot you in the heart?"

"I think so," Zebulon answered.

"You think so?" Toku said. "What kind of an answer is that?"

"Can we get this over with?" Delilah asked. "I didn't ask you to come up here and talk about him."

"One more thing," Toku said stiffly. "Your friend is a violent man who has done his share of killing and fooling around. He thinks doom is death and death is doom. That's why he wanders around like a ghost not knowing what trail he's meant to walk on."

Silently, he poked through the entrails, then nodded to Delilah. "You're the same. Just passing through. That's why you're drawn to each other and why you will never be together. Do you find that amusing? I don't. You have to find a way to help each other so you can be free of each other. Maybe that's what people in this country mean by love. Who knows? Not me."

He picked up his knife and dug out a narrow trench. Then he instructed them to lie down on their backs, head to head. After he had covered their bodies with dirt, except for their eyes and nostrils, he reached into his sack and took out a round mask of a grinning monkey. Then he buried the mask between their heads.

"This mask is your face and the face of everyone who has ever lived. When you understand that the separations between people are illusions, the spirits will go back where they came from. Right now the spirits are angry and confused. All they care about is sucking everything out from inside you and replacing it with greasy smoke. That can be very uncomfortable if you don't know the remedy."

He jumped up and down on Zebulon's chest and stomach, banging the drum and smacking his thick lips. Then he did the same to Delilah. Lighting up a half-smoked cheroot, he blew smoke in four directions, haranguing Delilah in his native language. She had no idea what he was saying as he continued to shout, more and more agitatedly. Finally, fed up and more than a little afraid, she pulled herself out of the trench and staggered to the creek, where she submerged herself in the water, only to have Toku drag her by the hair back into the circle.

"Oh…! Ah…! Ha…!" he cried, banging his drum and spitting into Zebulon's face and then into Delilah's. "Oh…! Ah…! Eh…! Ha…! Ho…! Ah…! Ha…! Eh…! Ho…!"

Suddenly Delilah dropped to the ground, rolling over like a snake shedding its skin. Zebulon fell down beside her, his arms jerking in spasms over his head as a current of energy rose violently up his spine. They remained flopping and writhing next to and on top of each other until the energies roaring through them stopped, and everything became flat and empty.

"The bad spirits have left," Toku pronounced. "Or most of them. If they come back, I'll need more than fifteen dollars to get rid of them."

He put the mask into his sack, bowed to the statue of the monkey, then to each of them.

"If you're lucky, you will never see me again," he said and walked away.

THE NEXT MORNING THEY WALKED BACK INTO SAN
Francisco. "If we're goin' on a long ride we should get
ourselves outfitted," he said, pointing to a clothing store.

"I should certainly hope so," Delilah said. "It's important
for a lady's state of mind to know that she's traveling with a
provider."

Delilah bought a pair of leather kid gloves, a pair of black
leather boots with high lace tops, two split riding skirts, and
finally, a .41-caliber derringer that she slipped into a leather purse.
For his part, Zebulon chose a broad-brimmed hat ornamented
with silver conchos and a fringed Mexican jacket with small
lapels that reached over his hips. His final purchase was a pair of
square-toed boots and a fancy set of spurs with silver rowels.

"So what do you think of my new-bought flasharity?" he
asked, turning around and examining himself in front of a full-
length mirror.

"You look like a judge or a lawyer."

"Now no one will know me," he said.

She held out her arms, twirling around in front of him.

"And me?" she asked.

"The wife of a judge. Or the madam of a high-priced
whorehouse."

She laughed. "Which do you prefer?"

She pranced away, swinging her purse and throwing him a

coquettish glance over her shoulder. "I suggest that we find out."

Their next stop was the waterfront and the Palace Hotel, where Zebulon impulsively booked a room on the top floor with a view of the harbor, a transaction that was made possible only after he represented Delilah as his slave; as people of color, even one as obviously exotic and indefinable as Delilah, were not allowed in the hotel except on terms of servitude.

They stood before the window inside the lavishly over-decorated room, staring down at the harbor and its hundreds of abandoned ships.

"Now I'm your slave," Delilah said.

"For one night anyway," he said. "Does that bother you?"

She turned away, sitting on the edge of the bed. "It bothers me that we're joined to a fate that we can't control. But then isn't that what fate is, a kind of slavery?"

The seriousness of her question unsettled him, even to the point of making him afraid, and then angry. "If you don't want to be here, maybe you ought to take off."

"I no longer know how to take off," she said. "And I don't know how to be here either, or anywhere else. When I saw you in the saloon I wanted to run away. And then in the hotel in Vera Cruz. But you keep showing up."

"Where does that leave us?"

"I have to see Ivan before he dies. He shot a man in the gold fields, in Calabasas Springs."

She stood up. "You don't have to come."

"I wish that was true," he said, and followed her out the door.

After they left the hotel, Zebulon purchased two horses and they rode south towards the Spanish town of Calabasas Springs, where Ivan was scheduled to be hung.

AS SOON AS THEY LEFT SAN FRANCISCO, DELILAH'S MOOD changed. Rather than urging him to press on, she started to drift and hang back, allowing them to proceed at a more leisurely pace over rolling green hills dotted with giant oak trees and clusters of well-fed cattle; the only sounds they were aware of were those made by their horses' hooves and their own breathing, and then gradually, as if they had entered into a silent and languid dream, not even those.

Their reveries were interrupted by a dozen cattle scrambling out of a gully followed by a *vaquero* in a wide-brimmed hat, shouting and swinging his *reata*. Once the cattle were out of the gully, the *vaquero* reined in his horse. He was old and had been through more than his share of hard times, but he had never seen anything quite like these two fancy pilgrims. Most likely a wealthy businessman and his slave, he decided, traveling to one of the great Spanish ranches that spread down the middle of the state like feudal kingdoms. Not wanting to find out, he tossed them a quick salute and rode off after the cattle.

Delilah spurred her horse in the opposite direction, smacking Zebulon's thigh as she galloped past him.

Laughing and shouting, they raced across a grassy meadow until they pulled up their horses by the bank of a slow-moving river. When she leaned forward, trying to catch her breath, he pulled her off her horse, dropping her kicking and screaming into the river. Rolling over on the muddy bank, they tore off their clothes, reaching out for each other in the weed-choked water.

Suddenly she stood up.

He looked up at her, not understanding.

"I can't," she said.

"What do you mean?"

"Do I always have to know what I mean?"

"I'll get some food," he said.

Without bothering to put on his clothes, he picked up his rifle and waded across the river.

After he had walked several miles with no game in sight, he sensed that he was being followed. There were fewer bird calls, and the land was too still, as if an unknown presence was moving through it. At first he thought it might be a Miwok, or a lone brave from a tribe he had no knowledge of, or maybe even a bounty hunter. He erased his footprints and circled back where he came from. Crawling through a clump of waist-high bunchgrass, he saw Delilah bending over, her eyes on the ground as she concentrated on his footprints. He watched her until she disappeared, then he circled ahead, waiting to surprise her in a clump of high grass. When she didn't appear, he circled back again.

When there was still no sign of her, he suddenly became worried and ran back to the river.

Delilah was leaning against a tree. A few feet away a wild turkey was roasting over a spit.

"When the wolf is silent," she said, "the moon begins to hunt."

~ ~ ~

That night they slept next to each other and yet apart. The following morning, after fording the San Joaquín River, they rode along the bank of the Tuolumne, through sparse country dotted with occasional oak groves, madrones, and manzanita shrubs.

Ten miles outside of Calabasas Springs they approached a collection of tents and shacks surrounding a half-finished adobe cantina. Any patch of earth not squatted on by prospectors was cluttered with mining equipment, wagon beds, spare wheels, barrels, and stacks of lumber.

"We'll need a stake," Zebulon said as they dismounted in front of the cantina.

Delilah hesitated, staring at two bearded men sitting on a bench, passing a bottle back and forth.

"The man wearing the bowler hat thinks he's seen you somewhere," she said. "Neither of them can figure out what you're doing with me, or what I'm doing with you, or if I'm for sale." She shut her eyes, her head shaking back and forth. "Bowler Hat hasn't told Yellow Rag about the nuggets he's keeping from him in his money-belt. Also, he hasn't heard from his wife in over a year. Mostly because she left him for someone else."

He looked at her as if she was mad.

"Lately I've become second-sighted," she said. "The way I was when I was a child."

As they walked towards the cantina, Bowler Hat leaned over and spat tobacco juice on Zebulon's boot.

"Ay know ye, dun' I?" he asked with a thick Scottish accent. "Ye be a bad un on the run."

"Bad enough to handle the likes of you," Zebulon said.

Bowler Hat stared at Zebulon with narrowed oily eyes. "Are ye makin' foon a' me? 'Cause if ya are, ya gaunna suffer."

Zebulon removed the man's bowler hat and stepped on it, grinding it into the dirt. "Ask your friend why he's hiding the nuggets he owes you. They're inside his belt. And forget about your wife. She's run off with someone else."

As they entered the cantina, they heard shouts, followed by a shot.

The smoke-filled room was loud and brimming with the usual collection of prospectors and whores. In the back, a rangy tow-headed farmer and a tall cadaverous man in a shiny black suit were shooting billiards.

"The one in the black suit is known as the Undertaker," Delilah said. "He's the one with money and the one you have to watch out for."

The Undertaker sliced his cue ball off two balls, and then another, not looking up as the farmer staggered towards the door.

"Game?" Zebulon asked.

"Your funeral," the Undertaker replied.

Zebulon put his last twenty dollars on the table, then won three straight games before he missed.

As the Undertaker bent over the table, Delilah sat down on a chair, staring at him and silently moving her lips.

Halfway into his shot, he stopped to look at her with eyes as cold and white as the cue ball.

"Don't stare," he demanded, then looked at Zebulon. "Tell your whore to turn her back when I'm lining up a shot, or I'll have her thrown out."

"She sits her own horse," Zebulon replied. "Nothin' me or anyone else can do about it."

"I'll second that," Hatchet Jack said as he walked up to the table, looking prosperous in a black three-piece suit, a narrow-brimmed hat with a braided horse-hair band, and a stringed tie. "If you let the witch break your stride, you're done for. You'll have to take up dominoes."

He sat down next to Delilah. "Go ahead. Take your shot. I'll keep things under control."

The Undertaker twisted both ends of his mustache, then slicked back his hair and slammed his stick into the cue ball, sending it ricocheting around three sides of the table before it nudged a ball into a side pocket.

They played two more games, the Undertaker winning all of them.

"Now you're done," the Undertaker said to Zebulon as he took the twenty dollars.

"Not just yet," Hatchet Jack replied. "The meal ain't over."

He dropped Delilah's gold and ruby necklace on the side of the billiard table. "One game. Your whole stake against the choker."

The Undertaker slid the necklace through his long bony fingers. When he realized that it was probably worth more than he had won in the last five years, he dropped thirty gold eagles on the table.

"Not near enough," Hatchet Jack said, "considering that this choker belonged to the Czar of Russia's cousin and before her, the Queen of Sheba."

The Undertaker dropped twenty gold eagles on the table.

"All right," Hatchet Jack said, clapping his hands and walking back and forth as if he intended to rearrange all the energies in the room.

"Sit or I'll walk," the Undertaker said.

Hatchet Jack sat, then stood up, staring at Delilah, until she gestured for him to sit down.

All of the Undertaker's considerable experience told him that he was being set up and that he should quit while he was ahead. The only problem was the necklace. Once he had it, his life would never be the same.

He took a deep breath and bent over the table as side bets flew around the room.

"You know why they call him the Undertaker?" Hatchet Jack asked the crowd as the Undertaker sank the first five balls. "Because he's five feet under, goin' on six."

"Under! Under!" Delilah mumbled. "Who will bury the

Undertaker when the Undertaker goes under?"

When the Undertaker's shot missed by less than a hair, Zebulon ran the rest of the points as easily as if he was playing a game that didn't matter.

"You set me up," the Undertaker said. "All three of you."

He picked up the gold eagles, then took out a pepperbox pistol from his vest pocket.

Before he could pull the trigger, Zebulon slammed his cue stick on the Undertaker's wrist, then over the back of his head, knocking him out.

He picked up the necklace, the Undertaker's pistol, and his fifty gold eagles, half of which he gave to Hatchet Jack, who ordered a round of wall-to-wall drinks for the room. Then all three sat down at a table and ordered a big sloppy meal of chicken mole and corn bread.

After they finished eating, Hatchet Jack removed a folded-up strip of newspaper from his jacket pocket and handed it to Delilah, who read it out loud:

> "And here among us was a living example of the Wild West! He was a man of the wilderness untrammeled by civilized constraints, primitive and unschooled in society, but spontaneous and generous in his conversation and behavior. The questions we asked! And the answers that we received as Zebulon Shook regaled us with his astonishing tales of the Colorado mountains and the vast southwestern deserts and the gold fields of California!
>
> "Imagine our surprise when we learned that Zebulon Shook was not only a famous outlaw wanted for murder, bank robbery, and horse theft with a price on his head, but that he was also a revolutionary sought by the Mexican government. After that, every passenger kept his cabin well locked.
>
> "The entire ship was relieved when he was ushered off at a small fishing town several hundred miles from

the Spanish port of Cartagena. As he stood looking back at us from a forbidding shore surrounded by dense jungle, there were few among us who believed we had seen the last of —"

Before she could finish, Zebulon reached over and tore the paper into small pieces, then slowly dropped the pieces one by one on the floor.

"Speakin' of breezy winds," Hatchet Jack said. "I ran into your Pa a month ago. He made a big strike on the Eel, then blew it all playin' stud poker."

"Where is he now?" Zebulon asked.

"Last I saw, passed out in the back of a feed store in Silver City. When I told him about you bein' in the newspaper and bein' wanted, dead or alive, he wanted to hunt you down and cut out your liver. 'A Shook should never be in no newspaper.' Those were his words. He didn't mind the outlaw part. It was you bein' a lyin' pecker-headed lunatic that rattled his pan. 'Course me bein' the one that told him didn't help. I offered him a horse to square things up, but he turned me down. Said he preferred me to owe him rather than accept an old rim-rocker just to square a debt he didn't want to settle."

Zebulon took the gold and ruby necklace out of his pocket and fastened it around Delilah's neck. "If you wait long enough things come around."

"And then around again," she said.

"Hold on," Hatchet Jack said. "I took that choker off two pilgrims in San Francisco who tried to rob me when I crawled into their shack to get out of the rain. By rights it's mine, considerin' I had to shoot both of 'em to get it."

"She gave it to me long before you had it," Zebulon said.

"What ends up, ends up with whoever it ends up with," Hatchet Jack insisted. "That's my say, and that's the way it is."

Delilah handed him the necklace.

Hatchet Jack hesitated, looking from Delilah to Zebulon.

Finally he shrugged and handed the necklace back to her.

"From you to me, and me to you."

"You're mixed in with him?" Zebulon asked.

"He was in the cantina when Ivan killed a man in Calabasas Springs," she said.

"Did he smoke someone over you?" Zebulon asked.

"Over a card game," Hatchet Jack explained. "When I saw her in that cantina in Calabasas Springs, she was playin' seven-card stud with that Rusky Count and a few others, a gold sniffer and a stagecoach driver. The Count was bettin' wild and crazy from all the gold he scooped up that week. I came downstairs after a little rendezvous of my own, and there they were, like when I first laid eyes on them, and then there was that shoot-out in the cantina in Panchito. I could see it all comin' like I'd been there before. I sat down at the table, bein' flush and wantin' to high-roll everything. You know how it is. It all came down to one hand. I had a full house and I swear to Wakan Tanka, the lady you're lookin' at pulled a queen-high straight flush. And then some drunk comes in yellin' that I stole his horse. Truth is, I had taken his horse to give to your Pa. And then all hell breaks loose – everyone duckin' for cover and shots fired from god knows who or where.

"I woke up in a ditch thinkin' I was dead. The Count had run off, havin' shot some poor bastard who called him out on his claim. When I come in, Delilah was sittin' at the bar. One thing led to another. That's why I come down here, to make it straight with the Count before he swings. He's a hard case, that Count. Wouldn't throw me a bone. Said it was my fault, which it weren't. Said I plugged the Aussie, which I didn't. Delilah is another story."

He paused. "Life dances on, don't it, little brother? I'll take you to where they got the Count locked up, and then I'm done with both of you."

"You ain't my brother," Zebulon said.

Hatchet Jack raised his shot glass. "Maybe not by blood. Maybe somethin' thicker than blood. Never mind. Here's to bein' on this side of the grass, brother or no brother, Count or no Count. The three of us yoked up and here we sit."

After they finished off the bottle, they rode off to witness Ivan's fate in Calabasas Springs.

ON THE OUTSKIRTS OF THE TOWN THEY WERE CONFRONTED by five drunken Australian prospectors who had arrived that morning from their diggings to witness the hanging of Count Ivan Baranofsky, who had killed one of their own in a card game. When one stationed himself along the flank of Delilah's horse and put his hand on her thigh, she lashed him across the face with her quirt.

Before his companions could react, Zebulon grabbed her horse's reins and all three galloped side by side into the town, where most of the population was still inside the eighteenth-century Spanish church celebrating the end of Lent. A few women in the square were preparing tables with platters of enchiladas, frijoles, tamales, grizzly steak, venison, and apple, mince, and cherry pies.

Hatchet Jack led the other two through a cluster of red-tiled buildings, then down a narrow alley behind the church to an adobe shed marked by a barred window. In front of the shed, a deputy sat on a bench with a shotgun across his lap.

"No one allowed inside," the deputy said. "Only one of you can speak through the window."

Hatchet Jack and Zebulon stood across the alley while Delilah approached the window.

Ivan sat leaning against the far wall, one of his ankles manacled to a long chain.

"Ivan," she called, peering through the bars.

He looked up. "I didn't want you to come."

"I had no choice."

He hobbled to the window and reached through the bars, one finger touching hers.

"You should have left me a long time ago."

"I tried."

"That's true. How you tried. I kept hoping…. Did you know they're hanging me tomorrow?"

"The day after tomorrow," said the deputy, who was listening from his bench.

"Can't you hurry it up?" Ivan asked the deputy. "I'm more than ready to depart. Anything to end all the drama."

"I'll ask," the deputy said. "But it's hard to rush a good party."

"Even without the gold we had enough to save ourselves," Ivan said to Delilah. "That's the great irony. We could have gone anywhere – Egypt, Tasmania, Brazil. Anywhere but this country…. But enough supposing and wishing and *what if's*. I prefer the hangman to those speculations."

He suddenly noticed Hatchet Jack and Zebulon standing across the alley, smoking cigars as they looked over at them.

"They came with me," she explained. "Or Zebulon did. We met the other one outside of town. Hatchet Jack. He said he had already seen you."

"He certainly did see me. Quite sloppy, he was, expressing his need to be free of blame or guilt. For what? I asked him. I was appalled at his whole approach. It made me feel that he actually might have shot the man they said that I shot. I didn't feel like granting him absolution. Or anything, for that matter. Not that that's in my power. And I certainly have no need to see Zebulon. If you hadn't gotten him thrown off the boat, I would have pushed him. I suppose now you'll go off with him. Hopefully he won't be as deviously sentimental as the other one. What's his name? Hatchet?"

"I'm not going off with anyone."

"Don't be absurd," he said. "You'll never survive alone."

"I've always been alone, and I've always survived."

"If you want to think that, go ahead. If that helps you."

"Forgive me, Ivan," she said. "I'm… I'm trying…."

"Oh dear god," he interrupted. "Spare me a pitiful goodbye. I thought you were better than that. Can't we just chat about the weather or the awful music they play in the town square, or say nothing at all?"

"There's no time, Ivan," she replied. "Please."

"Time? I'm yawning through time. I refuse to be consoled or offer reparation. I loathe that rubbish." He shook his head. "I won't forgive you or myself. There's nothing to forgive, and if there were, I'd lie and say I forgave you."

"Ivan…. Please."

She removed a long oblong root from inside her blouse and slid it to him through the bars.

"Chew on it before they come for you," she whispered.

"What a curious benediction," he replied, lowering his voice so the deputy couldn't hear. "It's easier for me, you know. All I have to do is die. You have to go on. Not that I wouldn't change places with you."

The deputy rapped on the wall with the stock of his shotgun. "Time's up."

"I'll come tomorrow," she said.

He removed a gold pocket watch from his shirt and slipped it to her through the bars. "Speaking of time. A reminder."

"I love you," she said. "I always have, even when I didn't."

"I know, I know," he said, his voice cruelly impatient, as if he was trying to drive her away. "Come tomorrow. But no slop."

"All right," she agreed.

He watched her walk down the alley with Hatchet Jack and Zebulon until they disappeared around a corner.

"Gone," he said to the deputy. "Gone before she ever arrived."

AS THEY WALKED PAST THE CHURCH, PARISHIONERS WERE streaming down the front steps towards the town square. Most were Mexicans, the women wearing ankle-length embroidered dresses and black shawls covering their hair, along with a few Chilean and Peruvian prospectors in red ponchos and leather chaps.

"I need a drink," Delilah pleaded. "Some whiskey. Anything."

She headed for a saloon across the square. When she suddenly sank to her knees, Zebulon and Hatchet Jack lifted her up and carried her to a table.

She sat without speaking, staring numbly at the crowd as if through a pane of smoky glass. The entire population of Calabasas Springs was gathered in the town square, as well as families and hands from the outlying ranches and the Australians and other Argonauts camping outside of town. Musicians played guitars and violins, and children ran in and out of the crowd and around the tables piled with food and drink. The Australians, who had mostly been rejected by the local women, danced with each other or by themselves.

An Australian ex-convict with an *X* branded on his forehead, stumbled up to the table where Delilah sat. Staring at her, he spread a hand through a mince pie and then slowly licked each finger.

"I have a bet you're for sale," he said.

"She's not a slave and she ain't for sale," Hatchet Jack replied.

The Australian shrugged. "That's not what I been hearing."

He sauntered off towards a bunch of newly arrived Argonauts from Alabama who were pulling down a Mexican flag from the top of a pole. As they stomped and urinated on the flag, they were joined by other miners, all singing:

Jimmy Cracked Corn And I Don't Care.

When Hatchet Jack and Zebulon walked over, several men threatened them with pistols, then pulled Delilah from her chair. They dragged her to an oak tree, where one of them bound her wrists while another threw a rope over one of the branches.

"Hold on!" Hatchet Jack shouted, pushing his way towards them. "This woman is not some mail-order slave you can do what you want with…. She's a princess with noble blood hailing from King Solomon's ranch down there in West Texas. She's the daughter of an English general, a purebred queen of the Amazon. More than that, she's a god-fearing Christian who knows how to cook and roll biscuits and pray to the Lord!"

Hatchet Jack pointed at Zebulon. "Does this man look like he would put his brand on a slave? Hell no! He's an *alcalde*! A man of the law from San Francisco. Do you particulate what that means? He's here on business, appointed by the Governor General of the State of Californie to fix the corruption of the mines, as well as to get himself hitched in the town's church to this woman whose neck you're about to stretch. If you people mess with an *alcalde* you're messin' direct with the State of Californie, or my name ain't Lorenzo de Calderón Vazquez de Gama."

The Australian spat on the ground. "And I'm sayin' that you're a horse-thieving half-breed. The only way this black whore will get herself hitched is in the court of hell."

His companion slipped the noose over Delilah's head while another carried over a chair for her to stand on. With a loud "Hurrah," they lifted her up.

Delilah spoke her last words to Zebulon and Hatchet Jack: "Let go whatever comes, good or bad. And when your time is up don't leave a mess behind."

Before the chair could be pulled out, four *caballeros* in black velvet suits embroidered with silver trim, entered the square from the cathedral, carrying an open Chinese palanquin on their shoulders. An ancient figure sat in the middle of the palanquin in an ornate armchair, his frail body wrapped inside a black cloak. A dozen well-armed *vaqueros* rode behind him.

Even though Don Luis Arragosa was over a hundred years old and half-paralyzed by a recent stroke, his presence commanded attention. As the last titled owner of one of the few remaining great Spanish ranches in California, he remained a beloved symbol of past glories to the Mexican population of Calabasas Springs.

After the *caballeros* lowered the palanquin to the ground, Don Luis sat quietly, contemplating Delilah as she balanced herself on the chair. Finally he spoke in a hoarse, barely audible whisper: "It is a sacrilege and sin to be disturbed in prayer, particularly at this sacred time of the year."

When several of the Australians objected, Don Luis raised a hand for silence.

"What crime has this woman committed?"

"She broke the law," replied one of the Australian ex-convicts.

"Whose law?"

"Our law," said another Australian. "The only law that counts. She struck one of us with her quirt for no reason. The woman is a slave and a whore. What else does anyone need to know?"

Don Luis turned to Delilah. "What is your response to this charge?"

Delilah straightened her shoulders, pointing at her accuser. "As I was riding into town, this man grabbed the reins of my horse and demanded that I engage in a carnal act with him. He treated me like a prostitute, so I slashed him with my quirt, and I would be pleased to do it again. It was not my intention, nor was it that of my companions, to cause trouble. We have more important matters to deal with."

"And what are those matters?" Don Luis asked.

"To witness the death of my husband, Count Ivan Baranofsky, who, as you must have heard, has been unjustly sentenced to hang."

Don Luis turned to the Australians. "You are sadly mistaken if you think that you can ride into this town like drunken San Francisco vigilantes and commit whatever outrage suits you. It is one thing to rape and pillage the country in a compulsive quest for gold – a quest, I might add, that will soon be exhausted – but it is quite another matter to violate a woman, no matter her color or race or religion. This woman was defending her honor. And you, Sir, obviously have no honor."

Exhausted, Don Luis sank back in his armchair.

The local population, along with the Chileans and Peruvians, surged forward, expressing their approval. For a moment it seemed that fighting would break out, but the *caballeros* held their ground, pointing their rifles at the Australians while Zebulon and Hatchet Jack removed the noose from Delilah's head and helped her down from the chair.

Don Luis sighed. "There will be only one hanging in Calabasas Springs, and that act will take place the day after tomorrow at six o'clock in the evening. To my mind, the decision is unfortunate: but it is the law, no matter if one agrees or disagrees."

An Anglo miner stepped forward.

"Know one thing, old man. There's a new bunch comin' to town, not to mention pourin' into this whole side of the country – immigrants, businessmen, scoundrels, all kinds, you can be sure of that. They're rollin' in every day. There's no stoppin' 'em, and none of 'em give a good goddamn what you think. Them old days when your people held the cards are over. Best thing for you is to stay out of the way."

"I don't disagree," Don Luis said. "This country has certainly been invaded by barbarians who offer us only selfish ambition and greed. But I will make you a promise. If my men ever see you or any of your companions in Calabasas Springs again, even once, they will shoot you like rabid dogs."

Don Luis' chin sagged to his chest. No one was sure if he was still breathing until he raised a claw-like hand, and four *caballeros* picked up the palanquin and carried it to a waiting carriage.

Before the carriage rode away, a *caballero* rode back to Delilah. "Don Luis asks that you and your friends join him at his ranch, where he will be pleased to welcome you for the night."

"You two go on," Hatchet Jack said. "After I grab some shut eye, I'm gettin' rid of this town and everything that goes with it."

He looked at Delilah. "Including you and your Count."

~ ~ ~

After the carriage drove off, Zebulon and Delilah were escorted to Don Luis' *hacienda*. None of the remaining Argonauts believed Hatchet Jack's explanation that Zebulon was an *alcalde*. A few even suspected that he was the outlaw, Zebulon Shook, recently written about in *The San Francisco Star*. And if that were the case, there was bound to be a reward for his capture as well as for that of his Abyssinian whore.

THEY ENTERED DON LUIS' ESTATE THROUGH AN ORNATE
iron gate and passed a guardhouse, tanning vats, a blacksmith
shop, several smokehouses, a butchering shed, and five outdoor
bake ovens. Further on, a forty-foot clock tower dominated the
end of an overgrown garden whose crumbling adobe walls were
covered with flowering bougainvillea. On the other side of the
garden, a long stately colonnade introduced an imposing two-
story Spanish adobe ranch house with a corroded red-tiled roof
and thickly latticed windows, most of which were in serious
need of repair.

A *vaquero* escorted their horses to a nearby stable, where a
stooped white-haired retainer led them through a massively
carved wooden door into a generous *entrada* lit by iron chandeliers.
At the far end of the *entrada* they entered a library.

Despite the logs blazing in the massive fireplace, an air of
gloom pervaded the musty high-ceilinged room with its cracked
and peeling walls lined with overflowing bookcases and portraits
of the Spanish court by Velásquez and Goya, as well as a mural
celebrating the *Conquistador's* conquest of Mexico.

Don Luis sat in front of the fire in the middle of a deep-
seated leather couch, his frail body almost invisible inside a
buffalo robe. Behind him in a far corner of the room, a three-
legged French clavichord stood next to a collection of lutes,

mandolins, and guitars, all hanging from the walls on sagging wires.

They sat on a row of armchairs facing Don Luis, sipping a dry red wine from his vineyard. After waiting an hour for Don Luis to speak, Zebulon finally broke the silence. "Maybe this ain't the right time to trample on your peace, Don Luis. We can pay our respects another day."

"In these dark days, every moment is precious," Don Luis replied. "Whoever you people are, wherever you are going, for this one night, *mi casa, su casa*. I am embarrassed that Calabasas Springs, a town my family has been proud to be part of for over nine generations, has now entered a state of anarchy and barbarism. In past years the entire town would have gathered at this ranch to celebrate Easter Sunday, but now…. Forgive an old man's ramblings about the ravages of time. But permit me to ask you: What is happening to this land? Why is it being raped and profaned and exhausted? But of course, how would any of you know the answer to such a question? You are obviously strangers here, and confused more than I about the way this country has always nourished itself, carried on its business, only to be – I don't know. God help me, it has all but disappeared."

He looked at Delilah. "Is it true what those savages said back there in the town square: that you're nothing more than an ambitious slave who will stop at nothing to get her way?"

"Perhaps at one time I could have been perceived that way," she said. "Certainly it was true for a short period in Africa, although that was due more to circumstances than character. But when Count Baranofsky made a proposal to me at an early age that I become his consort and eventually his wife, I was freed of any hunger for mere survival. He also saw to my education in many of the capitals of Europe. For his extraordinary generosity, I shall always be grateful."

Don Luis nodded, impressed by Delilah's diction and refinement. "A noble tradition, that of the consort," he said wistfully; "one that I have personally honored from time to time, even to the point of making a fool of myself – but that's another story."

"Certainly it has its advantages as well as its limitations," Delilah said. "On both sides."

"Of course," Don Luis said. "Why, not long ago…. Where was it? Madrid or Mexico City? Perhaps Venice. It doesn't matter. Another time, another place."

Don Luis shivered, pulling his robe around his shoulders as a sudden chill entered the room. "Let me add, my dear, that I was immediately struck by your courageous presence, by the way you stood on your chair calmly accepting your fate. Your resolve reminded me of my own situation – waiting… sinking… ready to depart…. I have made my final visit to Calabasas Springs. I will never go there again, not even to Mass; nor do I choose to go anywhere else…. In times past… before the insane *gringos* showed up… when my father was still alive… and his father and his father before him, they would have rescued your Count. No matter if he deserved to hang…. They knew how to please a guest in those days. Even if it meant arranging for his death, it would have been done in the right way. Precisely. With a certain amount of grace. Without this useless horseshit."

He slumped back inside his buffalo robe, his head sagging to his chest. "What I meant to say to you…. I talked to your Count last week. He told me many things about you, things that you yourself might not even be aware of. Things that were, quite frankly, disturbing."

No one in the room spoke or even moved.

"May I sing for you?" Delilah asked.

Don Luis' lips whispered a reply. "*Por favor, Señora. Gracias.*"

She sat down in front of the clavichord, closing her eyes. Slowly, with rising passion, she began to sing Tomás Luis de Victoria's "Ave Maria" from a Mass that Don Luis had requested that very morning to be sung at his funeral.

As she sang, the room filled with servants, *vaqueros*, and *caballeros*, all of them gathered around the old patriarch, who had fallen deeply asleep on his couch.

The song over, a retainer led them upstairs for the night.

They found themselves in a large vaulted room dominated by a king-sized bed. Silk robes had been laid out for them on a leather couch, and plates of freshly prepared food had been placed on a round table lit by candles.

After Zebulon changed into his robe he lay down on the bed, staring up at the ceiling as he smoked one of Don Luis' Mexican cheroots.

When he finished the cigar, he noticed Delilah standing on the other side of the room. She was naked, her robe around her feet.

As she slowly walked towards him, they heard a bell ringing from the church tower and shouts from the garden, announcing the death of Don Luis.

~ ~ ~

When they rode back into Calabasas Springs, they found the jail burned to the ground. Three Mexicans lay dead in the middle of the street; another was spread across a wagon wheel, two men horse-whipping his back and shoulders. Except for Ivan's dead body hanging from the branch of an oak tree, the square was empty.

Before they reached the end of the street, they were surrounded by a group of armed vigilantes.

"Don Luis is dead," Zebulon informed them.

"Good for him," was the reply. "Now you can join him."

As Zebulon was pulled roughly to the ground, Hatchet Jack rode down the street and grabbed the reins of Delilah's horse, and the two of them galloped off through the crowd of startled miners.

Zebulon's last image of Delilah was her long black hair streaming behind her as she and Hatchet Jack disappeared into the night.

No one bothered to mount a pursuit, there being no point in chasing after a whore and a half-breed with no price on their heads.

ZEBULON WAS KEPT IN A SMALL HOLDING CELL BENEATH
the Sacramento courthouse, half of which doubled as a
thriving saloon. Unfortunately for the Australian miners who
brought him in, the reward was only a quarter of what had been
advertised, and they returned to Calabasas Springs as outraged
as when they had first arrived.

The trial was jammed from the opening bell, mostly due to
Artemis Stebbins' front-page article in *The San Francisco Star*
reporting the capture of the celebrated outlaw. The first week
of examinations and cross-examinations proceeded at a slow
pace, as everyone, including the judge, was preoccupied with
rumors of a massive gold strike on the Feather River. Despite
this distraction, which had already emptied half the town, there
was no standing room left when the district attorney, a portly
one-armed man with ambitions for the senate, approached the
jury for his final summation:

"The story is simple, folks. Zebulon Shook rode into Calabasas
Springs pretending to be an *alcalde*, a man of the law hired by the
governor. His real intention was to aid in the escape of Count
Ivan Baranofsky, a convicted murderer. The same night that he
arrived, all hell broke loose. The next morning, the main street
of Calabasas Springs was littered with the bodies of five men
and two women. Gentlemen of the jury, I submit to you that
if Zebulon Shook goes unpunished for this heinous crime,

anarchy will have triumphed over law and order."

The district attorney was interrupted by a sparrow flying through a window. Circling the courthouse, the sparrow flew over the crowd, including Delilah and Hatchet Jack sitting in the last row and Stebbins seated on a fold-out chair by the door.

After another hysterical circle, the sparrow finally settled on Zebulon's outstretched hand.

Looking first at Delilah, then at Hatchet Jack, his fingers closed slowly over the quivering bird.

"One minute a man is flyin' free," he said to the room at large, "then he's caught. Then he's free again."

He opened his fingers, releasing the sparrow. The bird frantically flew back and forth, until finally, with the help of a few men waving jackets, it found its escape through an open window.

Everyone in the room, except for Delilah, burst into foot-stomping applause until the judge banged down his gavel and yelled for silence.

Order restored, the district attorney continued: "Gentlemen of the jury, storm clouds gather on the horizon. Our country's great and noble adventure is at risk and I fear for our safety, if not our future. If we don't protect the purity of this country from outlaws, renegades, and runaway slaves, as well as the influx of foreigners raping and pillaging our sacred heritage, then we are all to blame. I say to you, from my heart –"

He was interrupted by a drunk in long johns and a gun-belt, stumbling into the courtroom and announcing that they'd hit a mother lode on the Feather River, the biggest in the history of California.

When most of the room, including the lawyer for the defense, rushed outside, the judge ordered the jury to arrive at a decision within the hour, or he would be forced to postpone the trial.

Five minutes later the jury came to a decision: Zebulon Shook was guilty of manslaughter. The judge imposed a sentence of twenty years at hard labor, and Zebulon was shackled and led out of the courtroom by two deputies. He paused in front of Hatchet Jack, who stood by the door, Delilah behind him.

"I'll take care of her," Hatchet Jack said, "one way or the other."

Before Zebulon could answer, a deputy pushed him through the door and down the steps of the courthouse.

A T THE CITY JAIL, A CLERK ASSIGNED ZEBULON A PRISON number, then filled out a form with his name, nationality, occupation, and religion. Zebulon gave his real name but invented the rest of his answers: free-trapper for his occupation, Wakan Tanka for his religion, and The Big Sky Country for his native land. After the clerk methodically wrote down the information, Zebulon was led to a courtyard to be photographed.

A large crowd was waiting for him, most of them never having seen or even heard of a camera.

Zebulon was instructed to stand against a brick wall before the photographer, a short stocky man with sad drooping eyes, wearing a French beret. As the photographer disappeared beneath the camera's black hood, it occurred to Zebulon that he was about to be executed by some new-fangled weapon. Some of the old-timers had the same thought and made sure to stand several feet behind the strange contraption.

When the flash finally exploded, there was scattered applause and congratulations all around.

Wearing a convict's striped pants and shirt, he was driven in an enclosed wagon to *La Grange*, a French schooner anchored in the headwaters of the Sacramento River that had been transformed into a prison hulk after its captain and crew deserted her for the gold fields.

Zebulon was accompanied by the Warden's aide-de-camp, Master Sergeant Alva Bent, a peg-legged veteran of the Mexican War as well as several campaigns against the Comanche and Apache.

They rolled past a long line of schooners and paddle steamers tied up to an *embarcadero*, then along a wooden levee where dozens of Chinese workers hauled furniture and lumber through a chaotic congestion of newly arrived prospectors and overloaded wagons.

Bent lit two cigarettes, placing one in Zebulon's mouth. "A few years ago, this place had only a few saloons and a livery stable. Now it seems that every asshole in the world is paradin' around here, most of 'em with gold fever."

He pointed towards higher ground, where building lots had been staked out in parched fields strewn with offal, broken machinery, and dead cows. "Next year there'll be a hundred goddamn houses up there. Mark my words. But don't you worry, son. By the time you get out of the lockup or they decide to hang you, it'll be back to what used to be. That's the way life is."

He removed the last of Zebulon's cigarette from his mouth. "Tell me the truth. Were you bein' foolish with that reporter, or was that thievery and mayhem the straight tell?"

"Coming here by boat was true enough," Zebulon acknowledged. "That and bein' hired as a guide for the gold fields. Shootin' up the citizens of Calabasas Springs and startin' a jail break was a damn lie."

Bent took a flask out of his hip pocket and after a quick snort, offered it to Zebulon. "That's what I been sayin'. I can always smell a nosebag full of lies. It was all arranged: politicians puttin' the muzzle on all of the free-floaters, squeezin' the country, makin' it safe for business and greenhorns. 'Come on out to Paradise, folks, and get rich beyond your wildest dreams. Scoop up a few bowls of gold dust. Buy yourself a big hotel and fill it with easy women, or go back where you came from richer than your biggest dreams.' Those boys in Washington have put a noose around our necks. I know. I helped Fremont push the greasers back to old Mex. Fremont had his orders from back East: go for the gold and open up the sluice gates and watch the joint rip. Trains will run east to west and back. No sweat and no buffler and no red niggers and no good times. Them days is all gone. Hoe it down, boys. Plant your potatoes and tomatoes and to hell with what used to be."

Bent lit two more cigarettes and gave one to Zebulon, then both of them finished off his flask. "Your mistake was signing up with that Russian and his slave. That was wavin' a red flag at the bull. Now you're big time, son. There's a story on you. Guilty or not. I'll stake you to some advice: the Warden will twist your tail into a knot just for fun. When he starts bangin' on about god and the devil, let him talk. If you so much as bite your lip, he'll lower you into the drink slower than molasses and smile as you go under."

They traveled another two miles along the river, drinking and smoking, until they arrived at a newly built two-story shingled house with blue trim and an elaborate garden defined by a white picket fence. Directly in front of the house, Zebulon could see the prison hulk anchored in the middle of the river by rope cables attached to two sycamore trees.

"Here we are, son," Bent declared: "Your home away from home."

He led Zebulon past two guards stationed by the front door, then down a long hallway lined with presidential portraits of Washington, Jefferson, and Madison. Somewhere on the second floor a woman sang an Irish lullaby.

Bent knocked on a door and then knocked again. When there was still no answer, he opened the door and gestured Zebulon inside.

A thin middle-aged man wearing a white linen suit and wire-rimmed glasses sat behind a desk bent over a game of solitaire.

On the wall, Zebulon recognized a Hopi fertility mask hanging next to a Cheyenne war bonnet and two Crow tomahawks. A torn leather couch opposite the desk was piled with books, along with a scrimshawed whalebone, a fossilized walrus penis, a polished buffalo horn, and four Papago and Zuni baskets.

Bent cleared his throat: "The prisoner has arrived, Sir. Safe and sound."

The Warden gathered the cards into a deck and placed it back in its ivory box before he lifted his head and inspected Zebulon from head to foot.

"From what I read in the newspapers I expected a bigger man. Someone huge and grotesque, possibly even a Beowulf giant. Which is not to say that your appearance is marginal, Mister Shook. Quite the contrary."

The Warden turned his head, staring through a latticed French window at the looming silhouette of the prison hulk, which seemed, in the late afternoon light, to be suspended above the river. Then he reached into the top drawer of his desk and withdrew a small golden bowl. The bowl was no more than five inches in diameter and covered with a translucent dome, which was also made from gold and decorated with mastodon ivory carved with a barleycorn pattern.

It was the most beautiful and finely wrought object that Zebulon had ever seen.

The Warden began to recount the bowl's history and effect while Bent silently mouthed the words that, over the years, he had come to know by heart.

"A precious object, wouldn't you say, Mister Shook? Hellenistic, third century. Pure alchemy. Prima material, with no beginning and no end. All differences massaged within a roundness that acknowledges no boundaries. A vessel fit for the gods! Not like this appalling rubbish they dig up around here. I don't care about the karat count of a nugget; the entire pursuit, not to mention the end result, is cursed. Vulgar loot for ignorant minds. Reflect on the beauty, Mister Shook. A work such as this possesses enough elegance to overwhelm nature. Its transcendence has the power to stop time, to invoke rapture. Which brings me back to you, Mister Shook: If you wish to stop time, and I strongly suggest that it would be to your advantage to do so, then you must firmly commit yourself to the process of salvation."

The Warden carefully returned the bowl to its sanctuary. "Because of your reputation I was advised to transfer you to the penitentiary they've just built at San Quentin, across the bay from San Francisco. Fortunately for you, I was able to assure the governor that we are more than capable of keeping you here. Of course, if it had been up to me, I would have had you hung and been done with it. But that event will have to wait for a more appropriate moment."

Zebulon nodded, staring at a rattle in the middle of the Warden's desk.

"Sergeant Bent tells me it's Blackfoot," the Warden said. "Others suggest Ute or Crow."

"Lakota Sioux," Zebulon replied. "They use it to pray to Wakan Tanka, their Grandfather Spirit. When they have a problem to work out, they take it with them into a vision pit."

"I've heard of such things. And do you have any idea how long these vision quests last?"

"A few days. Sometimes a week. Sometimes more."

"Primitive, but commendable," the Warden said. "And if we are to believe some of what we hear about aboriginal behavior, rather mystical. But I'm afraid, Mister Shook, that your quest will be of a different order: your assigned pit being a dark and comfortless abode of guilt and wretchedness; a place designed for grief and penitence, according to the dictates of our Lord Jesus Christ; a place where time, as I have already suggested to you, might, if you are diligent enough, finally stop."

He signaled to Bent, who quoted from memory: "'Then

Joseph's master led him into the prison, into a place where the king's prisoners were confined, and he was there in the prison. But the Lord was with him, and showed him mercy, and He gave him favor in the sight of the keeper of the prison. Whatever he did, the Lord made it prosper.' Genesis 39: 20-23."

The Warden removed his glasses, massaging the bridge of his aquiline nose. "It is my conviction that even the most challenged and evil among us can achieve salvation, Mister Shook."

The Warden gestured to Bent, who jerked Zebulon's ankle shackles with both hands, sending him sprawling face-down on the floor.

"Do you have anything to confess before you're consigned to quarters?"

Zebulon shook his head.

"Good. Not only is silence golden, on this ship it's also practical."

The Warden pulled on his boots. "To survive, abide by the rules. The least display of anger, selfishness, or resentment will not be tolerated. The slightest tendency towards chaos or anarchy or any kind of trickery will be noticed and dealt with. Again, I refer you to the Old Testament. Any false statement or surly countenance will be punished with a straitjacket and a gag. If you indulge in stealing, fighting, or breaking ranks, you will be flogged and chained to a wall for an indefinite period. Any attempt at escape, or even an impulse to stray from your routine, and you will be hung from a block with only the tips of your toes brushing the floor. If you persist in a second attempt, you will be lowered over the side of the ship with only your nostrils above the water."

The Warden stood up, clapping his hands. "Order. Diligence. Cleanliness. The trilogy that we serve, Mister Shook. Otherwise, we would be faced with the abyss. As the book says, 'Whatsoever a man sows, so shall he reap.'"

Bent removed a bottle of brandy from a side table and filled two shot glasses, handing one to Zebulon, the other to the Warden.

"Fate has consigned us to Sacramento, Mister Shook. A name, by the way, that means 'sacrament,' a commitment to a sacred oath, or, if you will, a covenant between man and God. This is the last libation you will have for twenty years, or until your stay with us comes to an end."

He lifted his glass: "To salvation."

After they drank, the Warden took his cards from his ivory box and spread them out for a game of solitaire, leaving Bent and a guard who had been stationed by the door to escort Zebulon to the prison hulk.

The guard, whom Bent referred to as Snake Eyes, was a sallow-faced teenager with a struggling mustache. Once they reached the river, Snake Eyes established his authority by slamming his rifle against Zebulon's legs, then shoving him face-first into the small flat-bottomed boat that serviced the prison hulk.

~ ~ ~

Zebulon rowed while Bent and Snake Eyes sat opposite him.

"So you're one of them mountain men," Snake Eyes said. "Word is that you're an Injun killer, bank robber, gunslinger, and desperado. That's one hell of a big stack for just one man."

Zebulon didn't answer. He had never rowed a boat before with his wrists chained and he was having trouble with the oars.

"How many notches you got on your belt, Mountain Man?" Snake Eyes asked.

Zebulon raised the ante. "Fifty, more or less. After twenty you lose count."

"I notched my share," Snake Eyes said. "Last month I shot two prisoners tryin' to swim down the river. That gives me six in all."

Bent shook his head, embarrassed to have a man of Zebulon's reputation exposed to such crude braggadocio. "It's a shame all the real men are off in the gold fields and all that's left are young greenhorns dumber'n sticks."

"Haul it in, old man," Snake Eyes said. "Don't give me that 'I seen it all' bullshit. I'm talkin' to a real live bastard that's pullin' twenty years. He's mistaken if he thinks he can pull my johnson just 'cause he's more famous than the governor."

Snake Eyes lit another cigarette, blowing smoke into Zebulon's eyes as the prison hulk loomed up through the mist. "Manslaughter. Ain't that what you're in for? How come you weren't able to do some real killin' on your way out of that town? But maybe you did. Maybe you smoked them in the back and didn't have enough jingles to own up to it. One way or the other, I guarantee you'll end up under the grass sooner than later."

After the dory was tied up alongside the prison hulk, Snake Eyes and Bent led Zebulon up a gangplank, where a guard was waiting to take him below.

O NCE AGAIN, ZEBULON FOUND HIMSELF TRAPPED INSIDE
the stinking carcass of a ship. No sails billowed above or
water slid below. There was no past, no future. Only backbreaking
daily routine.

At night his legs were shackled to a bulwark below deck along
with twenty-two other lost souls. He knew their stamp: horse-
thieves, high-line riders, short-trigger men, bunko artists. Seven
women were quartered on the other side of the foc'sle, mostly
whores and thieves along with an ax-murderer and a cook who
had poisoned the owner of a Hangtown saloon after he insulted
her pork chili. Through the long suffocating nights, men and
women prisoners shouted insults and declarations of love back
and forth, pounding and throwing their broken bodies against
the bulkhead. At dawn they were transported across the river
under armed guard, the women in a separate dory to cook the
prisoners' greasy midday gruel or clean up the Warden's house
and wash his family's laundry. At night they rowed back to the
prison hulk. Too exhausted to speak, they were allowed a half-
an-hour on deck, where they stared with vacant eyes at the river
that never moved or offered the hint of a breeze.

Jammed head to toe on hard wooden planks, they were never
alone. Rats as big as possums scurried and sniffed across the
deck, wet with vomit and slop from blocked weep holes and
overflowing buckets of waste. Mosquitoes that felt big enough

to mount swarmed through open portholes to feed on raw, exposed flesh. At night, rinky-dink piano music from one of the city's saloons drifted across the river, invading their wretched dreams like a drunken surgeon scraping flesh from bone. Every sound and movement seemed designed to encourage their longings for early death.

Zebulon dealt with despair the way his Pa had taught him: by beating up the first man that crossed his path or dared to step on his shadow. In this case, rather than some lost mountain man gone *loco* from lack of stimulation, the target available on the neighboring bunk was a twisted sack of venom by the name of Plug. He was a scrawny bank clerk convicted of killing a stagecoach driver and two female school teachers when their combined savings didn't measure up to a steamship ticket to Brazil, much less a stake to Mexico. Due to a shortage of manpower to help build the booming state capital, Plug's execution, along with that of three others, had been delayed until further notice. Zebulon didn't give a damn about Plug's past. What bothered him was Plug stealing his tobacco and using his waste bucket when his own was only half-full. Not to mention Plug's nightly screams for a whore named Lucy Goosey who had left him to run off to Hawaii with a shipping clerk. The final straw, one that made Zebulon jam his knee into Plug's stomach and smash his nose into his forehead with an open palm, was waking up with Plug's fingers around his neck, whispering to his darling Lucy Goosey that when he broke out he was going to track her down, wherever she was, and nail her fat whore's ass to the outhouse door. It was a satisfying solution, smashing up Plug, but the result wasn't worth it.

From then on, Plug treated him like a savior, or at least someone he feared was crazier than he was; it was as if all the anticipation and dread Plug had projected onto the Warden, he had now switched to Zebulon. To his dismay, Plug began to follow him around like a whipped dog, offering tobacco and scraps of food and whatever else he thought Zebulon might appreciate, including a rattlesnake skin and a broken arrowhead he had found clearing brush on the riverbank. Plug also revealed a secret: any day now, wait and see, he planned to uncover a hole he had dug near his bunk and then, hallelujah, sink the entire fucking ship and everyone in it.

"It takes a Plug to work a plug," he declared. "The job will be done when we come back from work detail. Everything is ready. I got other holes drilled just in case. A few of the women know about it. Large Marge, that big Irish snatch that chopped and pickled her boss, she's dug herself some holes. You wait, all hell will break loose. When the guards experience water risin' over their ankles, they'll jump like chickens runnin' from the ax. Ain't one of them can swim. That's the beauty. We'll grab their rifles and shoot one or two to show we mean business. If the Warden is around, we'll skin his righteous ass or take him hostage. *Glug, glug, glug.* Know what I mean? Before they know it we'll be in that little skiff. Just the two of us. It'll be night, and we'll slide down that fat river like Egyptian pharaohs with the stars above and freedom just ahead. We'll row all night until we float into San Francisco. When we pass a steamer carryin' a load of gold-suckin' pilgrims headed for the gold fields, we'll stand up and shout: 'You'll be sorryyyyyy, sorryyyyyy, sorryyyyyy!'"

Plug turned over on his side, chuckling and chewing his lower lip, congratulating himself on the efficiency of his plan.

A week went by. Then two. Then a month. The prisoners measured the passage of time by marking incidents and occasions on the side of the bulwark: the arrival of a prisoner, an execution, an accident. Otherwise time would stop, and a day would become a year.

The list always changed and was always the same: a card cheat committed suicide by falling onto a pick ax he had propped up on the side of the road, three runaway Chinese suffering from opium withdrawal hung themselves from their long pigtails, a Samoan whore was caught giving a blow job to Snake Eyes behind the chuck wagon. The Warden shot the whore out of hand and relieved Snake Eyes of his duties, a rejection that incited him to rob two well-heeled prospectors from Virginia of enough to make a run for the gold fields.

As the days went on, Plug fell into an increasingly dark and deluded lethargy. Unable to summon enough nerve to execute his plan, he retreated to a closed-off section of his mind and a defensive silence that was broken only by bursts of maniacal laughter and further threats to his true love, Lucy Goosey.

The Warden remained a distant and ominous presence. Occasionally he and his wife journeyed to San Francisco for a few weeks to attend the opening of an opera or music hall, or to promote himself to the Eastern businessmen that were continually staking out the city. On his return, the prisoners would often see him at dawn, standing in a nightdress in front of his house, staring at them through a spyglass as they rowed to work across the river. On one occasion as they approached the shore, oars raised, they floated past the Warden bathing waist-deep in the river. Cupping his hands, the Warden poured water over his head, smiling at them as he waved a salutation.

Plug grabbed Zebulon's arm. "Look at that slime-coated bastard. He knows what I'm up to. And you, too, for bein' an accomplice. He'll cut off our heads, that's what he's thinkin'; he'll place them on stakes in front of the courthouse. A warning to all malcontents."

Rowing back that evening, they saw the Warden and his family swinging in a hammock beneath the branch of an oak tree. A uniformed Large Marge stood in attendance before them, waiting for them to stop swinging long enough to offer cookies and lemonade from a silver tray. The Warden wore cream-colored linen pants and a long-sleeved blue-and-white striped French jersey; his wife wore an ankle-length white dress. Their son sat squirming between them as if a platoon of ants were crawling up his sailor suit.

On holidays the Warden hosted lavish picnics attended by the city's elite. Kites were flown along the riverbank, and a band from Sacramento or Sonoma played lively marching tunes and Scottish and Irish jigs. At the Warden's fiftieth birthday celebration, his son ran along the riverbank dressed as a miniature George Washington with a long white wig and a general's peaked hat, slinging rocks at the prisoners as they rowed slowly back to the prison hulk. When a rock struck Zebulon in the forehead, the band celebrated the boy's marksmanship with a triumphant drum roll and bugle blast while the guests clapped hands, applauding the boy's spunk and spontaneity.

Plug laughed hysterically, then shouted:

> *Onward Christian soldiers,*
> *Marching to War,*
> *With the cross of Jesus going –*

Before he could continue, a guard clubbed him on the back of the head with the butt of his rifle.

Minor transgressions such as Plug's were punished by a ritual flogging or a week's visit to the dungeon: an airless black box filled with water and waste-slop at the bottom of the ship's hold.

Escape attempts were treated as acts of sedition. When a guard caught an escaped Miwok horse-thief hiding outside the city at the bottom of an outhouse, the unrepentant heathen was bound hand and foot and forced to stand on deck contemplating his fate for the rest of the day.

A few minutes before sundown a drum rolled as the Warden, followed by Bent, appeared on the poop deck. Beneath them the prisoners stood at attention – men lined up in front of the women, the guards standing behind them in full dress uniform, their rifles held at port arms – as the Miwok was lowered over the side of the ship by a series of groaning pulleys. Ten minutes later the Warden ordered the prisoner raised to the deck, only to discover that he was still breathing

Shaken, the Warden turned to Bent. "We have witnessed an act of either divine intervention or, God help us, of Lucifer. The only moral solution is for the bloody heathen to be submerged again. If he survives, it will be by the will of God and I will give him his freedom."

As the Miwok was lowered once again into the river, the Warden searched his Bible for an appropriate scripture dealing with heathens and non-believers. On deck, the prisoners and guards whispered bets, the odds being twenty-to-one against the red nigger. There was no movement except for swallows swooping across the river for insects. Somewhere a frog croaked. Then silence.

Zebulon was the only one to notice two riders appearing along the riverbank. One of the riders was Delilah, the other, Hatchet Jack.

Half-an-hour later, the Warden snapped his Bible shut, and the Miwok was cranked out of the water. Once his lifeless body was laid out on the deck, the Warden, satisfied that neither the Lord nor the devil had intervened, ordered himself rowed back to his home, where dinner was waiting for him.

That night, Zebulon lay on his bunk, dreaming of water spirits rising above him like swaying anacondas. The water spirits were wrapping him inside a curse that was somehow connected to Delilah, the drowned Miwok, and from the distant past, the Shoshoni half-breed, Not Here Not There. He felt himself lifted high in the air, then dropped down a long slope, finally rolling to a stop in a ditch. Unable to move, not knowing if he were dead or alive, he was dragged out of the ditch and hitched to a wagon pulled by Delilah and Hatchet Jack.

~ ~ ~

In the days that followed, the Warden appeared before the prisoners more frequently, inspecting their progress as they shoveled dirt or broke up piles of rock for one of the new capital's ambitious networks of roads. Holding a parasol over his head against the unbearable heat, the Warden would drink from his canteen and then pour the water over his head and shoulders. When he ordered a water break for everyone else, he gave his canteen to Zebulon to refill from a water bucket. He would keep his own body as hydrated as Zebulon's was dry, so that finally Zebulon would come to understand that water was the Warden's to control and Zebulon's to be grateful for – a surrender, the Warden promised, that would ultimately lead to deliverance.

One night in the middle of a thunderstorm, a newly arrived Chinese prisoner picked the manacles that bound his ankles and wrists. Unseen and unheard, he crept across the deck towards Zebulon's bunk. Kneeling before him, he gently touched Zebulon's forehead, his fingers as delicate as the feelers of a praying mantis.

Grabbing the Chinaman by the throat, Zebulon tried to choke off his windpipe.

The Chinaman sighed, offering no resistance, then pressed his elbow into the pit of Zebulon's stomach until the pressure made Zebulon let go of his throat.

"I am Lu Yang," the Chinaman whispered. "I see you before, in Dream Palace. I open door. You are looking for dragon woman, Delilah. Special customer. Remember?"

Except for his tiny bottle-thick glasses, Lu was unrecognizable with a raw red scar running down the length of one cheek.

"Delilah say 'Hello,'" Lu said.

Lu's words were painfully pronounced, as if he had learned English from a children's book. "I walk to Sacramento to find prison boss. Everyone in Sacramento talking music and making fun. Except when I pull out sausage and splash prison boss.

Soldiers and prison boss became angry and bring me here."

He looked at Zebulon with a quizzical smile. "You ready to fly coop, outlaw man?"

Outside, they could hear the wind howling across the river and waves slapping against the creaking hull.

"Listen to big wind," Lu said. "Maybe you don't like wind. Delilah's mind empty. Not like wind. Like ocean. Your mind like pig running from ax. Noisy. Always thinking maybe you are dead. When dead, nothing happen. When nothing happen, then thinking comes. Now you a dead man in between too many worlds. Who tell you, be happy? Who tell you, listen? Everything okay. Then we stir soup."

Zebulon had no idea what the Chinaman was saying.

Lu smiled, as if understanding Zebulon's confusion. "No worry. Lu, Hatchet, Plug, we stir soup. We drink. Plenty spice. Then we fly coop."

Next to them, Plug's arms and legs thrashed out in the middle of a nightmare, his screams waking up the rest of the prisoners, including the women on the other side of the bulkhead. All of them began yelling and banging on the partition, convinced that someone was being killed or raped.

"I tell Plug, stir soup very slow," Lu said. "But he no listen. He go too fast and bad happen."

He sighed, then reached over and pressed a thumb into Plug's neck until he passed out.

He waited for the prisoners to quiet down before he spoke again.

"Are we bustin' out?" Zebulon asked. "Or cookin' or what?"

"First soup." Lu nodded towards Plug, who had opened his eyes. "Then Plug fly coop. Then outlaw man, Chinaman, everybody fly coop. Not now. Later. Now nothing. Very difficult, nothing."

Plug sat up on his bunk. "If you ever put your paw on me again, I'll cut it off and use it for live bait."

Lu looked across the rows of sleeping prisoners, thinking it over.

"Good idea."

He floated back to his bunk as silently and ghostly as he had first appeared.

"Don't say nothin' to nobody about nothin'," Plug said to Zebulon. "And stay the hell away from me until the soup boils over on the stove. I jumped too soon. That damn Chinee gave me the wrong signal."

He turned over on his side and went back to sleep.

~ ~ ~

Three days later, as if she, too, were involved in Lu's plan, Large Marge busted out, or more accurately, went berserk. She was working at the Warden's house, a job she'd had for over a year, when Abigail, the Warden's wife, yelled at her to separate the white from the colored laundry and to fold each article of clothing – not to just shove them into a drawer, but to pile them neatly, socks and underwear next to jerseys and shirts; if Large Marge was not up to this simple task, she could be replaced.

"Fair enough," Large Marge said. She picked up the ironing board and clobbered Abigail over the head, knocking out two of her front teeth. After rampaging through the house and breaking several windows and a Chippendale table, she was finally captured swinging in the hammock by the river, finishing off a bottle of the Warden's hundred-year-old Spanish brandy.

The following evening, true to form, the prisoners were lined up at attention, the Warden standing above them on the poop deck. In the lineup of prisoners, Lu and Plug had managed to position themselves on either side of Zebulon.

"Soup's boiling," Plug whispered. "Now it's my turn to take care of that cold-hearted bastard."

Before Large Marge could be lowered over the side, Lu

suddenly lurched backward and collapsed. Banging his hands on the deck, he screamed in Chinese for justice, salvation, and a one-way ticket to Shanghai until two guards wrestled him below.

"It's all set," Plug said. "Now all he's got to do is slip his chains and pull the cork."

Large Marge's huge bulk was lowered inch by groaning inch over the side. Halfway to the water, the plug Lu removed below began letting in a torrent of water, causing the prison hulk to groan and creak, then slowly list to starboard. The ropes binding Large Marge gave way, and with a loud yell she plummeted straight down, landing in the middle of a dory that was tied up against the ship's stern.

From then on, everything happened at once.

Zebulon held onto the railing as Bent slid past him, his mouth open in a silent scream, his peg leg at a right angle. Prisoners followed him over the side, a few sinking beneath the water while others hauled themselves into the dory or swam to shore. Plug climbed up a ladder to the poop deck and, waving a butcher knife, rushed towards the Warden, only to have the Warden shoot him in the leg. Plug kept on anyway. He grabbed the Warden around the waist, locking them together in a violent dance until Plug's leg gave out and he rolled across the deck into the river.

"Die now or stir soup," Lu said, appearing beside Zebulon. He was completely naked, his body skeletal enough to push a finger through.

They turned as the Warden ran towards them, his pistol raised. Before he could fire, Lu grabbed Zebulon by the hand and pulled him into the river.

~ ~ ~

Quién es?" a voice inside him asked.

Who was he, and where was he going? And who was there

to save him? He wasn't in a ditch, he knew that much. And he wasn't sinking. His hands were reaching out, asking to be saved.

It was Lu, dragging him out of the river and into a stand of sycamore trees, where Hatchet Jack stood waiting with three horses.

They saw Bent leaning against the trunk of a cottonwood tree, his rifle pointing at them.

Before he could pull the trigger, Hatchet Jack fired his pistol.

"Well, what do you know?" Bent looked down at the hole in his shoulder. "I'm dead meat."

He looked up at Zebulon. "One small favor, Zeb. A pay back for the drinks and smokes…. Tell 'em you kilt me straight up. You against me. Not some fuckin' half-breed no-account horse-thief shootin' me lyin' down…. That way I'll be part of somethin' big, maybe a song or two."

As they rode off along the shore, Large Marge stumbled out of the river, her wet clothing hanging from her bulk in shreds, her hair matted with mud.

"Room for one more?" she asked, hauling herself up behind Lu and wrapping her arms around his neck.

When they reached the Warden's house, the second story was on fire. Highlighted against the flames, prisoners ran in and out of the front door, throwing household goods into a carriage and over the backs of horses. More prisoners were fighting on the lawn over Abigail's jewelry and the Warden's collection of esoteric objects, including Syrian vases, antique French clocks, German hunting rifles, Peruvian and Mexican jewelry, and dozens of English pocket watches arranged in felt-covered boxes.

On the lawn, Hatchet Jack tried on one of the Warden's linen suits, then a high-collared London shirt and Spanish leather vest with pearl buttons. Lu chose a silk blouse and a boy's sailor outfit while Large Marge struggled into a full-dress military uniform.

After Zebulon changed into one of the Warden's cream-colored linen suits, he pushed past them into the burning house.

The Warden's office was full of smoke, and flames were spreading over the couch and floor. He pulled out the desk drawers until he found the Warden's small golden bowl, Lakota Sioux rattle, and fossilized walrus penis.

As he staggered out of the house, he tripped over the front steps. Above him, crouched on the sill of an upstairs window, the Warden's wife, Abigail, pressed her son against her breast. For a moment their eyes met before she turned towards the prison hulk, where the Warden was pacing back and forth on the bridge, waiting to be rescued by an approaching rowboat.

"Jump!" Zebulon yelled to Abigail. "I'll catch you."

As she picked up her son and inched her way forward, the floor collapsed and they disappeared.

ZEBULON, LU, HATCHET JACK, AND LARGE MARGE GALLOPED along the south fork of the American River, guiding their horses in and out of the water to minimize their tracks. Where the river was shallow, they rode across and rode back again.

By late evening they'd found an abandoned hunter's shack within a grove of cypress trees. Too exhausted to speak, they collapsed inside, their odd clothing making them look like runaways from a traveling theater or lunatic asylum. Newspapers had been nailed on the walls for insulation, with headlines announcing highlights of an era: "Mexican War Ends"; "Zachary Taylor President"; "California 31st State"; "San Francisco Burns"; "Gold Discovered In Sonoma!"; "Biggest Strike Ever!!!!"; "Confederate Troops Capture Independence, Missouri!"

Hatchet Jack stepped outside, lying flat on the ground to listen for pursuing horses. Satisfied that no one was on their trail, he produced a bottle of tequila from his saddlebag, took a long pull, and went back inside. He handed the bottle to Zebulon, who drank and handed it to Lu, who did the same and handed it to Large Marge, who took a slug and passed out, the Chinaman curled up against her thigh.

"You been nothin' but trouble ever since that cantina in Panchito," Hatchet Jack said to Zebulon. "If I was you, and I ain't, thank god, and I'll always be grateful, I'd point my muzzle to another trail. That woman, Delilah, is demonized. Take it from me. I been travelin' lately through her partic'lar valley, and nothin' is like it seems. She's up the river at Sutter's Fort. The same place where they first discovered the gold. Now it's all gone to ruin and I could care less."

"Did she get you to spring me?" Zebulon asked.

Hatchet Jack shook his head. "If it was up to her, you'd still be in the calaboose. That Mex healer-dealer, Plaxico, he told me to break you out. You might remember. You saw him at that *pueblo* we went to with your Ma. The same one I been learnin' the spirit business with in Mexico. He said my job is to work the graveyard shift and rescue the dead, or those that don't know they're dead. Startin' with you. You ask me, a bad job all the way around."

"I don't want to know about it," Zebulon said.

Hatchet Jack slugged back some tequila. "I don't blame you."

He tossed the bottle to Zebulon. "I'm off to the diggin's. Heard there's a strike up in Placerville. And don't give me no *yessir, nossir, depending.* Now that I've sprung you, our case is closed. You can ride where you want to."

He spat out the door. "I ran into your Pa again. He's still the same crazy old coon. Came down with a bad case of gold fever in Virginia City. Made another big strike, then lost it all to some cheap low-bellied bone-stripper. Now he's down to eatin' rocks. Can you believe, I offered him another horse, and this one was prime stock. He still wouldn't take it. Some things don't never add up. I should have left you in that stinkin' arroyo."

"I thought you did," Zebulon said.

Hatchet Jack laughed. "Too late to get into that. Go ahead. Ride up to Sutter's Fort and rope the witch in, and good luck to you. If we're lucky we'll never meet up again."

When Zebulon woke the next morning, Hatchet Jack was gone, along with Lu.

Large Marge was sitting on a log, rubbing the raw welts criss-crossing her shoulders and neck, a result of her near drowning.

"Don't talk," she warned. "I don't know where they took off to and I don't give a damn."

LARGE MARGE AND ZEBULON DRIFTED ACROSS THE Sacramento Valley towards Sutter's Fort. The only signs of life were an occasional herd of deer, and once, a startled bear gazing at them from the middle of a berry patch. Entire farms were deserted, vineyards and orchards neglected, fences broken. All that was left of once-golden wheat fields had been grazed over by stray cattle and sheep.

When a line of riders appeared in the far distance, moving in and out of rain squalls and shafts of milky light, they galloped in the opposite direction, ending up at a deserted farmhouse sheltered by a mournful stand of half-dead oak trees. Leading their horses through the front door, they squeezed into a narrow low-ceilinged room, thick with dust and straw from a collapsed roof. The dirt floor was covered with mice and weasel droppings, the cupboard empty except for a leftover slice of bread covered with blue mold.

"We'll pad our bellies, then rest up," Large Marge said, then walked outside. A few minutes later she returned holding a headless chicken.

Not wanting to advertise their presence with a line of chimney smoke, she plucked and cooked the chicken in a deep pit.

"I've had my run-ins with old man Sutter," she said, tearing into the half-cooked meat. "Rolled him biscuits, made dough for him, burned his grease, wet his whistle – you name it. I cooked for him one winter when no one else would. Pleasured him when he was too roostered to know I wasn't one of them San Francisco whores. Anyway you cut it, I comforted him better'n anyone had a right to."

She threw the chicken bones over her shoulder, wiping her lips on a sleeve of the Warden's jacket.

"Tell you what, Mister Shook. You go on alone to Sutter's, unless you prefer to head up to Oregon, just the two of us. I'm talkin' partners, not *esposa*, although that could change. We'd be a team. But count me out with Suttter. He's used up. Overrun and plowed under. A thousand Argonauts up there squattin' on his land, I guarantee you. A stampede. Time is money. That's what you'll hear up there…. Used to be the man had himself an empire, the biggest and best stretch of land from the Sierras to the Pacific: fruit trees, pastures like billiard tables, a thousand head of horses. The man would trade with anyone – Ruskies, Spanish, Mormons, all kinds of pilgrims. Gave 'em what they wanted and took what he needed. The biggest sawmill in California. Biggest parades. Biggest barbecues. Biggest fandangos. Slickest women. Made his Injuns wear uniforms and start a marchin' band. He was the biggest cock-a-doodle-doo from Mexico to the North Pole. Now look at him. You don't want to know."

She stood up. "So how about it, Mister Shook? Are you ready to stretch a blanket with me and plow a furrow all the way up to Oregon?"

Zebulon shook his head. "I'm on my own trail."

"Well of course you are," she said, more relieved than disappointed. "A famous outlaw like you. Not to mention that foreign whore you're stuck on, the one that everyone is flapped up about."

She mounted her horse. "Don't give me that look. People talk. I been around the dark side of the barn long enough to know when a man is pulled by his whizzle string."

"Call it any way you want," he said.

She thought it over. "I'll ride with you to Sutter's because maybe I owe you, having sprung me from that prison hulk. But then you're on your own."

They rode on until they topped a rise and Large Marge reined in her horse. Her arms crossed, she gazed at Sutter's Fort silhouetted against the granite peaks of the Sierras like a destroyed Crusader's castle.

"There's no way I'm haulin' my freight to that pile of stone. I don't care what we have goin' between us."

She dismounted and lay back in the tall grass, staring at a parade of black clouds drifting across the sky. "I'll take my *preciosa* carcass over to Sonoma. There's a saloonkeeper there who owes me favors, enough for a ticket back to where I used to be."

She looked over at him: "If you was smart, you'd ride with me. Sonoma's a pretty little town. On a boom right now."

When he didn't answer she mounted up.

"It's your loss, Mister Shook. Somethin' has gone to your head, maybe bein' hunted for and talked about so much. But I know better. I know who you are and who you ain't. And you ain't weaselshit. No matter what that wild witch might say or the lies that newspaper feller's always writin' about you."

After a snort and wave, she rode off towards Sonoma.

He hadn't gone more than a few miles when she galloped up beside him. "I remembered what it is about that saloon in Sonoma. The oily bastard that runs it is most likely six feet under feeding worms. Or if he ain't, he should be. Not only that, but it's me that owes him, and I ain't in no mood to settle up. Not with the way things are goin'. Maybe it's time for Sutter. It's not like he don't owe me a stake after all I done for him."

A mile later she changed her mind again, deciding on Hangtown, where an ex-lover had a brother who ran a feed store. "I can start something big up there. If not with him, someone.

Hitch myself to some pilgrim or store-bought flatlander, and if that rides south I'll turn into a shanty queen. Experience counts, Mister Shook. Twenty dollars a poke, plus extras. Hangtown is a favorable place. No one will recognize this old sow among all them busted bushwhackers and down-and-outers. I don't know what I was thinkin' about, throwin' in with you. 'Specially now that you have a fancy price on your head."

With another shout and wave, she galloped away.

Zebulon was relieved. He preferred to be alone. It was a condition that he had longed for ever since his days on *The Rhinelander*: to know that his feet were once again planted on the earth; to stare into his own campfire, or, if his mood shifted, ride back to Colorado or Mexico or some place off the map. He was finished with people and their wants, who says what, who's going where and why. It was enough to survive. The chasing and finding was for others. The problem was.... But the thought evaded him.

He rode past an Indian's severed head displayed on a stake beneath a faded sign:

BAD HOMBRES AND DOINS NOT
TOLERATED PAST THIS POINT.

In the fading light, dozens of ghostly figures were floating around campfires in front of the Fort. "Like soldiers from a defeated army," the Count had said. He remembered Delilah on the steps of the Vera Cruz hotel, staring at him as if he was a ghost. *Save me*, her eyes had implored. *And if you know what's good for you, stay away.*

~ ~ ~

A mile from the fort, he joined a weary procession of Pennsylvania Quakers – the men walking beside half-dead oxen, the women sitting on battered Conestoga wagons, their heads bowed under bonnets, their shoulders covered with thick shawls. They had started their journey over two-hundred strong, and now they were reduced to less than fifty, having been decimated by Indian raids, a Platte River flood, and bouts of cholera and dysentery.

What was left of the fort's iron-studded gate lay on the ground, most of it having been used for firewood. The stench of sewage and rotting food made it almost impossible to breathe. In front of them, a sprawling cluster of shelters and tents had been thrown together from whatever was at hand: old blankets, pants and shirts, wagon slats, broken tables and chairs, and the usual strips of torn, mildewed canvas. The fort's three-foot-thick adobe walls were riddled with bullet holes. On the crumbling bastions, a row of dismantled cannons pointed blown-up muzzles towards an empty sky. Everything else was in motion: cursing women, banging dinner pots, howling dogs, tents raised and dismantled, wagons repaired, mules braying, horses and oxen unyoked and fed.

Further inside the compound, half-naked Indians, all that remained of Sutter's farmhands, knelt in front of a long wooden trough shoving feed and cornmeal into their mouths. On either side of them, drunken men rolled in the dirt, wrestling and slashing at each other with bowie knives and tomahawks. A gunshot was followed by a woman's scream and maniacal laughter. A naked man ran out of a barn waving a frying pan only to be clubbed to the ground by a Peruvian miner. A horse bucked out of a barn. Mormons sang hymns and shouted praises to the Lord, ignoring three prospectors dancing on top of a busted wagon, braying at the full moon.

Zebulon stopped at the edge of a crowd, where a one-armed man in an English top hat held up a shiny new shovel. "Only five of these fine beauties left! Never been used. Pure metal from Vulcan's forge. Can't dig for gold without a shovel, gentlemen. Thirty dollars! Do I hear more? It's good business, gentlemen. Forty to the handsome gent sitting underneath the wagon! You know what it takes to get a box of shovels overland or by sea? Fifty! Do I hear fifty? Who knows when one of these shovels will come this way again. Maybe a month! Maybe six! Maybe never! No shovel, no gold. No gold, and I guarantee it's a long way back to Tiperary. There! At the rear. Fifty dollars. Sold!"

For his next item, the hawker held up a painting of a lascivious ebony nude lying on a sofa surrounded by three Egyptian eunuchs. The roundness of her thighs and breasts reminded him of Delilah.

"The best for last, gentlemen! Cleopatra, Queen of the Nile, in her most intimate lair. A welcome companion for the diggings, where a man can go for months without the sight of a woman. This beautiful vision of exotic lust and romance was owned by a Russian count murdered just last week in Calabasas Springs. Before him, she was the proud possession of an English lord. Before that, she was hung in the Queen of Spain's boudoir! We start at a hundred dollars. Over there! Under the wagon. The man in the leather vest. One-fifty…? Two…! Do I hear three?"

The hawker pointed at Zebulon. "You, Sir! In the fancy linen pants! You're obviously a gentleman who knows how to appreciate a great work of art!"

Zebulon kept going, heading towards Sutter's headquarters, the Casa Grande, a crumbling two-story adobe structure with its upstairs windows shot out. Approaching the twenty-foot oaken front door, he stumbled over a Mexican slumped against a wall.

"*Quién es?*" The Mexican glanced up from underneath his sombrero, revealing a toothless face marked by an empty eye socket. "You ever get the feelin' that the faster you ride, the longer it takes to get there?"

The Mexican slapped his thigh, doubling over with laughter at Zebulon's startled expression. "You ain't sure if I'm that old Mex from the *pueblo*, or just another down and out greaser."

"You're Plaxico," Zebulon said.

"And you're Zebulon. The one that's so stuck inside his own

nosebag that he can't figure out if he's comin' or goin'. That happens more than you think."

"Hatchet said that?"

"That and other things, like not knowin' the difference between a straight flush and a ditch full of frogs. *Quién es*? Know what I mean? Who's out there? And if you is out there, where are you headed? Maybe it's time to quit all those questions."

"Where's Hatchet now?" Zebulon asked.

"Most likely lookin' for you. Now that he's done his best to deal with your Pa, you're next in line."

"You're here for the gold?" Zebulon asked.

Plaxico laughed and stood up.

"I ain't here, and I ain't there. Ain't that how the song goes."

He slapped Zebulon on the back, then walked straight across the compound as if he knew where he was going.

Zebulon sat down against the wall. Around him, men and women were spreading out bedrolls, discussing a mudslide near Grizzly Flats, a mother lode on the Yuba, and a hanging at Morgan's Flat. A small boy led a crippled horse into a livery stable. A door opened and slammed shut. Then silence, followed by a song drifting across the compound from the Casa Grande:

> *Amazing grace! How sweet the sound*
> *That saved a wretch like me!*
> *I once was lost, but now am found.*
> *Was blind, but now I see.*
>
> *'Twas grace that taught my heart to fear,*
> *And grace my fears relieved;*
> *How precious did that grace appear*
> *The hour I first believed.*

It was Delilah.

HE PUSHED OPEN THE HUGE OAK DOOR OF THE CASA GRANDE and walked down a dimly lit *entrada* to a banquet hall. A stern white-haired woman in a high-necked black dress sat at a dining table in the middle of the cavernous room, her head between her hands. Next to Frau Sutter sat her son, August, a plump young man in a Tyrolean hat, drinking whiskey and smoking a curved ivory pipe. Behind them, a large-bellied man with a thick brush mustache and knee-length buckskins strode back and forth, slapping a riding crop against his massive thigh.

Delilah sat behind a clavichord on the far side of the hall. As Zebulon paused inside the door, her eyes found him, then shifted to August Sutter as he slammed his pipe on the table.

"You are not the only one that wants to buy my father's land, Herr Kehoe. I will tell you once again: My mother will never sell without my father's consent."

Azariah Kehoe took a deep breath, trying to remain calm. "You must understand that I am here to help, not to make matters worse. It was my distinct impression that Captain Sutter wished to sell what was left of his land to settle outstanding debts."

Frau Sutter looked at him, speaking with a halting German accent. "You must understand, Herr Kehole. I am newly arrived in this country. I am tired. I have sick stomach. I am not seeing my husband in seventeen years. Imagine how I am suffering when he has business somewhere else and is nowhere to wait for me in San Francisco. I have left a son and a daughter to wait for him, and then I journey with one more son, August, to find my husband, and we go over a terrible, wild country, and now I am seeing his fort of ruins. Imagine all that!"

"My dear Lady," Kehoe said. "I am deeply sympathetic to your difficulties and sufferings. Having spent half my life on the frontier, I know very well what you're going through. For your own sake, please allow me to help."

"And everywhere this gold madness!" Frau Sutter continued, not having heard a word he said. "In Switzerland, I hear of my husband and California and his orchards and vegetables and cows. For many years, I am hearing my husband is a king in this land. That he is being loved by everyone, even native savages, and that everything is arranged for me and my children to come here and be loved with him. We are not business people, Herr Kehole. We are family people who want a life with cows and food and happiness. That is the promise I am hearing in Switzerland, and that is why I am coming here."

"What you say is certainly true about your husband, Frau Sutter," Kehoe said. "Or it was, anyway. A fine man, Captain John Sutter. Courageous. Inventive. Energetic. Even though, alas, foolish in business as well as his choice of, shall we say, leisure pursuits. But we won't indulge in spurious gossip. Above all, we must remain calm."

As Zebulon approached the table, Delilah stood up from the clavichord and walked over to him. Her eyes never left his as she sang to him in Spanish:

> *Sublime gracia del Señor*
> *Que a mi pecador salvo*
> *Fui ciego mas hoy miro yo*
> *Perdido y él me amo.*

Zebulon stood in front of the table, repeating the verse in Navajo:

Nizhonigo jooba' ditts' a'
Yesdashiitinigii
Lah yooiiha k'ad shenahoosdzin,
Doo eesh'ii da nt'ee.

"I am sad," Frau Sutter said, wiping away tears. "I am crying. What is this meaning?"

"An expression of gratitude," Delilah explained, "gratitude for redemption, for being saved by grace."

"Who is this Grace?" Frau Sutter asked. "Am I knowing her?"

"You know her," Delilah explained. "But if you ask for her, she will never come. And if you don't ask, she won't come either."

"Yes," Frau Sutter exclaimed. "Yes. Yes. I am understanding. You are Grace, and the man you have been saying to me all about is Redemption! The man who goes away and comes back and goes away."

"This is the man." Delilah continued to look into Zebulon's eyes. "Or what passes for him anyway. He goes by another name than Redemption."

Frustrated by these bizarre interruptions, Azariah's riding crop began to slap against his thigh like a runaway metronome.

"Frau Sutter, I beg you – no, listen to me, I *implore* you: can we please return to the business at hand?"

"Frau Sutter is not calm, Mister Kehoe," Delilah stated firmly. "She is not happy, and she is not patient, and until she sees her husband, she will not decide if she will return to Zurich. She has done her best to explain her situation to you, and she will not make any business arrangements or deals about Captain Sutter's land with you or with anyone else."

"Excuse me, Madam," Kehoe said, breaking his riding crop in

two. "I have no idea who you are or by whom you're employed, but I find it inappropriate and rude that you speak for Captain Sutter, or, for that matter, for his wife or son or anyone else."

Frau Sutter pulled herself up from the table to her full height, which was not more than five feet. "Countess Baranofsky is not a servant, Herr Keyhole. She comes from Russia to Mexico and then to this fort to ask my husband for help. Her husband, Count Baranofsky, we have talked to in Zurich, Switzerland, to be friends with us and have business in California, a land which I was told is green like God's Eden, which, I am learning, is not true. Now her husband Count Baranofsky is killed by outlaws. I am not saying who is doing what, Herr Keyhole. This is not my fort. It is my husband's fort. I am not here to sell land or chickens or cows."

August Sutter looked around the room with glazed eyes. He struck a match to his pipe, only to stub it out with his thumb, then light it again.

"Can we please finalize this situation? If we're lucky, Mother, some cowboy or prospector or savage red brute will cut off Papa's head, along with that of his Hawaiian mistress. Then we will be able to arrive at a practical solution and not have to depend on people such as Herr Kehole. We will sell everything at a good and fair price and get the hell out of here."

Frau Sutter held her hands over her ears. "August, you are saying against God. You must never speak these terrible words."

"It is not for me to know about God's will or what goes on in Sacramento or San Francisco," Azariah Kehoe said. "But I can assure you, Frau Sutter, that unless you come to terms right now, this very minute, I will leave, and you will be faced with ruin. Please understand: this country is on a fast roll. Soon there will be a train from coast to coast carrying thousands of immigrants into every corner of the state. Unless you make suitable arrangements to distribute your holdings while they still have value, you will be left behind."

Frau Sutter made a desperate effort to concentrate. "You are making me become madness, Mister Kehole. You are looking at my husband's land and you are making plans. My husband owns many hectares. He will arrive with friends and then he will eat and talk with you. Now I only want to sit in a fruit tree with Countess Baranofsky, and speak where we have been and what we have lost, what we will not become or see. I have a dream to come here, a dream of finishing things up. What happens to that dream? Maybe it is the dream of another? Maybe it is not a dream. Maybe I am dreaming there was a dream."

She turned to Delilah. "That happens. You and I are knowing that."

"Yes, we are." Delilah reached over to hold Frau Sutter's hand. "We know all about that."

Azariah Kehoe had heard enough. Bending down, he briefly passed his lips over Frau Sutter's limp hand. "If you will excuse me, Frau Sutter, I have overstayed my visit. Unfortunately, I've important business matters in San Francisco that need attending to. Let us hope for both our sakes that we will never have to discuss business matters again. Please extend my deepest salutations to Captain Sutter. I believe he has my business card."

Delilah looked at Zebulon, then at Kehoe. "Do you know the old saying? 'If you want to make God laugh, tell Him your plans.'"

"Indeed," Kehoe muttered, and strode out of the room.

Frau Sutter sighed. "I am always thinking Herr Keyhole will not go away. Now when my husband comes here, he will know if he will stay with me and my children and grow fruits and vegetables and cows. He is no good for business. And now you, Countess, with your nice young man! So strong! So quiet. Do not have him running off to make business!"

She kissed Delilah's hand. "Now, Countess, I am asking you to go away from this fort before it is too late. My husband is failing me. He is always failing me and my children, and he will fail you, Countess, if you have business with him. There is nothing here for you, nothing here for anyone. Are you understanding what I am saying? Go to China or Portugal or India. Go to Switzerland. But always be going from this bad country. What am I saying to you?"

"You're tellin' her *vamanos*!" Zebulon said.

"*Sí*," she nodded, one hand reaching for a glass of wine, the other hand waving them towards the door. "*Vamanos* far away."

ZEBULON FOLLOWED DELILAH ACROSS THE DARK COMPOUND, maneuvering around drunks and Argonauts passed out between wagons and mining machinery, then over a crumbling wall and around a corral towards a tent pitched at the far end of a field.

Inside the tent, they listened to thunder rolling down from the Sierras, followed by gusts of rain slamming against the fragile shelter like tiny fists.

"I knew you would find me," she said.

"Did you want me to?" he asked.

"Off and on," she said.

As suddenly as it had begun, the rain stopped.

She guided his hand to her breast, then to her stomach. Her belly was larger and rounder than he remembered. And there was something else, something that he wasn't sure about that filled him with fear.

Suddenly all that mattered was his horse. For all he knew the horse was dead or had been stolen. Not that anyone would bother to steal a sway-backed strawberry roan on her last legs.

He stood up. "I got to check on my horse."

She reached out to hold onto his leg.

He knelt before her, placing his head on her belly as she stroked his head. Then he was inside her and they were silent in the center of everything that moved.

Until she pushed him away.

Through the open tent flap they saw the Warden and a half-a-dozen men riding towards them. Behind them and in front of the fort, Frau Sutter stood with an older man wearing a bright red uniform and cockade hat, who Zebulon figured must be Sutter. As they stumbled out of the tent, pulling on their clothes, more men and women appeared on top of wagons and along the fort's bastions.

He took the Warden's small golden bowl from his vest pocket and placed it in her hands.

"You can sell it back at the fort, or San Francisco. You'll have enough for wherever you need to go."

"I need to go with you."

"I'll find you," he said.

He ran across the field, circling towards the fort.

As the Warden rode up, she grabbed a stirrup, her other hand pointing east.

"The bastard raped me," she moaned. "He's run off to the mountains."

The Warden shoved her to the ground and galloped off with his men towards the high Sierras.

By the time Delilah reached the corral and had the gate open, Zebulon had cornered a horse. In one leap, he mounted and rode past her.

A shot rang out, a bullet creasing his scalp. Another bullet tore into the fleshy part of his arm.

He managed to hold on to the horse's mane until he was riding free and out of range.

ZEBULON RODE THROUGH THAT NIGHT AND INTO THE DAWN until his horse gave out. He walked another three miles before he fell asleep near a small stream. When he woke, the sun was directly overhead and he wasn't being followed.

He walked on, towards a range of humpbacked mountains. The only signs of life were isolated bunches of stray cattle and once, in the far distance, a line of riders. He waited until they disappeared, then walked through the night and the next day.

It was almost dark when he approached a large sign nailed to the trunk of a tree:

> WELCUM TO GREASY SPRING
> GATWAY TO H

As he stumbled on, his legs buckled and he passed out.

~ ~ ~

He woke up in a ditch. His ribs were bruised and there was a knot on his head. A frog croaked and a few feet away a goat was chewing on garbage.

"Who's down there?" a voice called out.

Nobody but old Zebulon Shook, he thought. Humpin' his broken ass down a washed-out street of pain.

The goat made him think of his Pa. He wondered what the

old bastard was up to. Most likely working another claim. "The higher the country the better": that's what he always said. Far away from the likes of flatlanders and sodbusters.

"If you ain't dead, say somethin', Mister," the voice called out.

Was that his voice, or someone else's? He remembered another time, in another ditch. He wasn't dead. He was sure of that. Not that it would be so bad to be dead. Anything to be shut of being... on the drift ever since — He heard a roll of drums, or maybe thunder, followed by rifle shots. Some kind of celebration, he guessed. The goat moved closer, staring down at him with melancholy eyes. If he had a pistol he'd shoot it, just to be one up.

A barefoot kid wearing torn overalls walked up to him holding a burlap sack in both hands.

"Are you that man that was holed up in the saloon?" the kid asked. "The one that was playing cards and then they shot him? That ain't you, is it?"

Something was squirming inside the kid's sack.

"A mess of rattlers," the kid explained. "I sneak up on 'em when they're goin' for frogs. But I got to be careful not to get bit."

The kid turned around, listening to more shots coming from the town.

"We got a big shoot-out going on. I seen three, not counting the one that killed my Uncle Ezra, who had it comin'. Did you know Uncle Ezra?"

The drumming sounded as if it was coming from inside his head.

"Are you a ghost, Mister?" the kid asked.

"Maybe," Zebulon answered. "What's your take?"

"I think you are. But I ain't afraid, if that's what you're askin'."

"That's good," Zebulon said. "Now you won't become a

ghost yourself."

"Is this what happens when you get shot?" the kid asked. "You wake up and you're a ghost?"

"Only if you're afraid or don't know what you're doin'."

"Like you?"

The kid followed him as he crawled up the side of the ditch and walked towards the town of Greasy Springs, a muddy street of wooden buildings bunched around a saloon, jail, and blacksmith shop. Beyond the street there were green fields as flat as billiard tables, stretching to foothills and snow-peaked mountains.

At the far end of the street a dozen men crouched behind farm wagons and piles of stacked lumber. All of them were pointing rifles, shotguns, and pistols at the Last Chance Saloon, a large two-story building also serving as a hotel and barber shop.

Occasionally someone would fire a shot, then duck behind a wagon to reload – or take a pull from a bottle, or eat a chicken leg, or grab a slice from one of two roasted pigs.

Zebulon and the kid sank down behind a wagon next to a portly man with gray side-whiskers and a sheriff's badge pinned on red long johns.

"I need a doc," Zebulon said.

"The doc's inside," the Sheriff said. "You want him, be my guest."

He looked Zebulon over, confused by the fancy cut of his linen pants and silk shirt. "Business man, are you?"

"Bounty hunter," Zebulon replied. "Got creased chasin' a rack of prisoners that broke out from that prison hulk in Sacramento. A few broke ribs. Maybe part of a slug somewhere past my pump."

"Heard about that breakout," the Sheriff said. "Zebulon Shook, I think it was, and some other desperadoes. A bad bunch all the way around."

A bullet from the saloon split the wagon's tailgate, sending a splinter through the Sheriff's leg.

"Who's holed up?" Zebulon asked.

The Sheriff methodically took off his pants and removed the splinter. "Some mountain man. He rode into town last night with a bad tooth. When the doc pulled the wrong one, he went *loco* and shot the place up. Kilt two. Maybe three. Now he's holdin' the doc and the town artist hostage."

"What's he want?" Zebulon asked.

"Free passage to the mountains. That ain't possible as long as I'm sheriff."

When several men fired off another round, their volley was answered by a shot from the saloon.

"What's he usin'?" Zebulon asked.

"A shotgun and a Sharps rifle. Most likely a few handguns from those he shot."

"I can take him out," Zebulon said. "But it'll cost you."

"Tell you what," the Sheriff said. "You take out that mountain cocksucker and the town will stake you to a free room and three meals a day for a month. Plus any whore you so choose and whatever the doc charges to patch you up."

"Throw in a horse and saddle and I'm your man."

"Done," the Sheriff said, not taking his eyes off the saloon.

Zebulon turned to the kid. "I'll need your sack of rattlers."

The kid thought it over. "Ten cents for the little ones. Fifty for the bigs."

The Sheriff handed the kid two silver coins. "You're lucky to get this much, Chester. Now take yourself home. And don't keep huntin' snakes or you'll turn into one."

The kid dropped the sack and ran down the street.

Zebulon had more requests for the Sheriff: "I'll need two bottles of whiskey, a loaded shooter, and some 'baca to parlay with."

After the Sheriff gave him what he asked for, Zebulon

hobbled to the rear of the saloon and heaved the rifle and the bag of snakes through a side window.

A few minutes later, there was a scream from the saloon, followed by a shot, then a curse and two more shots.

As Zebulon inched over the windowsill, he saw his Pa staring up at him from beneath an overturned table. Before Zebulon could speak he fell to the floor, passing out.

When he woke, his Pa was lying a few feet away, shoving a cartridge into a rifle – a hard task considering that part of one leg was blown off, and a rattlesnake was sliding across the floor a foot away from his head. Parts of other snakes were scattered near the bodies of two men. Aside from his shot-up leg and the blood oozing out of his gut, Elijah hadn't changed. A crooked scar ran down the right side of his face, slanting one eye and pulling down the corner of his mouth. The same curtain of white hair fell over his shoulders, and he was wearing the same greasy buckskin jacket and otter cap.

Elijah peered at his son through startled half-lidded eyes. "Was it you that pitched in them snakes?"

"They told me there was a mountain lunatic shootin' up the place," Zebulon said. "I didn't figure on you."

"Well, you should have."

Father and son stared at each other, unable or unwilling to measure the distance between them.

"What the hell business is it of yours, tryin' to save this worthless town of egg-suckin' sodbusters?" Elijah asked. "That ain't what Shooks do. We bring a town to its knees, not stand it up."

"I'm on the run, Pa."

"I ain't surprised. That's what you get for slopin' down from the mountains. 'Course, I could say the same."

Elijah shut his eyes, coughing and spitting out a stream of blood. "Hard times, son. Pelts a plew a plug. Powder's worse. Gold fever is what done it. A damn curse all the way around.

Lost a mother lode bigger than Midas. Got shot up. Rode off to the mountains and tried again, ridin' down on the spring flood with two mules loaded with prime pelts. But they watered my likker, son, cheated me worse than bad. Just to top off the foam, that sawbones over there jerked the wrong tooth."

He nodded towards the other side of the room, where a short bald-headed man stood on top of a billiard table, wearing a bloodstained white smock. His hands and legs were bound tight with belts: one end of a rope was tied around his neck, the other around Elijah's waist.

"Your teeth were rotten," the doc yelled, "every last one. I'm tellin' you, let me go and I'll give you new choppers."

Elijah jerked the rope, sending the doc howling to his knees.

"Don't mind the little jaw-cracker," he said. "He's skeered he's about to be dead meat."

"Ma's gone under," Zebulon said.

"Gone under?" Elijah sat up, shaking his head.

"Got herself shot when me and Hatchet went back home to help with the winter haul. You'd taken off, so we rode to Broken Elbow. All hell broke loose when some pencil-pusher tried to pull a fast one and she demanded her fair price."

"She never was one for business."

He groaned, biting down on his lower lip. "Hatchet tried to tell me, but before he could get to it I chased him off for cheatin' me on a horse. He had the nerve to come back, but I was on a bad run, one cold deck after another... then I land me a full house, and some wolf-eyed half-dick savage deals one off the bottom for a straight flush to my full house. I called him out and next thing I know, I'm belly up in a stinkin' ditch."

When Elijah's head sagged to his chest, Zebulon thought he was dead.

"Your Ma and me had our times," Elijah finally whispered. "Truth is, she couldn't wait to see me off... and me bein' the righteous stand-up man that I am, I obliged her."

He looked up. "Did she get to plug any of them store-bought vermin on her way out?"

"She took down seven or eight," he lied. "Maybe more."

"She always could shoot better'n you or me."

Zebulon handed Elijah the bottle and pouch of tobacco, which he was glad to have, swallowing and chewing all at once.

"I always figured to go back home one last time," Elijah said. "Make it up to her with a big sack of gold dust. Enough to buy some female fineries. God bless her. I'll be seein' her soon enough."

A voice spoke up from the other side of the room. "Well, well. If it ain't Zebulon Shook. Last I saw, you was takin' a jump off that devil ship, and I was floatin' my stick to San Francisco."

Plug sat slumped against the bar, holding a snake-bit ankle with both hands. A rattler was curled a foot away, its crazed head swaying back and forth.

Plug pointed at a mural of several scenes running above the length of the bar. "How do you favor the artwork, Zeb?"

The mural showed a series of images: Zebulon plowing his horse down a snow-peaked mountain, then riding across a high plateau, a posse galloping him. At the end of the mural, a full-rigged schooner sailed through heavy seas. Other scenes showed San Francisco destroyed by fire, a wanted poster for Zebulon Shook in large bold letters, and finally, Zebulon jumping into a river of flames from the deck of a sinking prison ship.

"They paid me good money for this art," Plug said. "Soon as I'm shut of this place, I'll paint your story from Hangtown to Mariposa, and who knows, maybe back East."

Elijah loaded up the Sharps and pulled back the hammer, aiming it at Plug.

"Hold on," Plug yelled. "I still got to paint the scene with the two of you. Then they'll come from all over. This town won't never be the same. Guaranteed."

He screamed as the snake buried its fangs into his foot.

Elijah pointed the Sharps at the snake, then at the doc. Unable to make up his mind, he dropped the Sharps on the floor.

Zebulon picked it up. "I ain't exactly partial to the Sharps. Stock's too heavy. Chamber overheats."

"It's you that's overheated," Elijah said. "Ever since you was a little pecker-head."

Zebulon fired, blowing the head off a snake sliding across the floor towards them. Another bullet took care of the snake coiled next to Plug; not that it mattered as far as Plug was concerned, his face having turned blue as his breath left him.

Before Zebulon could shoot again, he was interrupted by a yell from outside:

"Halloo the saloon!" the Sheriff called out. "Anyone alive in there?"

Zebulon crawled to the window.

"We're shootin' snakes," he yelled. "Hold your fire. I'm comin' out."

He turned to Elijah. "I'll make a deal."

"Too late for deals, son," Elijah said. "I'm past comin' and goin'. But if those pilgrims are dumb enough to put a rush on me, I'm happy to shoot out their lights."

Zebulon walked out the door.

The Sheriff and most of the population of Greasy Springs were gathered behind the overturned wagons, drinking whiskey and eating what was left of the barbecue.

"I need you to hold your fire for the rest of the night," Zebulon said to the Sheriff. "Otherwise he'll take out the doc and the artist and most likely some of us, me included."

"Take it easy," the Sheriff said. "As long as you take him."

"One more thing," Zebulon added. "If I bring him out alive, he goes back to the mountains."

"Done," the Sheriff said.

Zebulon nodded, his eyes on the prison photographer from Sacramento. He was standing behind a wagon loading a glass plate into his box camera.

He looked up as Zebulon walked over. "I won't say nothing to nobody about who you are," he said. "As long as you don't interfere with me taking your picture."

"How long do I have?" Zebulon asked.

"Two days. No more. Not with the Warden and half the state lookin' for you."

"It has to be until I get out of town," Zebulon said.

"All right." The photographer swiveled the camera towards Zebulon. After he arranged the bellows, he held up his hand, then ducked underneath the black cloth.

"Wait," the Sheriff called out. "You forgot the most important thing."

The Sheriff and the town's citizens arranged themselves around Zebulon, all of them staring straight at the camera. Behind them, inside the saloon, Elijah was singing his death song:

> *Heya heya heya yo-ho, ho yo*
> *Yeha hahe-ha-an ha-habe ha-wana*
> *Yo ho ho-ho ha-ha ha-he ha-an*
> *Wana yeya hey.*

By the time Zebulon lowered himself back over the windowsill, Elijah's song had ended and the last rays of evening sun were sliding across the saloon's floorboards, highlighting the dead snakes, the mural, and Elijah, still leaning against the overturned table, spitting up clots of blood.

"Did you make a deal?" Elijah asked.

Zebulon shook his head.

"Tell me, son. Are you still foolish on shootin' billiards?"

"Of and on," Zebulon replied. "Enough to keep my stroke oiled."

Elijah sighed. "You recall that little spit of a town, Repose, I think it was, and that stiff-backed Swede that run the table on you? He cleaned you out with no more than a broom handle. Took your belt buckle, shotgun, boots. Lucky he didn't take your topknot. He plumbed your bones, that Swede. Your Ma was there. And Hatchet."

"I remember all that," Zebulon said.

Elijah looked across the room with dying eyes. "There are things that me and your Ma never told you. How when you was little we thought you was demonized, all time speakin' to critters and seein' spirits no one else did. We took you south of Pueblo to an old Arapahoe squaw with second sight. She said you was born in some in-between place. Between the worlds, she said…. Another thing: I never told you how I won Hatchet from a bean-eater half-breed Mex down in Corrolitos who had him trained head to tail as a slave."

"I know that, Pa," Zebulon said.

"Not all of it," Elijah said. "I won him with a high straight flush. The Mex couldn't pay, so he gave me Hatchet. I packed him home, thinkin' he could be useful. When I asked the Arapahoe what went down, she said that the Mex put a curse on me. There's more that I can't hardly recall. But so what? We're all cursed when we come into this world. Same as when we leave."

Elijah shifted his head to Zebulon's stomach. "Is Hatchet followin' you? Or me? If it be me, tell him we're all squared up. No hard feelin's."

In front of the saloon, two fiddlers and a harmonica player began to play a lively jig as the population of Greasy Springs made the best of what promised to be a long night.

Elijah nodded his head with the music, then jerked the rope tied around the doc's neck, making him scream and howl.

He reached for the Sharps and propped himself up.

"I come into this town wrong," he announced. "I'll go out right-side up."

"Hold on, Pa," Zebulon said.

Elijah hesitated. "Hold on to what?"

"I made a deal for you to ride off."

"Nowhere to ride off to, son. Them days is gone."

When Zebulon tried to hold him back, Elijah slammed the stock of the rifle into his chest, sending him to the floor. "This dance is mine. I started the ball rollin' and I'll see it through. We all be pilgrims slidin' down life's chute, but now is my time to howl. Your turn will come soon enough."

Elijah took off his otter cap and dropped it on Zebulon's lap. "Elk's elk and meat's meat, son, and nothin' matters, and to hell with the rest of it. I seen air whistle through rocks, and water turn to fire. I lived hard and wasn't afraid to look straight at the misty beyond. I don't give a damn who or what is waitin' for me on the other side. I'll deal with that party when it happens. Or not."

He leaned down and kissed his son on the head, then hobbled to the door, returning to his death song:

> *Heya heya heya yo-ho, ho you*
> *Yeha hahe-ha-an, ha-habe ha.*

There was a moment when Zebulon wanted to join the old bastard, to go out the old way, both of them straight up with their socks on. But there was a deeper pull that kept him on the floor, watching Elijah stagger out the door, firing his Sharps with one hand, the pistol with the other, yelling out a last mountain cry: "Waaaaaaaaagghhhaaahh!!!"

Every weapon in Greasy Springs fired back, the bullets slamming Elijah through the door and across a table, and then to the floor where he landed on top of Zebulon.

None of the crowd looking through the saloon windows spoke until the doc was untied and Zebulon was carried over to the billiard table.

After the doc tore open Zebulon's shirt, the Sheriff handed him his medical bag and a bottle of whiskey; together they forced a slab of cowhide between Zebulon's teeth and poured whiskey over his wound. Then the doc took a knife out of his bag and probed for the bullet.

"I'll be damned," he said. "There's a slug in there all right, but it's an old one."

The bartender, convinced that he was witnessing a miracle, poured drinks for the Sheriff and the doc, as well as for the photographer and the rest of the town, who had lined up cheek to jowl at the bar.

"We'll need proof about what happened," the Sheriff said. "Otherwise people will think we made it all up."

Opinions flew back and forth:

"A slug tore through him."

"It was the old man that shot him."

"It was the artist. He shot him."

"Hell, we all shot him. Every last one of us."

"Three bullets right through his pump."

"He ran out, then he was hit. Twice."

"Then the other one got hit. The one that went in to get him."

"Do you people know who's lying on the billiard table?" the doc asked after the crowd quieted down and were concentrating on their whiskey. "Zebulon Shook, that's who. I saw his picture in Sacramento. You're lookin' at the biggest damn outlaw in the entire state of California. There's a five-hundred-dollar reward on his head, dead or alive."

As his name rippled through the saloon and out to the street, the photographer rushed outside to get his camera.

The Sheriff shook his head, trying to understand. "You're sayin' he's that same outlaw that broke out of jail in Sacramento?"

The doc nodded. "That's what I'm sayin'."

"I don't care who he is," said a voice from the bar. "The man's a goddamn hero."

"He saved us and saved the town," voices shouted.

The doc turned to the Sheriff. "If he pulls through, then what?"

"Lock him up. What the hell else can I do?"

"You'll be run out of town," the bartender said. "Or worse."

"All right," the Sheriff said, backing down. "We'll take care of him until he's ready to leave. We owe him that. We'll give him a room upstairs and three squares."

The crowd cheered.

The photographer placed his camera in front of the billiard table and lined up a shot of Zebulon, who had been propped up, his arms arranged around his dead father.

The camera's flash was followed by the largest celebration Greasy Springs had ever experienced.

ZEBULON WAS AWAKE WHEN HE SLEPT, AND SLEEPING WHEN he was awake, his mind dissolving into dreamy shadows and visitations that he had no control over. Voices whispered and echoed around him. During the day, rays of light circled him. At night, dark shapes crouched by the foot of the bed. There was a bear and a two-headed eagle and a croaking frog sitting underneath a one-eyed goat. Mountain lunatics appeared, sitting cross-legged beneath the window, spinning windy tales of disaster and deliverance. Sioux, Comanche, and Crow drifted by with faces decorated in war paint, their lances and tomahawks raised. Greasers, red niggers, and Chinese celestials showed up. And Delilah, sitting on the edge of the bed, rubbing his heart. Pigs rooted for turnips beneath the bed and curved-beaked shorebirds flew over the windowsill. And there, right in front of him, were his Ma and Pa and Hatchet Jack, arguing about separation and loss and how to stand your ground. Behind them, gamblers and outlaws drifted by wearing long canvas dusters and scarves pulled over their faces. Did they know there was a price on his head? Dead or alive.

~ ~ ~

The doc probed a finger into Zebulon's chest. "Everything I learned about gunshots says you should have been dead a long time ago. Your scar is old. If I open you up to bone out the slug, I might slice into an artery. Best thing is just to go on. There are plenty of men walkin' around with enough lead inside 'em to fill a saddle bag."

He pushed harder. "Pain?"

"No."

The doc reached for his scalpel and pressed it into Zebulon's leg. "Feel that?"

"No."

"Odd." He probed harder. "How about that?"

"Nothin'."

"Do you remember getting shot?"

"I recall yesterday, and not much of that."

"The only cure is not thinking about it," the doc said, and left the room.

~ ~ ~

Days later, or maybe it was that afternoon, Zebulon stood in front of the photographer and his camera, wearing a clean shirt and pair of pants and a leather vest, all of which had been donated by a special fund of well-wishers.

"I guess you're aware of your reputation," the photographer said. "Everyone's talking about you. They might even appoint you mayor."

The camera's flash left Zebulon momentarily blind.

Working quickly, the photographer handed Zebulon a tomahawk. "Raise it like you're about to scalp someone."

When the camera's flash went off, Zebulon threw the tomahawk into the wall, missing the photographer's head by a few inches.

The photographer handed him a Mandan war club.

"Think about how many men you've killed, and how many want you dead."

Zebulon slammed the war club at a pillow, sending feathers flying around the room.

For his last shot, the photographer handed Elijah's rifle to Zebulon.

"Aim at the camera the way your Pa did when he came through the saloon door."

Another flash.

Zebulon lay back on the bed, closing his eyes, imagining that he was soaring over the town.

"Beautiful. Don't move." The photographer set up another shot of Zebulon sleeping. "Remain as still as a mountain. We're not only gonna make history, we'll make more money than you can imagine. More than any gold strike! I'll sell these pictures to newspapers, picture books, magazines. Seventy for me. Thirty for you."

Zebulon shook his head. "I want nothin' to do with that. All I want is to ride off and be forgot."

"Too late," the photographer said. "Your horse is out of the barn. There's a price on your head and they're singing songs about you from here to New York City. If it was me, I'd make a dash for the cash."

"Fifty-fifty."

"Sixty-forty."

"All right," Zebulon agreed.

The photographer shook his hand, closing the deal, and went out the door.

~ ~ ~

Zebulon sat in front of the window with his eyes closed, imagining a wooden bench stretching across an empty desert. Lost and bewildered men sat on either side of him, not knowing who or what they were waiting for, or running away from.

He didn't look up when the Sheriff opened the door.

"Tell me what to do with you?" the Sheriff asked. "People say you ain't worth the trouble, and that I should hand you over. Others say I should keep you around. You ask me, it would be easier to shoot you."

"Your choice," Zebulon said.

"Not hardly," the Sheriff said. "They'd tar and feather me if I plugged you. And they'd be right. You saved the town and put us on the map. Last week Greasy Springs meant nothin' but cheap whiskey and worse grub. Now people come all the way from Hangtown and Mariposa to see that painting over the bar. Now we got entertainment – fiddlers, mouth organs, and accordion players. Shanty queens and floozies. Yesterday a woman came all the way from New Orleans. She sings like she's plugged into God's choir. We're big time, Mister Shook."

The Sheriff lit up a cigar, blowing a fat smoke ring towards the ceiling. "The other day another pilgrim come in, wantin' to buy the painting. Said he wants to haul it to San Francisco, the bar and everything on it, ship it to London and hang it in the biggest dance hall in the Western world. Of course, I didn't go for it."

He unrolled a newspaper. "Here's what they're saying about you in the state capital":

> "Two weeks ago, rage, violence, and fear swept through the state capital when a band of desperate prisoners escaped from a prison ship anchored on the Sacramento River. The breakout was initiated by Zebulon Shook, the outlaw whose exploits have become so well known throughout the Far West. Shook was serving a twenty-year sentence for manslaughter. At the time of his escape, several other charges of bank robbery, horse theft, and murder were pending against him in Texas and Colorado.

> "According to eyewitnesses, the breakout was the result of a simmering resentment that Shook harbored

towards the prison's Warden, Major Ashton Bigelow. A revered public figure who had just announced his intentions of running for governor, Warden Bigelow served in the army under Colonel John Prescott in the recent war with Mexico. A native of Boston, Warden Bigelow is a graduate of Harvard Divinity School.

"In the middle of the prison's evening roll call, Shook produced a revolver and stormed the officer's deck, seeking to kill Warden Bigelow. Unable to overpower Bigelow, who had barricaded himself inside his cabin, Shook jumped into the river and swam to shore, where several accomplices were waiting for him. In the chaos that followed, several other inmates overpowered the remaining guards, killing three and wounding four. Other prisoners managed to commandeer the ship's lifeboats and were last seen rowing down the river. Eight other prisoners, half of whom were females, made their way to the shore only to be captured the next day by troops sent out from the army garrison in Sacramento.

"Zebulon Shook, aided by his small band of desperadoes, looted and burned the Bigelow's house, killing the Warden's wife and son before riding off.

"Now that this dangerous outlaw is once more on the loose, citizens have one more reason to lock their doors at night. Local militia groups have joined the Warden in a concentrated effort to track down Zebulon Shook and bring him to justice."

The Sheriff folded up the newspaper. "I been tellin' folks that you've gone to Colorady or Texas, but one of these days some likkered-up fool will spill the beans. Then the law will ride in and string you up. You ask me, you're better off on the run."

The Sheriff paused at the door. "I never knowed a man as famous as you, and I hope I never will again."

~ ~ ~

That night, Zebulon heard a song drift up from the saloon:

Hard times come again no more.
'Tis the song, the sigh of the weary.
Hard times, hard times, come again no more.
Many days you lingered around my cabin door.
Oh hard times come again no more.

A sigh that wafts across the troubled wave,
A wail heard upon the shore,
A dirge murmured around the lowly grave –
Oh! Hard times come again no more.

~ ~ ~

The next morning he woke to find Delilah beside him, rubbing rose petals over his wounded heart.

Her fingers trailed across his stomach. Then lower.

"Where's Hatchet?" he asked.

"Waiting for us."

"Forget about Hatchet. We'll head to Mexico. Or north. It don't matter where."

She eased herself on top of him, straddling his waist and biting her lower lip as she felt him rise inside her. He closed his eyes. "You never sang about grace, and I didn't see you inside that *hacienda*, and you didn't head off the Warden so that I could ride free, and I never saw you before."

"That's true." She leaned down and kissed his throat, and ears, and eyes. "It was all a dream."

She arched her neck and maneuvered her hips over his, then leaned over and pressed her hands on both sides of his heart. Not moving, she joined her breathing to his until he calmed down, enough to let her guide him gently to another edge of himself, and then slowly reel him back again, a sensation that he had never experienced before. In the past he had always been the guide, the one who marked the trail, the one that was always in control, who came and went as he chose.

"Are we dreaming each other?" she asked.

"No." He thrust into her so violently that she screamed. "Now?"

"No," she whispered, guiding him back.

"Now?"

"Yes," she moaned. "Now."

Later that night, as they lay side by side, her voice was so distant that he had to hold her in his arms in order to hear her:

"A long time ago, in a faraway land, there was a girl who spent all her days playing by the side of a big muddy river. The girl had been born with special powers and knew how to speak to all the life forms that lived on the river, including fish, frogs, snakes, and insects, as well as several mischievous water spirits who considered themselves very special and in control of everything that went on.

"One day, the girl made fun of the water spirits, telling them that she knew more about the river than they did and that they weren't doing a very good job of handling the floods and the greedy fishermen that were making the river a dangerous place. She advised them that if they knew what was good for them, they should consult her, as she possessed a special gift. The water spirits, most of whom were old and cranky, became angry with the girl's vanity and decided to teach her a lesson by placing a curse on her.

"The curse made the girl so afraid that for three years she was unable to leave her bed. One night in the middle of a thunderstorm, an old dwarf appeared in the village and told the girl's mother and father that she had been imprisoned in the shadowy realm that existed between life and death. To break the spell, the old man told the girl to stand by the river every night and pray for the water spirits to guide her back to life. Several months later, after listening to the girl's wild and hysterical songs, the river spirits finally agreed to lift the curse, but only if she accepted three conditions: that she never forget that she was an ordinary human being who could never understand the mysteries of nature; that she leave the village, the river, and her family behind; and that she never spend more than a few days in any one place. When the girl began to weep at her terrible fate, the river spirits took pity on her and told her that one day, after many adventures, she would meet a man in a strange and violent land who had also been imprisoned by a curse. If they had compassion for each other, they would have a chance to be released from their in-between worlds – even if it meant that one of them would die so that the other might live, and that a child would spring from her loins."

~ ~ ~

Later that morning, roused by a commotion of hooves and shouts, they stood together at the window, looking down at the Warden who sat on his horse in front of the saloon, along with Stebbins and a ragged platoon of mounted soldiers and prison guards.

The Sheriff and the doc came out of the saloon, along with the photographer and a few whores and drunks who weren't ready to give up celebrating the birth of Shookville, as the town had been renamed.

"We know that Zebulon Shook was wounded when he took off from Sutter's Fort," they heard the Warden say. "And we know that he rode up here and raised all kinds of hell."

More people came out of the saloon to listen.

"Shook was here all right," the Sheriff said. "He came here to deal with his Pa after he killed three men and shot up the saloon."

The bartender spoke up. "If he hadn't done what he did, a lot of us would be dead and the saloon burned to the ground."

Incredulous, the Warden shook his head. "Are you saying that Zebulon Shook killed his own father? I find that hard to believe."

"If he hadn't killed him, I wouldn't be standing here talking to you," the doc said. "And I'm not the only one."

"That's right," said a voice from the crowd. "He saved our bacon."

"The man is a saint," said one of the whores.

"Where is he now?" Stebbins asked.

"Dead, most likely," the Sheriff said, "or if he ain't, he's in Colorady or Mexico."

"He shot a man called Plug," the doc said to the Warden. "I think he was one of your prisoners."

"I took a photograph of Zebulon Shook holding his dying father in his arms," the photographer added. "If you like, I'll show it to you."

The Warden dismounted and walked up to the steps of the saloon, then turned to address the crowd. "Let me make this very clear to you people. Zebulon Shook is an outlaw. He has caused damage and suffering across the entire state. Because of him, innocent people have died, including my own wife and son. This man lives with the devil on his shoulder. Anyone found harboring him or withholding information about his whereabouts will be arrested."

When no one spoke up, the Warden pushed his way into the saloon.

On the street, Stebbins pulled the photographer aside. "My newspaper will pay a good price for your photographs. I've been filing reports on Zebulon Shook since the start of his outlaw career. I came out to California with him and wrote my first dispatch about him for *The New York Herald* and two Philadelphia papers. I know more about Zebulon Shook than any man alive."

The photographer was interested. "I'll take your portrait where the shoot-out happened. You can stand in front of the bullet holes and the busted tables, none of which have been removed. You pay me if you send a picture to your paper."

"Of course," Stebbins said as they walked into the saloon. "I wouldn't have it any other way."

~ ~ ~

The Sheriff and the Warden will make a deal." Zebulon said as they struggled into their clothes. "Then they'll bust down the door and shoot us."

As if to verify what he said, there was a shot from the saloon, then another, followed by a scream.

Halfway down the hall, he hesitated.

"North," Delilah said, as they hurried down the stairs two at a time.

Then they ran for a stand of trees, where Delilah had horses waiting for them.

THEY RODE BENEATH A COLD SHIVER OF METALLIC STARS, their horses' hooves thudding over the black earth. Before dawn they reached a lean-to, a strip of canvas nailed between two oak trees. In front of the lean-to, three saddled horses were hitched to a log near the remains of a small fire.

Hatchet Jack stumbled towards them, pulling on his pants and reaching for a gun-belt hanging from a branch.

He looked at Delilah. "I figured you and him for old Mex."

"He wanted to. I didn't," she said.

Hatchet Jack pointed to Elijah's otter cap pulled over Zebulon's forehead. "I know that bonnet."

"Pa's dead," Zebulon said. "He got himself shot."

Hatchet Jack turned away, kicking dirt on the fire. "It was gold that done it, that and leavin' the mountains."

Hatchet Jack disappeared into the lean-to. He came out carrying his rifle and two saddle bags that he cinched over a horse.

"I should have left you in that ditch," he said. "It would have saved me and everyone else a lot of trouble."

"Who's leavin' who in what town?" Large Marge said, swaying out of the lean-to.

She slowly hoisted herself onto a horse. "I guess you know they're comin'. But I ain't stayin' to find out."

She galloped off, followed by Hatchet Jack.

Delilah walked over to her horse, then stopped, looking back at Zebulon.

"Go with them, if that's what you want," he said.

"I was thinking we should head for Mexico," she suggested.

"I'm finished with all of that," he said. "And maybe with you, too."

"If only that was true," she said, mounting her horse and riding after the others.

He sat down against the trunk of an oak tree waiting for her to return.

Quién es? he asked himself.

The answer was a confusion of voices that sounded like marbles poured over a dishpan.

He waited through the morning for the voices to stop. When they became louder and even more confused, he rolled on the ground, pounding his fists on the earth.

Quién es? he asked again.

Finally he got up and rode after Hatchet Jack and Delilah. After a few miles, he became worried about falling asleep in the saddle. The last thing he needed was to wake up inside a dream that wasn't his.

Dreaming was easy, he thought. Being dreamed was the problem.

HE FOUND THEIR CAMPFIRE AT THE FAR END OF A NARROW ravine. It was dark. The air was cool from a recent rain and the wet earth smelled of pine cones. Halfway into the ravine, he dismounted and hitched his horse to a stunted pine tree rooted in a boulder.

An owl hooted and he answered with a long mournful two-note. When a sharp pain exploded through his chest, he dug his fingers into the earth and bit his lip until he tasted blood. Again, the owl hooted, this time from a lower branch. "Shook!" the owl screeched: "Shoook... Shooook... Shooook!"

When he stumbled into the camp, everyone was asleep.

He lay down next to Delilah, who was sleeping on the other side of the fire next to Hatchet Jack, her head on his chest, one arm around his shoulder.

He hesitated, looking from Hatchet Jack to Delilah, then placed a hand on the small of her back, inhaling the scent of her musty mud-caked hair.

"I knew you'd come," she said, not opening her eyes.

He hesitated, looking over at Hatchet Jack. "Maybe it's too late."

"Maybe you should find out," she replied.

She didn't resist when he slipped off her pants.

As he entered her, she pulled her arm away from Hatchet Jack, whose mouth was stretched open as if in rigor mortis.

"Don't move," she instructed as she let him settle into her, breathing with him until he felt a pressure rush up his spine, followed by waves of pulsating heat.

The sensation over, he felt suddenly abandoned, as if he was falling towards the waves of a dark turbulent sea. *Come closer*, the towering waves howled, *closer to* – There was no way of knowing what waited for him. When he opened his mouth, he was no longer breathing. He imagined his lungs full of water, and the more he struggled to breathe, the more he felt fear overwhelm him.

He prayed to Wakan Tanka and to all the spirits who live and dance where the sun goes down, who take care of all the in-between creatures trapped in all the waters of the world. The old people were talking to him. His Ma and Pa were calling out to him and to the two-headed eagle who lives where the giant supports the world on his shoulders; they were all calling for him.

"Hee-ay-hay-ee," he called, the cry loud enough to wake the others. "Hee-ay-hay-ee-ee!"

When he opened his eyes, Hatchet Jack was leaning on an elbow looking down at them, his Colt .44 pointed at Zebulon's forehead.

"Ain't you carryin' this ride too far, little brother?" he asked, with a curious half-amused smile.

Zebulon recognized the Colt that he had carried when he had been shot in the saloon and thrown into the arroyo.

"I didn't steal it," Hatchet Jack said. "And I didn't take it off a dead man. Not my style. The Colt was on the table. Since you weren't around, I figured it might as well be mine."

"Go ahead and shoot him." Large Marge was looking over at them. "And her, too. He'd do the same. Or if you lose your nerve, shoot me. Or yourself. Anything that shuts down all this stupid goddamn palaver and poochin' around with each other."

Disgusted with a situation that was more than she could or

wished to understand, she pulled a blanket over her head.

Hatchet Jack handed the Colt to Delilah, who shifted it from one hand to the other. Then she handed the Colt to Zebulon, who handed it back to Delilah.

Hatchet Jack stood up, pulling on his pants. "Tomorrow we'll ride after Plaxico. He's waiting on the Yuba. He drew me a map."

He removed a slab of cowhide from his shirt pocket. CALFORNIE was scratched above a line of arrows pointing to the northwest, ending in a three-masted sailing ship. Another scratch of letters was marked ORAGON.

Delilah pressed the Colt between her breasts with both hands.

"Is that all we need? A map? Is that why we're here? To ride on, and then ride on some more, and then some more again after someone who rides after us, or maybe ahead of us, because we don't know how to ride after ourselves? If that's true, then let's ride up to Oregon and find whoever it is we're looking for. Maybe Plaxico, whoever he is, will tell us what we're doing, even if he doesn't know, or if he does, but can't say why. You choose. I don't care."

She fired a bullet into a tree trunk and stalked off into the night.

When she returned they were sleeping, or at least pretending to be. Choosing a spot away from Hatchet Jack and Zebulon, she curled up alone with her arms crossed over her breasts.

Above them, dark clouds swept beneath a full moon, like blotches of spilled ink. Somewhere a wolf howled. Then two more, until the whole pack joined into one mournful chorus.

They slept through the night, together and apart, too exhausted to dream, or hear the howling of the wolves.

HATCHET JACK LED THE WAY OVER GRASSY HILLS DOTTED with goldenrod and manzanita berries. To the east, a rainbow, thin and pointed as the end of a cue stick, hovered over a waterfall. Above, eagles soared. At the sound of their horses' hooves, antelope and deer scattered ahead, then stopped to stare back with huge startled eyes.

After crossing the headwaters of the Sacramento River and Cottonwood Creek, they negotiated a series of hills covered with tangled alder and thick groves of maple. Further on, as they emerged from a stand of spruce, they saw a thin column of smoke curling against the horizon.

They climbed towards a rocky outcrop. The thin air left them speechless, their minds empty, as if they had entered a stillness that had always been there, a magical land free of stagnation and death, where nothing had ever happened nor was yet to come.

Their dreamy preoccupations were interrupted by the *clink*, *clink* of pick axes and shovels. Beneath them, through strips of foamy mist, a mining camp of shacks and tents had been set up along the bank of the river – a roaring cascade that plunged down the middle of a steep gorge.

The only shack with four walls stood apart from the others on a small rise. A sign across the door read:

SUPPLIES AND GEAR – AFFORDABLE PRICES.

Delilah pointed to Cox, the Englishman from *The Rhinelander*, as he walked up the rise towards the shack, followed by three Miwoks carrying heavy sacks of grain on their heads and shoulders. After Cox directed the Miwoks inside, he sat down on a bench near the door, lighting up a hand-rolled cheroot.

Beneath him, a line of exhausted men worked tailrace ditches and flutter wheels. Further downriver, half-naked Chinese, Mexicans, and Indians stood waist-deep in freezing water, shifting gravel back and forth in wooden rockers.

Suddenly a Miwok let out a low cry. Kneeling down, he pressed an ear to the ground. Immediately the other Miwoks working upriver threw down their rocker pans and ran into a dense stand of silver fir, just ahead of the Warden as he galloped into the camp.

A slanted cockade hat was pulled over the Warden's forehead. His frail body, bent with dysentery and choleric rage, was covered with a torn red cloak. Behind him, the Sheriff led a ragged platoon of guards and three horse-drawn supply wagons. Further back, struggling to keep up, Stebbins and the photographer pulled two mules loaded with camera equipment and several racks of Spanish wine.

"We're looking for the outlaw, Zebulon Shook," the Warden shouted. "We know he rode this way. If any man has information about his whereabouts, now is the time to speak up."

No one spoke. Most of those present had never heard of Zebulon Shook – not that they would have betrayed him if they had, or any other outlaw, given their own problematic histories.

"One last chance," the Warden shouted again.

When no one came forward, he nodded to the Sheriff, who pulled out his pistol and shot a Chilean miner through the foot.

Except for Cox, who had run into his shack at the first sign of the Warden, everyone else shouted what they knew, or thought they knew about Zebulon, even if most of their information was invented: "He went to ground, General.

Who knows where –"; "New Mexico or Colorady –"; "Oklahoma –"; "El Paso is what I heard –"; "People seen him on the Brazos –"; "He took down a bank in Sliver City, shot up half the town –"; "Killed a man in Placerville –"; "Set up camp on the Frazier River with a bunch of renegades –"; "Halfway to Vancouver –"; "That mulatto whore leading him by his nose ring –"; "On the way to Oregon, with some Minnesotans –"

"Apprehend that man!" the Warden shouted, pointing towards a Chinaman crouching behind a sluice gate, his face half-hidden beneath a split-bamboo hat.

As two soldiers ran towards him, Lu wrenched a board from the gate and waded into the river. Holding onto the board, he let himself be swept over the boiling rapids, his long black queue trailing behind him like a snake as he disappeared down the river.

Everyone ran in different directions except for a dozen Chinamen holding rocker pans in front of their faces. Two were shot out of hand, then three more running into the trees. The rest stood in the water, hands raised in surrender.

The Warden rode furiously back and forth as his men spread out through the camp, bursting into shacks and tents and shooting anyone that resisted, and even a few that didn't. When a large stash of gold was discovered beneath one of Cox's floorboards, he was clubbed, his gold confiscated, and his shack burned to the ground.

The violence stopped as suddenly as it had begun, leaving in its wake the roar of the river, which was almost loud enough to drown out the cries and moans of the wounded.

As if nothing out of the ordinary had occurred, wagons were unpacked and a table and chairs were set up for lunch by the river for the Warden, who was joined by the Sheriff, the photographer, and Stebbins.

While they drank wine and smoked cigars, waiting to be served a warm meal, the photographer set up his tripod.

"Hold it right there, gentlemen," the photographer shouted. "Perfect.... Warden, if you would be so kind as to move to your left three inches. That's right, your left.... Perfect.... Now, if you could all look straight ahead, towards the river.... No one move.... Beautiful."

"We ought to shoot 'em all and get it over with," Hatchet Jack said as the camera flash went off.

"I can drop a few with the Sharps," Zebulon said.

"No point in stirring a hornet's nest," Large Marge advised. "Otherwise, I guarantee, vengeance will hound us forever, or at least until we get to Oregon."

They stayed where they were, looking over the edge of the rocky outcrop until the Warden and his men rode off with the rest of his troops. They were followed in a wagon by Stebbins, the photographer, and the Sheriff, all of them too drunk to mount their horses.

BY THE TIME THEY REACHED THE CAMP, MOST OF THE ANGLO miners had fled and the remaining Chinese, Mexicans, and Indians were either dead or wounded.

Delilah tore up shirts for bandages and fashioned crude splints while Large Marge cooked a thick gruel of potatoes and mashed-up corn.

Hatchet Jack and Zebulon found Cox lying with his head against a grain sack, a line of blood oozing from his thigh like a fat worm.

"Gold is what I had," he muttered. "Gold is what I lost. A whore's dream slopped on a saloon floor by all the demons of hell."

Zebulon wandered off towards the river. He remembered other gunfights and massacres: a rancher and his wife and five children scalped and decapitated, an old trapper starved to death a mile from his cabin, an Arapahoe village wiped out from plague, settlers and prospectors drowned, hung, or shot. All of it seen and taken for granted.

As he looked at the row of bodies lying near the river, the roar of the rapids exploded into his heart.

~ ~ ~

The next day the dead were buried in a long ditch on a small rise facing the river. Archibald Cox offered the eulogy, an act he was well suited for, having studied for the ministry in the north of England.

"Life has gotten out of hand. It has become bigger and uglier and, at the same time, more beautiful and more precious than we first knew it to be. Gone are our dreams. Gone is the irreverent and irreplaceable spirit of youth that gave us the blind courage to journey here in the first place. As we stand in solemn contemplation before these graves, we can no longer take our lives for granted. But the Lord protects us by lowering a veil over our suffering. In His mercy, He provides us with enough grace to survive, and soon we will turn away from the dead and we will go on because we have no choice. To be born is to die and soon enough all that will be left of us will be memories of who we were, and then, not even those. Our tears cannot produce the green of May or make love bloom again. But it will, just the same. That is what we live for."

He sat facing the river, unable to speak until he was handed a bottle of whiskey. Then he proceeded, along with the rest of the survivors, to drink himself into oblivion.

~ ~ ~

The next morning, Cox and the rest of the Argonauts agreed that there was still gold to be found in the valley and that others would be coming soon enough to make their own grabs. They decided to hold on and defend what they had, rebuild what was left of their shacks, work their claims, and then get out before it was too late.

For their part, the Mexicans chose to head back across the border, except for a youthful fruit farmer from Chiapas who was determined to find Plaxico, convinced that the old *brujo* could see into the future and point the way to a mother lode, or at least a big enough score to stake him to another fruit farm south of the border.

The remaining Chinese set out for San Francisco, where they planned to earn enough wages for passage back to China, or, failing that, to remove themselves forever from the gold rush and all that it stood for.

HATCHET JACK LED ZEBULON AND THE OTHERS TOWARDS the coast, avoiding Redding and Plumas City, as well as the Applegate Trail with its new settlements and mining camps. Three days later they crossed the Feather River and proceeded due west, passing Mount Shasta at dusk, its snow-covered cone barely visible through luminous layers of melancholy cloud.

The next morning they came upon the deep ruts of wagon tracks, followed by a trail of household goods – a smashed Chippendale dresser, a leather couch, broken chairs and china dishes, torn pages from a leather-bound Bible, an upright piano, and an array of mining and farming tools – all scattered across a grassy meadow. The slashed portrait of a Puritan minister and his equally severe wife leaned against a wagon wheel near the mutilated bodies of five men and women. Further on, half-hidden in high bunchgrass, a young girl holding a rag doll in her arms lay sprawled across the chest of a black woman wearing a ripped and shredded high-necked gingham dress. Both of them were dead.

A voice rose up behind them: "Mad. All mad. The Warden and his merry band of lunatics."

Stebbins crawled out from underneath a wagon and collapsed at Delilah's feet, coughing up clots of blood.

"They thought the woman was you and they rode in shooting. I told them... I told them... they had it wrong, but they shot her anyway. Then someone shot me."

Delilah held Stebbins in her arms until his breath left him. Then she laid him on the ground, walked over to the dead girl, took the doll from her hands, and wandered off into the bunchgrass.

Zebulon and Hatchet Jack found her sitting on the ground, rocking the doll in her arms. As she started to sing, dark clouds moved slowly above them like a lonely funeral procession:

> *Once I had two sweethearts*
> *And now I have none,*
> *They've both gone and left me*
> *To sorrow and moan.*
>
> *Last night in sweet slumber*
> *I dreamed I did see*
> *My two precious jewels*
> *Still smiling at me.*
>
> *But when I awakened*
> *And found it not so,*
> *My eyes like some fountain*
> *With tears overflowed.*
>
> *I walked across America,*
> *From Africa to Spain;*
> *And now all that is left*
> *Is a child's broken doll*
> *To be cast on the watery main.*

After they buried Stebbins and the pilgrims, they rode for a few miles until dusk, when they made a small fire. No one spoke or ate. That night they all slept together, Hatchet Jack and Zebulon on either side of Delilah, Large Marge curled up next to the Mexican fruit farmer.

~ ~ ~

At dawn they pushed on, encouraged by a warm breeze that carried a hint of the sea. When they reached Goose Lake, an expanse of ice-blue water as calm and flat as glass, they stripped off their clothes and waded into the cold water, splashing and waving their arms like children.

That evening they stayed compulsively busy, as if they were protecting themselves from unknown dangers.

Large Marge prepared a meal of biscuits and horse meat while Delilah led the horses to the lake, rubbing them down with handfuls of wet grass. The Mexican fruit farmer sat on a rock, fishing with a crude hook fashioned from the prong of his belt buckle. Further away, Zebulon stood on the shore, watching a blue heron with a damaged wing try to launch itself over the water. Over and over the heron flapped its wings, only to fall back and try again.

A shot rang out, a bullet blowing the heron's head off.

Hatchet Jack walked up to Zebulon.

"A bird can't fly with one wing," he said, shoving the Colt inside his belt. "Never has, never will."

"Are you sayin' I can't fly with one wing?" Zebulon asked.

"I'm sayin' one of us will fly and the other one won't."

"Won't what?"

Hatchet Jack shrugged, not having thought that far ahead.

He walked towards a canoe half-hidden in a copse of tall reeds and water lilies. When he climbed in and started to paddle the canoe into the lake, Zebulon waded into the water and held it back by the stern.

Hatchet Jack lifted the paddle over his head, neither of them moving as each waited for the other to make a decision.

"Are you comin' or goin'?" Hatchet Jack asked, putting down the paddle. "Maybe you're spooked, bein' in water? Tell you one thing. If you drown, they won't have to hang you."

Zebulon climbed into the canoe and sat in the stern while

Hatchet Jack paddled into the lake. Finally he let the canoe drift.

"How long we been knowin' each other?" he asked.

"Long enough," Zebulon answered.

"Except when you tried to kill me, or me you, we managed to get along. I pushed you onto your first whore, pulled you out of a beaver trap, fixed your busted leg, and kept you from gettin' scalped more'n once."

"You also pushed my head underwater a few times," Zebulon said.

"All right," Hatchet Jack said. "And you slammed me out more'n once. That makes us even."

"Is that what Plaxico told you to say?"

"He told me I had to make it up to you, and Elijah and Annie May."

"What business is it of his?"

"Otherwise, he said – Do you want to know or not?"

Zebulon didn't answer, but Hatchet Jack told him anyway. "It was Plaxico that lost me in that poker game to your Pa. He tracked me down to tell me. Ever since, he's been tryin' to get straight with me, teachin' me things. Otherwise he says it won't sit right with him and he'll have a bad ride into the misty beyond. He says he ain't got much time left on this earth. Him bein' a *brujo*, who's to say he don't?"

They sat watching the setting sun slide behind the mountains. When the light was gone from the lake, Hatchet Jack removed the Colt from inside his belt, shifting it from one hand to the other. "You think it was me that drilled you back in that saloon?"

"Well, was it?"

"What do you think?"

"I think it was."

"Well, it weren't."

"Maybe you wish it was," Zebulon said.

"That's different."

Hatchet Jack lowered the Colt. "You left her and I never did. That's why she favors me more'n you."

He handed the Colt to Zebulon. "Go ahead and smoke me. I'm tired of chasin' and bein' chased. Tired of not knowin' what's a dream and what ain't. Tired of you, tired of what Plaxico is layin' on me, tired of poochin' or not poochin' your witch, and tired of ridin' down lost trails to the middle of nowhere."

Zebulon raised the Colt, more out of frustration than anger, and then handed it back to Hatchet Jack, who shoved it in his belt.

"We're fixed on the wrong target," Hatchet Jack said. "It's Delilah. No matter what Plaxico says, one of us should blow her away. Plaxico knows things we don't, but he don't know how bad she's been twistin' our tails. But we won't do that, will we?"

"No," Zebulon agreed.

"And I won't blow you away."

"True enough."

"So maybe we ought to let her decide who she favors?"

"She ain't capable," Zebulon said. "That's clear. Not when her belly's ready to spring loose and not knowin' who the Pa is. It could be you. Could be me. Or maybe the Count, or someone else. We didn't ask for it and neither did she, and that's just the way it is."

They beached the canoe and were walking along the shore towards the camp when Zebulon stopped.

Without warning he slugged Hatchet Jack on the jaw, then hit him in the stomach and pushed him backward into the lake.

"That was for bringin' up all that stuff, and for makin' it worse with Delilah. Bein' pushed into the lake was just for old time's sake."

Hatchet Jack waded out of the water, pointing the Colt at Zebulon's head.

Zebulon smiled, spreading out his arms. "Go ahead. Find out if the Colt fires when it's wet. Smoke one into me. You'll be doin' me a favor, somethin' you ain't never done before."

When Hatchet Jack pulled the trigger, the gun didn't fire.

He dropped the Colt, then brought Zebulon to his knees with a furious punch to the side of his head.

They stood toe to toe, slugging back and forth, neither of them giving in until Hatchet Jack pulled Zebulon into the lake and held his head under the water with both hands.

Zebulon knew that somehow it would end this way, his head underwater, the way Hatchet had tried to finish him off when they were kids – which was, of course, what he had tried to do to Hatchet in other ways, more than once.

Then his head was yanked to the surface and Hatchet Jack left him to make it to the shore by himself.

~ ~ ~

When they staggered back to the camp, the Mexican fruit farmer and Large Marge were cooking up a large mess of trout.

"We found a canoe," Hatchet Jack explained. "We went out on the lake and the canoe sank. It took some time to get back."

"I'll bet," Large Marge said, looking at their swollen faces.

"Where's Delilah?" Zebulon asked.

Large Marge shrugged. "She ain't with you?"

Without a word, Zebulon and Hatchet Jack walked back to the lake.

They stood waist-deep in the water, shouting Delilah's name over and over, but all they heard was dense unforgiving silence.

~ ~ ~

The next morning, Delilah was still missing. Hatchet Jack and Zebulon searched around the lake while Large Marge and the Mexican fruit farmer rode into the woods, stopping every fifty feet to call out for her.

By the evening of the following day, everyone except Zebulon had given up. He rode inland, retracing the way they had come. When there was still no sign of Delilah, he considered riding to San Francisco, thinking she might have returned to Lu's Dream Palace, but after a few miles he realized it was hopeless and turned back.

When Delilah showed up the next day, they were sitting around the fire, eating rabbit stew. Her clothes were torn and her face and neck were full of bloody welts and scratches. She sank down next to Large Marge, dropping her gold and ruby necklace on Marge's lap.

"Maybe it will bring you more luck than it's brought me," she said, turning her back to them.

She never mentioned where she had been, nor did anyone ask her.

A HUNDRED MILES FROM THE COAST, THE SKY TURNED AN ominous slate gray and then let loose a relentless downpour that left them so ornery and full of spite that they were unable to speak or look at each other. In the middle of the third night of rain, the Mexican fruit farmer realized he had made a wrong turn with the wrong people and rode off towards the Mexican border with a horse, two rifles, and a blanket. When Large Marge tried to shoot him, her pistol was so caked with mud that the barrel exploded, leaving powder burns across her chest and face. Despite the fruit farmer's thievery, his departure proved auspicious. As if a curse had been lifted, the rain suddenly stopped and the sky exploded into fiery streaks of northern lights.

At dawn they crossed a valley covered with cedar and stands of alder. In the distance, giant redwoods stood framed against the horizon like a line of towering cathedrals.

As they approached the forest, now almost invisible behind layers of dense fog, Hatchet Jack jumped off his horse and dropped to the ground, his hands pointing towards the trees.

"Listen to me, wood spirits," he called. "We're a bunch of lame fools. Not only that, but nothin's been goin' right for us and we can't offer you more than a big 'Howdy.' There's no blame if you turn us down or make trouble, but we need a break because we ain't sure who we're lookin' for or where we're goin' or what's waitin' for us when we get there."

They pushed on through shafts of brittle light into a forest as gloomy and wet as the bottom of a rain barrel. Overhead, there was no birdsong or living creature, only a soft rain dripping through thick carapaces of waterlogged branches.

Zebulon's heart began to pound like a drum.

In fact, there was a drum. It was coming from somewhere ahead, as if urging them on. Or, as Large Marge suggested with a wry smile, warning them of approaching doom.

The drumming was coming from all sides, growing louder and then almost inaudible, sometimes ahead and then behind them. Finally, when they had given up on any sense of direction, they were greeted by what sounded like a series of exuberant exhales:

"Oh...! Ha...! Ho...! Oh...! Ha...! Ho!"

Through a narrow avenue of trees, they saw the low silhouette of a wooden longhouse facing a narrow bay. The roof was supported by two rows of wide posts and covered with roughly hewn planks. A row of totem poles, several feet higher than the roof, stood on either side of the longhouse, decorated from top to bottom with carved figures painted in dark reds, apple greens, and blacks. Two Indians sat slumped on a bench on one side of the twenty-foot door. Both of the Indians wore army pants and bowler hats with eagle and raven feathers sticking up from the brims.

The drumming and chanting grew louder as Plaxico emerged from the longhouse, looking almost comical in a knee-length buttoned blanket with a red eagle on the back and a conical hat fashioned from a spruce root. Lu followed behind him, wearing a long sack-like yellow robe, his black queue tied into a knot with long strips of bark.

"Well, well," Plaxico said, looking them over. "I guess things ain't what they seem after all, nor, if you want my opinion, be they otherwise."

He walked up to Hatchet Jack and slapped him on the back with such surprising force that he fell to his knees. "So, my long lost son, all the ducks are finally in the noose. Another day and I would have lit out for home."

He looked at Zebulon. "Did you bring your cards with you?"

"I'm finished with cards," Zebulon said. "And I wish I was finished with you."

"You will be," Plaxico said. "Sooner than you know."

"Will this do?" Delilah reached into her pouch and held up the queen of hearts.

"When you come up with a whole deck, we'll play," Plaxico said. "Dealer's choice. No marked wild cards or dealin' off the bottom, the way you've been known to do."

The sight of the queen of hearts, together with the mix of *gringos* and their mention of poker and dealing off the bottom of the deck, convinced the Indians sitting behind Lu that, at the very least, they were in for a wild night.

Their excitement faded when a huge gray owl swooped over them and settled on the head of a carved wooden eagle on top of the longest totem pole. The eagle was painted dark green and was further distinguished by a long curved red beak. Its eyes were fashioned from abalone shells and were the same colors as Hatchet Jack's: one black, the other blue.

The owl swiveled its head in a circle, staring first at Plaxico, then at Zebulon and the Indians.

"Hooo, Hooo, Hooo," the owl cried, flapping its huge wings.

"Hooo, Hooo, yourself," Plaxico answered, flapping his arms.

Unnerved by the way these strange people were communicating with each other, the Indians retreated into the longhouse.

"Owls see things," Plaxico said. "But you can't count on 'em.

Sometimes they're just bored and want somethin' to do, so they make a lot of mischief."

Large Marge decided that she had seen more than enough mumbo-jumbo and walked over to her horse.

"My peace is gone," she sighed, "and my heart is sore."

"And you shall find it nevermore," Delilah said, finishing the poem.

Hoisting herself into her saddle, Large Marge became suddenly aware of what it might mean to ride off alone into country she knew nothing about. With a shrug, she dismounted and walked over to the bench, her eyes on the owl as it settled on the roof of the longhouse, its head tucked beneath one of its wings.

Plaxico sat down on the bench next to Large Marge. "The owl ain't sure if it's at the right place. And to tell the truth, I ain't either."

"Amen to that," Large Marge said.

Plaxico pulled out a tobacco pouch and rolled two smokes, handing one to Large Marge. "I don't know what goes on with these people, whether they're Kwakiutl or Tlingit or Haida, or what they're up to. For our purposes, it don't hardly matter. Most of 'em know enough English from whalers and prospectors, so we'll make do."

Inside the longhouse, the drumming grew louder, followed by shouts and what sounded like hobnail boots kicking the walls.

Plaxico sighed and stood up. "Time to strut our stuff on the dance floor."

He pointed to a bunch of wild flowers and abalone shells piled beside the door. "Don't touch or smell or look too hard at 'em. They're to fool the spirits, the ones that ain't allowed in. Of course, that ain't us. Not yet, anyways."

He turned back at the door. "Once you're inside, you can't come out. But what else do you got to do? In my experience, it's like this when you're faced with losing who you think you are, or what you're doing, or where you think you're goin'."

Zebulon stared up at the totem pole. Just below the carved eagle, three sea monsters were joined together, their heads staring in three separate directions.

For a moment, he was sure that one of the heads was his own and the other two belonged to Hatchet Jack and Delilah.

Then the heads became sea monsters again and he found the courage to follow Plaxico.

THEY SAT AGAINST THE WALL OF THE CAVERNOUS LOW-
ceilinged room hung with skins and strings of seal and whale
teeth. Plaxico stood in the center of the room, wearing a frog
mask with grinning copper teeth. Near him, on the other side
of a fire pit, a large flat stone supported a display of eagle and
hawk feathers, piles of hard candy, a polished human skull, and
a large wooden statue of a blue heron standing on one leg with
a broken wing.

Children ran around the room and up and over the outstretched legs of men and women puffing on large hand-rolled
cigars, shaking rattles, and banging on box drums. Most of them
wore ceremonial shirts made of cedar bark and decorated in red
and cobalt blue with hand-sewn wolves, eagles, and ravens.

"This is your house," Plaxico cried, strutting around the room
in ankle rattles made of clam and mussel shells.

"There is no other. I am a guest. You are the hosts and I am
the host and you are the guests."

"Oh…! Ha…! Ho!" he cried

"Oh…! Ha…! Ho!" the room answered.

He paused, looking at each face. "There are things I've been
asked to do, people I'm here to help. I came all the way from old
Mex to be here and I thank you for takin' this old fool into your
lodge. Some of the people I brought here might look strange,
and they are, but inside this lodge we are all the same."

"Oh…! Ha…! Ho!"

"Oh…! Ha…! Ho!" the assembled responded, all of them excited and curious about this old spirit doctor who had come such a long way with the first Chinaman they had ever laid eyes on.

Plaxico continued to strut around the room, smacking people on their heads and chests with his hands. Lu followed behind, waving sticks of smoking sage.

"We are all here: the dead and the living and those folks who are caught in-between. We are all here, and we are all the same. Tell me if that ain't true?"

"That's true," shouted the reply.

"We are nowhere but here. Tomorrow, everything will be different. And the day after that and then the day after that. But in this place, even if we are separate, we are the same; even our enemies who want to steal our power and kill us; even the outlaw who runs for his life and doesn't know that he's headed for death. All of us are headed for death, and we are all the same. Fathers and mothers, brothers and sisters, black, white, yellow, and red. We are all the same!

"All sit down!" he cried.

"All sit down!" the room replied.

Plaxico smacked Hatchet Jack on his head and shoulders.

"This one in front of me is a coyote. He'll steal your woman, and sell off your children, and take your boat, and your horse, and your chickens and goats."

Plaxico spread out his arms, rolling his eyes and howling like a coyote.

Children cried and hid behind their parents, who laughed and clapped their hands but were still careful to keep their children close by.

Plaxico stopped in front of Zebulon. "Look at this one who is caught between the worlds. He suffers because he thinks there's a way to shake loose, that there's someone here with the power to free him. He believes a woman can help him, but that woman is as lost as he is."

"Oh...! Ha...! Ho!"

"Oh...! Ha...! Ho! As lost as he is."

Plaxico jerked Delilah to her feet. "Look at this woman! She has come from the other side of the world only to find out that she never had to go anywhere! She, too, is caught between worlds. She has been told that one way for her to get loose is to free others from the same glue. Another way is to know that all trails are dreams and that there was never anything to try for or do; only to be."

"Oh...! Ha...! Ho!"

"Oh...! Ha...! Ho! Only to be."

Plaxico lowered Delilah to the floor and nodded to Lu, who placed his palm on her stomach.

"This woman will have a son," Lu pronounced.

"A son!" Plaxico shouted.

"A son!" everyone replied.

The crowd cheered and shouted. The drums pounded so long and hard that people thought the paddles and fishing gear stuffed in the rafters would fall on top of them.

"Oh...! Ha...! Ho!"

"Oh...! Ha...! Ho!"

"Who's the Pa?" Hatchet Jack shouted.

"The Pa?" Plaxico shouted back. "Who cares about the Pa? This boy belongs to everyone."

"Oh...! Ha...! Ho!"

"Oh...! Ha...! Ho! This boy belongs to everyone."

The men pounded their fists on the floor while the women pulled their children even closer.

"Oh...! Ha...! Ho!"

"Oh...! Ha...! Ho!"

A bowl of whiskey was passed around the circle. Gusts of rain swept across the sea and poured into the longhouse through large cracks in the supporting wall posts and between the roof planks. When the wind knocked over the lamps of whale oil, candles were lit and placed around the room on flat stones.

Plaxico continued his prowl around the room with bulging eyes, as if a fire were smoldering inside his head. Stopping in front of Zebulon, he grabbed the bowl of whiskey from Lu, took a swig, and sprayed it into Zebulon's face and eyes, shaking his rattles and crying out.

Then he slammed his fist into Zebulon's heart, sending him to the floor.

When Zebulon came to, Plaxico was kneeling on the floor, laughing at him.

"Before you went out, you sounded like an old whore suckin' on a stick of ice."

Zebulon grabbed him by the throat, trying to strangle him, an act which made Plaxico laugh even harder.

"Oh…! Ha…! Ho!"

"Oh…! Ha…! Ho!"

Again, he slammed his fist into Zebulon's heart.

"It ain't your pump that's broke. It's your spirit. You think it's all over when it ain't even begun."

The crowd shouted and clapped their hands.

"Oh…! Ha…! Ho!"

"Oh…! Ha…! Ho! His spirit is broke, and it ain't even begun!"

Plaxico continued around the room, shaking his rattle and crying out.

"Oh…! Ha…! Ho!"

"Oh…! Ha…! Ho!"

Zebulon floated above the floor, staring at the parade of figures dancing across the ceiling. He knew them all: outlaws and mountain men, Comanches, Arapahoes, Shoshonis, and Sioux, all wearing headdresses and war paint. There was a water spirit with pendulous breasts rising from an angry, howling sea, goats, frogs with snake-like tongues, ravens, and thunderbirds, and struggling not to be left out, Sergeant Bent, Snake Eyes, his Ma and Pa, the Warden and his wife, Stebbins, and Captain Dorfheimer.

"Oh...! Ha...! Ho!"

"Oh...! Ha...! Ho!"

As the night wore on and visions waned and roared back, objects were exchanged. Plaxico gave Delilah a turquoise belt buckle and she gave him her gold and ruby necklace that had been given back to her by Large Marge. Indians handed out and received fishhooks, beads, rifles, shirts, bowls, and chisels. Zebulon tossed the Warden's gold pocket watch to Lu, who gave him a Tlingit knife with a carved sea otter handle. Large Marge handed an ornate French pen to Plaxico, who slipped a beaded African necklace to Hatchet Jack, who gave him his Green River bowie knife, and so on and on around the room.

The Colt was passed from Hatchet Jack, to Delilah, to Large Marge, to Plaxico, who exchanged it with Zebulon for the fossilized walrus penis that Zebulon had taken from the Warden's desk. Zebulon gave it to a Tlingit, who gave him an oyster-shell necklace. He gave the necklace to Lu, who handed Delilah her gold and ruby necklace, who kept it hidden inside her blouse.

The orgy of giving and receiving rose to a frenzy as objects were pushed, thrown, negotiated, and handed back and forth. Drums pounded, rattles shook, children screamed and laughed, men and women pouted and cried and clapped their hands. Soon no one cared or remembered the origin of the gold nuggets, knives, rifles, beads, mirrors, copper plates, boots, paddles, cards, dominoes, bullets, belts, long johns, chisels, fishing gear, Lakota Sioux rattles, or sacks of flour and food that passed from hand to hand around the room.

"Waaaaaaaaagh!" Zebulon cried, holding the Colt in his hands.

"Oh…! Ha…! Ho!"

"Oh…! Ha…! Ho!"

Zebulon recognized Captain Dorfheimer as he appeared on the ceiling, dealing cards to a bandy-legged man and Azariah Keyhoe; and there was Hans, the German from *The Rhinelander*, shooting a cue ball into the side pocket of a billiard table floating on the ocean; and Cox and Plaxico, comforting Frau Sutter; and the Sheriff; and Stebbins, who was holding Miranda Serenade in his arms, rocking her back and forth as he read his latest dispatch to her; and there was Delilah, sweeping by, arm and arm with the Count and Hatchet Jack, and then just as suddenly, floating apart.

Zebulon joined the crowd, stomping, whistling, and shouting, all of them crying out:

"Oh…! Ha…! Ho!"

"Oh…! Ha…! Ho!"

Delilah offered him the queen of hearts and then took it back as her face dissolved into that of an old crone and then into a bleached skull. The skull could have been Miranda Serenade from Vera Cruz, Rosita from Denver, Suzy from El Paso, Louisa from Alamosa, or Not Here Not There – all the women from all the lost times, dead and alive. There was his Ma, pulling him out of the river by his hair. And there was Hatchet Jack, sitting on the bank, laughing and laughing.

The Warden loomed up, bowing before him, along with his wife and son. He was followed by the photographer, who was lining up his camera for a shot of the room. The Sheriff smoked a cigar, blowing smoke into the doc's eyes and then into Plug's. They were all posing – the Count and Vanderbilt, Large Marge and Ivan, the bandy-legged man and the doc, the Finn, the Seminole, Toku, Not Here Not There, Captain Dorfheimer, and the Irishman from Belfast – all congratulating each other as the camera flash went off and they danced and danced, grinding their spit and sweat and booze and urine into the floorboards.

"You'll be sorryyyyyy," Plug was yelling as he slid backward out the door.

"Oh...! Ha...! Ho!"

"Oh...! Ha...! Ho!"

Delilah crawled into his arms, listening to his heart pound with the drums. Before they passed out, they heard Stebbins' voice report news of Zebulon's capture, or maybe it was his death, or a reward of one-thousand dollars. Or more likely, they were dreaming.

When Zebulon woke, Delilah wasn't next to him and his heart wasn't beating. And yet, he was breathing. In and out. A faint pulse. Out and in. Then a thump. More breaths. More thumps. Life and death and life.

"Quién es?"

He looked at Hatchet Jack, who was standing by the door with Plaxico and Lu, all of them moving their jaws back and forth like pensive goats. Near them, two small boys and a girl sat on the floor playing with the Colt. One of the boys pointed the Colt at the girl and pulled the trigger, only to find the chamber empty. Then the other boy took the Colt and pointed it at Delilah, who still lay on her back in the middle of the room, her lips moving as if she were trying to explain something to someone, maybe to herself. When the girl pulled the trigger, the chamber was still empty.

Zebulon stood up and exhaled, then slowly inhaled. He tried again, and his breathing still worked. He tried once more, in and out as he walked towards Plaxico, who was still standing by the door with Hatchet Jack and Lu.

"Quién es?" he asked Plaxico.

Or was he speaking to himself?

"I did what I come to do," Plaxico said as Zebulon approached. "Some of it worked and a lot of it didn't. One way or the other, you and your made-up brother got some business to finish. Lucky for me, because if these old bones weren't headed to a rendezvous with the misty beyond, I might be dumb enough to hang around."

Across the room a few people were beginning to stir, moving their heads around and stretching out their arms and legs. Others were still sleeping or sitting dazed on the floor, staring at the walls or up at the ceiling.

"One last thing," Plaxico said to Hatchet Jack and Zebulon: "Don't either of you hold on to whatever was said or done, even if it comes from me or that power witch over there, or anyone else. If you're foolish enough to hold on to what don't exist, one of you might go up in smoke and the other find himself driftin' between the worlds, not knowin' how to shake loose. If someone pushes your head underwater and laughs about it, or you snake a card off the bottom, or you get suckered from behind, let it go. And even if you don't, let it go anyway. Not that either of you two fine mountain *locos* would ever do such a thing as gettin' stuck in your own fun."

"Oh.... Ha.... Ho," he said wearily.

"Oh.... Ha.... Ho," Lu repeated with a long sigh.

Thunder rumbled, followed by lightning and gusts of rain pouring through the planks and underneath and above the door.

"Which way you pointed?" Hatchet Jack asked Plaxico.

"To the border, then south until I get rid of all the aches and pains I've gathered tryin' to make things right with you."

"I'll ride along," Hatchet Jack said.

"I won't stop you," Plaxico said. "But know that I'm headed for the land of no big deal. There'll be no scratchin' for gold. And no chasin' or bein' chased. There'll be nothin' to do and no one to do it with."

"Fine by me," Hatchet Jack said.

Plaxico studied him for a long moment, not sure that he was getting through.

"I never figured you and me would get this far," he said. "But now that we have and we're done with who we been and who we ain't been, and you knowin' I'm your Pa, ready or not and all of that, maybe we can put it to rest."

"Fine by me," Hatchet Jack repeated.

Plaxico sighed, still not convinced. He started to say something to Zebulon, then thought better of it and walked after Lu, who had gone out the door.

Hatchet Jack looked at Delilah, who was still passed out on the floor.

"I'm done with her," he said to Zebulon. "And maybe if Wakan Tanka throws me half-a-bone, with you, too. One more thing: If we ever have the bad luck to bump into each other again, we'll most likely start the ball rollin' and we'll both lose. Or wish we had. So let's hope we don't."

Then he walked out the door after Plaxico.

~ ~ ~

When they woke the next morning, Zebulon, Delilah, and Large Marge were the only ones left in the longhouse.

They spent the rest of that day waiting for the rain to stop. When the rain continued and they still hadn't come to a decision about where to go, they decided to head north, not wanting to return south, and not knowing where else to go.

"North," Zebulon concluded. "Everywhere else is used up."

ZEBULON, DELILAH, AND LARGE MARGE RODE OVER STEEP eroding cliffs, then turned inland, proceeding in a line roughly parallel to the coast. After three days they reached a narrow river. As they followed the river towards the sea, the rain turned into a soft mist, making the dense green of the surrounding forest seem untouched, as if no one had ever lived there.

Forced to dismount, they led their horses through thick groves of hemlock and cottonwood. The river widened and became sluggish as it merged into a large estuary. At the lee side of a large peninsula, they saw the tiny specks of buildings clustered around a saw mill. Further on, where the estuary flowed into the sea, a fierce wind blew curtains of white sand high into the air.

Walking their horses around a bend in the river, they heard rifle shots.

Four Russian sailors wearing oversized tunics and baggy pants stood in the middle of a sewn-together canvas longboat, shooting at a herd of sea otters feeding in a kelp bed.

A large otter sat on a rock, staring at the sailors. As if pleading for mercy, the otter held up a front paw, covering and uncovering its eyes. A dozen others lay dead on the shore, their front paws crossed gently over their breasts, as if, at the last moment, they had come to terms with their fate.

Delilah cried out, but not for the otters.

It was *The Rhinelander*, announcing her arrival from a cannon booming from her stern as she sailed through the mouth of the estuary. She was freshly painted, displaying new sails and a row of bronze swivel guns protruding from her bow.

They watched the ship from the riverbank until all they could see were her running lights moving across the black water. Even for Zebulon and Large Marge, who had vowed never to set foot on a ship again, *The Rhinelander* offered an unexpected ray of hope, enough, in any case, to press on.

By the next afternoon they reached the peninsula, where they discovered a line of rutted wagon tracks leading to a sprawl of shacks and salmon racks. A full moon was rising while the sun sank, making it seem, in the last drop of daylight, that moon and sun were on a collision course.

The settlement's only street was deserted except for a few drunks sleeping in doorways or sprawled across soggy planks. A dog barked as cold fingers of fog swept across the estuary, sliding around the corners of a trading post and the half-finished frame of a church. At the far end of the street, past the sawmill and several large storage sheds, a piano pounded out a dance tune from The Trail's End Saloon, a ramshackle two-story building made out of shipwrecked timbers and freshly cut cedar planks.

A roof over a long porch fronting the saloon was propped up on a row of narwhale tusks. On either side of the front door, narrow windows faced the estuary and a dilapidated wharf, where *The Rhinelander* was tied up bow to stern. Next to her, two Russian fishing boats were lined up behind a sea-going canoe with a high-curved prow dominated by the widespread wings of a carved eagle. Further up the shore, barely visible in the fog, a line of groaning logs shifted back and forth like an undulating road.

A burst of laughter reached them from two men smoking cigarettes on *The Rhinelander*'s stern.

"The only boat I been on was that prison hulk," Large Marge said. "They'll have to strip me naked and cut out my heart before

I set foot on another one."

The wind shifted and *The Rhinelander* disappeared inside a thick blanket of fog.

The only way to the saloon was over a narrow plank laid across a wide ditch. As Zebulon stepped on the plank, a frog croaked beneath him. Looking down, he saw a goat staring up at him, methodically chewing on garbage.

He was unable to move. Once across, there would be no way back.

"Who's out there?" a kid yelled from the far end of the plank, his small body a vaporous outline in the fog.

"Are you from the boat?" the kid asked. "'Cause if you ain't from the boat, then where are you from?"

On a plank stretched between worlds, Zebulon thought as he took another step.

A rock hit the plank in front of him, bouncing into the ditch.

"Say somethin', Mister," the kid yelled, "so I know you ain't a ghost."

Zebulon took a small step. Then another, then stopped.

"What the hell," Large Marge muttered behind him. "Do I have to hold your hand?"

A frog croaked in the ditch.

The kid's words floated in the fog.

"Can you hear me, Mister?" The kid's words seemed to be floating somewhere above him.

"We're from California," Large Marge replied.

"Did you come up here to fish?"

Zebulon took another step. Now he saw the kid. He was wearing a rain slicker, rubber boots, and a black sailor's toque pulled halfway over his head.

"Hey kid," Large Marge called out. "Do they serve food in that saloon?"

"They have food, but my Ma won't let me go in. She says

people get shot in there and all kinds of things."

"You mean they get shot because of the food?" Large Marge asked.

"My Ma says people go in there to play cards and fool around, and some shoot at each other and some of them never come out because they're dead."

The kid threw another rock, then two more and ran off into the fog.

Zebulon took a few more steps and suddenly he was across.

A small bandy-legged man in a sheepskin coat stood before him on the edge of the saloon's porch, taking a leak.

"Never mind the boy," he said. "He thought you might be a bunch of ghosts. He gets scared when a boat comes in and there's strangers lurkin' around. Last week he saw someone get shot and thrown into the ditch. Ever since then, he sees ghosts. When the fog is in, I make him stand out here, just so he knows there ain't no such thing as a ghost. That way he can shake hands with his fear."

He paused, looking at Zebulon. "Do I know you?" He reached for a pistol inside his belt. "Wait now. I seen your likeness. It was on a wanted poster on that boat that come in, *The Rhinelander*. The poster was hung up in the Captain's cabin. A thousand-dollar reward for the outlaw, Zebulon Shook. And he looks just like you."

Delilah walked up behind Zebulon. "Maybe you didn't hear what happened to Zebulon Shook. They hung him in Calabasas Springs, in California. The whole town turned out to see him hang. It was in the papers."

"I know what I seen," insisted the bandy-legged man. "That's all I'm sayin'."

"Anyone can make a mistake," Zebulon said. "But if you're gonna dry-shoot someone, me included, do it with your whizzle in your pants."

He pushed past him into the saloon, not giving a damn, one

way or the other.

The bandy-legged man looked at Large Marge and Delilah, then at the two whores laughing at him through the window.

"Damn ferriners," he said as he shoved his whizzle into his pants. "Who cares who he thinks he is or who he thinks he ain't. Not me. But I know what I seen."

As Large Marge lumbered past him, she allowed her shoulder to slam into his back, causing him to fall face-forward into the ditch.

TWO OIL LAMPS HANGING FROM A LOW CEILING CAST A flickering glow over the gloomy smoke-filled room. Another row of lamps was empty or had been shot out. As they headed for the bar, they passed a rattlesnake coiled up inside a glass jar on top of a piano. The piano player glanced at them through rheumy half-closed eyes, then struck a series of rumbling dissonant chords that shook the top of the piano, causing the snake to wave its head back and forth as if looking for a way out or someone to sink its fangs into.

At the bar they drank several rounds of screech, a local whiskey that burned into their guts like branding irons. In back of the bar, an unfinished mural showed two Kwakiutl fishermen standing at the prow of a war canoe, their spears raised as they approached a spouting sperm whale. In the distance, under a dark gloomy sky, a three-masted schooner beat her way across a sun-splashed sea under full sail, four swivel guns protruding from her bow and stern. The ship was sailing towards two men and a woman sitting on a rocky shore. All of their faces were blank. Above the mural, five moose heads were lined up in a row, staring over the room with shot-out eyes.

"I been here before," Zebulon said, staring across the room where Dorfheimer and Hatchet Jack were playing cards.

"I know the feelin'," Large Marge said. "Only I don't remember when or who I was with. Not that it matters. I didn't bust my hump all the way up here to remember where I come from. I'm here to forget."

Delilah pushed back her shot glass and walked over to the piano player as he began another tune. The snake was still moving around inside the bottle, its tongue darting in and out. As Delilah kept her eyes on the piano player's hands sliding over the beaten-up keys, Zebulon drifted past her and sat down with Dorfheimer and Hatchet Jack.

"Look who's here," Dorfheimer said as Zebulon shoved his money on the table. "I thought you were dead or locked up. In fact, I bet on it."

Zebulon smiled. "Maybe I am dead."

"Or about to be," Hatchet Jack said.

"Are you tellin' me the ducks are in the noose?" Zebulon asked.

"Unless you figure another way."

After Zebulon lost three straight hands, he went over to the other side of the room and joined two sailors from *The Rhinelander* who were playing billiards.

Closing her eyes, Delilah improvised a song, the piano player struggling to find the right chords to keep up with her:

> *I've been here before,*
> *Or so they say.*
> *So don't look for cover*
> *From your backdoor lover,*
> *Don't hold on*
> *When he's already gone.*

Large Marge, who was beginning to be overwhelmed with unsavory premonitions, placed the Warden's small golden bowl in front of the bartender and booked the most expensive room in the house – including food, drink, and laundry.

As she lumbered up the stairs, Delilah finished the song:

So don't ask me to love you
After the fool I've been.
And if you don't believe I'm sinkin',
See what a hole I'm in.

She started another verse, then thought better of it and walked over to Dorfheimer and Hatchet Jack.

"I thought you'd be in Mexico by now," she said to Hatchet Jack.

"I tried," he replied. "And then I tried again, even though Plaxico told me I was a fool and that I should quit while I was ahead."

"How did you find us?" Delilah asked.

"I didn't find you. You found me."

Across the room, Zebulon made three straight caroms into the same side pocket. After he picked up his bet, he walked over and sat down opposite Delilah.

"I thought you gave up on cards?" he asked.

"Some things change," she replied. "Even when they don't."

Zebulon paused, looking across the room, then back at Delilah and then at Hatchet Jack. "Choose. Him or me."

"Lately I've had trouble with choices," she said. "I'm resolved never to choose again."

"Choose anyway," Zebulon said.

"I don't know what you people are up to," Dorfheimer said, "but my advice is to stick to cards. What's done is done. No one owes anyone anything. Up here we have a chance to leave the past behind. After all, isn't that the nature of the frontier? Isn't that what the promise is? We all come with baggage, but now we can pitch it overboard. I suggest a game of chance to help us relax and not take things too seriously."

Dorfheimer shuffled the cards. "I warn you that I'm on a dangerous roll and I have no intention of taking prisoners."

Hatchet Jack looked at Delilah. "I know about that. Prisoners slow things down."

Dorfheimer picked up the deck. "Seven card stud. Nothing wild. Play it fair and square or take your problems outside."

For the first dozen hands the betting remained more or less even, with no one falling very far behind except for Dorfheimer, who bet every card as if it were his last. When Zebulon lost the biggest hand with three tens to Hatchet Jack's low straight, he pushed back his chair, sending it to the floor.

"You dealt that one off the bottom," he accused Hatchet Jack.

Hatchet Jack's hand settled on the butt of his pistol. "If you think that's true, which it ain't, we might as well take it outside."

"Your call," Zebulon said.

Hatchet Jack stood up, then slumped down again. "I came all the way up here to deal with you two and now I can't get to it."

"When you figure things out, let me know," Zebulon replied.

He walked over to the billiard table. After he won four straight games, doubling his money, he made his way back to the card table.

Hatchet Jack took a pull from a bottle of screech and handed the bottle to Zebulon. "I've been thinkin'. Maybe the two of us should ride back to Colorady. Rustle up some pelts or whatever comes to hand. Let it all bust loose like old times, maybe head down to that rendezvous on the Purgatory." He paused. "Unless you got another idea."

"Nothin' comes to mind." Zebulon drained the last of the bottle. "And I ain't about to go back to the mountains."

"Let the cards decide," Delilah said. "Winner takes all. The losers promise to go away and never come back."

"You people are crazy," Dorfheimer said. "Poker isn't a hundred-yard dash with a brick wall at the end of it, or some dumb shoot-out. It's a marathon. A game of skill and endurance. Otherwise, why bother?"

When neither Hatchet Jack nor Zebulon replied, she shuffled the cards.

"One hand." She dropped her gold and ruby necklace and all of her money on the table. "All or nothing."

"Count me out." Dorfheimer gathered up his winnings and marched towards the door.

"One winner," Delilah repeated. "Two losers. Or one loser and two winners, depending on your view."

Delilah shuffled the deck and placed it in front of Zebulon, who slowly cut the cards and shoved the deck to Hatchet Jack, who cut them again.

"Why do you have to be the dealer?" Zebulon asked Delilah. "Why not cut for high card to see who deals?"

"I'm the dealer," she said. "I have been from the beginning, whether you know it or not."

Zebulon placed the Warden's fossilized walrus penis on the table, along with all the money he had just won from playing billiards. Hatchet Jack matched him with Ivan's pocket watch, the Warden's Lakota Sioux rattle and Mandan war club, and finally, the Colt.

From the moment Delilah slid the cards across the table, Zebulon felt caught inside a repetition that he was unable or unwilling to back away from. He had been trapped here before, over and over, ever since he had first seen Delilah in the Panchito saloon. Once again he was in the same dimly lit cantina with most of the oil lamps smashed or burned out, the same restless piano chords, a mural of an unfinished journey over the bar, a deck of nubbed and bent cards, two whores staring at them from their bar stools, and now, Delilah dealing a hand where winning or losing had already been decided. And there was something else. Something that he felt doomed never to be able to realize or acknowledge.

The thought made him laugh rather than run out of the room, as if he and everyone else were part of the same joke: not knowing what they or anyone else was really up to.

When the saloon door opened, letting in a sudden blinding

shaft of sunlight, he slammed his hand on the table, causing a glass to shatter on the floor.

"*Quién es?*" the kid at the door asked as his Pa rushed up behind him, holding him back.

Zebulon answered out loud: "One who comes, and has already gone, and is not ready to come again, but is goin' to anyway."

When his eyes finally focused on the door, the kid and his Pa had disappeared.

"You've cracked wide open," Hatchet Jack said.

"That happens when a crack lets in too much light," Zebulon said.

Hatchet Jack studied Zebulon's eyes, the line of his mouth, and finally, his hands. There was no sign of confusion or doubt.

"It won't play, messin' with my head," Hatchet Jack said. "Not when you're holding an empty hand."

Everything, including life itself, was on the table.

As Delilah dealt the last card face down, Zebulon noticed a shiver travel down her sleeve, then flow through her fingers.

Hatchet Jack turned over a ten of spades, giving him a full house with three tens and two eights.

Delilah showed a queen of hearts, giving her a queen-high straight flush.

"Why ain't I surprised?" Hatchet Jack said.

Zebulon's last card was a seven, filling a low straight.

Delilah took her time looking at each of them, then scooped up everything on the table and stood up. "I'm leaving, and I won't be back. Now you two will have nothing left to fight over."

As she walked towards the door, the bandy-legged man stumbled past her, firing a pistol at the ceiling.

"It's Zebulon Shook, all right," he shouted. "In the goddamn flesh. Wanted dead or alive for a one-thousand-dollar reward, and this old coon is here to pick it up!"

Hatchet Jack's hand reached for the Colt lying on the table, but before he could pull the trigger, the bandy-legged man shot again, blowing out an oil lamp.

Zebulon was aware of picking up the Colt and firing a blind shot towards the bandy-legged man. Then two more shots were fired, followed by screams as another oil lamp exploded.

Then the room went black.

ZEBULON LAY ON HIS STOMACH IN THE MIDDLE OF A DITCH full of whiskey bottles and stinking fish guts. He didn't see the layers of fog floating over him like torn blankets, or the goat feeding on the garbage, or the silhouette of the kid standing at the end of the plank peering down at him.

"Is anyone down there?"

He turned over on his back, his head pounding as if locked inside a giant church bell.

"I saw you in the saloon," the kid said. "Are you dead, Mister, or are you a ghost?"

Who was he anyway? he asked himself one last time. And where was he coming from? And where was he going? He sat up, wiping the blood from his eyes. A man lay next to him, surrounded by smashed bottles, his mouth stretched open in rigor mortis. There was a hole in the man's forehead. Zebulon looked closer. A fly was crawling across one of Hatchet Jack's eyeballs. It was a long journey, the way the fly was crawling, then stopping, then crawling on. Caught in the middle of nowhere, he thought, drifting between worlds, from life to death and back again. He shut his eyes. He remembered a full house and a queen of hearts, then a shot followed by more shots. At least he wasn't dead. Not that it would be so bad to be dead, the way things had been going. And if he really was dead, and it had been that way all along, then he no longer gave a damn which way the cards played out.

The kid's voice floated through the fog. "Can you hear me, Mister?"

Could he hear? Could he speak? Could he smell? He had always been able to track changes in the wind; to smell the wet earth and his horse beneath him, the horse pounding on, always on; and he knew by heart the ritual mumbles of drunken high-rollers as their cards slapped across the table; and the bartender's windy tales; and the musky scent of Delilah as she surrendered her body to his. On the road to nowhere, he thought, drifting between worlds ever since – He remembered Not Here Not There, as her eyes found his before she disappeared through the ice. And now he, too, had disappeared. Suddenly he knew that he was no longer trapped between the worlds. That he had lost all that he had ever been attached to, and there was no going back to what no longer existed. The goat stepped closer, calmly staring down at him, as if reminding him that his string had run out, and that it was time that he accepted that fact and got on with it. He didn't bother reaching for his Colt, but stumbled to his feet and crawled up the side of the ditch towards the kid, who was running down the street, laughing and laughing, as he pretended that a ghost was coming after him.

ZEBULON WALKED TOWARDS THE SALOON WHERE LARGE Marge was sitting alone at the end of the porch, smoking a pipe and drinking from a nearly empty bottle of screech. The morning sun had burned away most of the fog, and the saloon was covered with milky light. Two planks were nailed across the saloon door, and a KEEP OUT sign was painted to one side in large red letters. He looked in one of the blown-out windows. The only signs of a shooting were two shot-out lamps, a bullet hole through the piano, and another bullet hole through the shot-out eye of a moose.

He sat down on the bench next to Large Marge, who wasn't surprised to see him.

"They told me you was dead," she said. "'Course I didn't believe it. They been sayin' that ever since I had the misfortune to meet up with you. I can't say the same for Hatchet Jack."

"Who shot him?" he asked.

"You don't recall?"

"I remember a queen-high straight flush to Hatchet's full house. Then a shot. Maybe two. And a lamp blown out. Nothing else."

"You didn't shoot nobody?"

"I might have. It went by like a dream."

"Ain't that the truth?" Large Marge said. "Lately I come to see life like that, one damn dream after another."

Large Marge sighed and looked out across the harbor, where the last strip of fog was drifting over the horizon.

"When I heard the shots, I took my time comin' downstairs. No sense gettin' myself killed over a card game. Everything was dark when I come in the room. One of the floozies was kneelin' behind the bar havin' a fit. When I asked about you, she said you and Hatchet Jack had yourselves a shoot-out. No one had a clear picture about what went down. The barman said Hatchet shot that bow-legged man comin' for the reward, and then someone shot you as you followed Hatchet out the door, or maybe it was the other way around. One of the Ruskies said it was you that shot Hatchet, but the pianer player says it was Delilah who picked a gun off the floor, plugged you, and then went after Hatchet. The whole thing happened too fast for anyone to know who was doin' what to who."

She sighed and drank a last long gulp of screech. "I always knew one day you two would go at each other. Crazy mountain lunatics. That's what you all do. Shoot each other straight to hell. Now the whole place is zippered up and everyone's spooked. Looks like you got away with it, ornery and stubborn bastard that you is."

"What about Delilah?" he asked.

"She sailed away on *The Rhinelander*. You'd think she would have waited to see if you was dead or not, but I guess she knew all along, bein' a witch and all. Anyway, she had all that money from the poker game to pay for her passage."

Zebulon pulled the planks off the door and walked into the saloon to the billiard table, where he picked up a cue stick and knocked a few balls around, just to see if he still could.

An hour later, when he still hadn't come out of the saloon, Large Marge peered through the window. There was no sign of Zebulon, and she didn't have the courage to try to find out what happened to him. The way things had been going, she suspected that she might have imagined him, and that he might not have been there at all.

She never told anyone about seeing Zebulon on the porch, preferring to keep at least one part of the legend for herself, out of old-time sentiments, if nothing else.

WHEN THE WARDEN RODE UP TO THE TRAIL'S END SALOON a week later with the Sheriff, the photographer, and a half-a-dozen soldiers, there was no sign of Zebulon. Reports of his whereabouts varied. Some said that he had gone up to Canada to the newly discovered gold strike on the Frazier River, which by all accounts promised to be the biggest in the history of the world. Others were convinced that he had returned to the high mountains of Colorado. And there was another rumor that he had set sail for the Aleutian Islands with a renegade band of Kwakiutl or Tlingit cannibals.

The Warden and his soldiers, along with the photographer and the Sheriff, rode back to San Francisco.

Large Marge, who had avoided capture by hiding in a storage shed, became the madam of the whorehouse above the Trail's End Saloon; it was a successful enterprise that was staffed almost entirely by Asians and Negro runaway slaves.

Delilah died on the Isle of Wight at the age of one-hundred and five, having lived a reclusive life translating Sufi poetry from Arabic into French and Portuguese, and growing medicinal herbs in the sanctuary of an enclosed garden. She was survived by a son, an actor and theatrical entrepreneur celebrated in most of the major capitals of Europe, as well as New York, Boston, and San Francisco.

Ten years after Delilah sailed away with Captain Dorfheimer, the photographer's portraits of Zebulon, along with a dozen landscapes of the Far West, were shown to enthusiastic acclaim in a New York gallery. The most famous portrait was bought by a French collector and showed Zebulon sitting on a billiard table in the Last Chance Saloon, staring into the camera as he cradled his dead father in his arms.

The photograph was later sold to a San Francisco museum, where it was never shown, the image having faded to such a degree that Zebulon's face had become blank.

The End